"You nee[...]
Vanessa [...]

She'd seen it too many times with family members trying to do it all and ending up getting sick themselves. She'd done it herself.

"I've survived worse," he said. Only, this time, it didn't sound as though he was joking.

"How would Ellie feel about a professional who's no longer a stranger and who does care stopping in to check on her every once in a while?"

Who really needs eight hours of sleep anyway? There would be time for structure once she and PJ were back in Cheyenne and she started working a regular schedule.

Austin didn't answer. He just looked at her, but she understood. Even the small decisions could have huge consequences in such matters.

As much as she wanted to explore the sadness behind those eyes of his, she would keep this on a professional level. It was her policy to not get involved with clients or their family members. That was how her failed marriage had begun. And how it ended.

Dear Reader,

Anyone who has been a caregiver for a loved one knows how unpredictable yet rewarding it can be. For those who haven't, it's a journey I highly recommend. It's also one that the hero and heroine must navigate in *And Cowboy Makes Three*.

Vanessa spent her childhood as the caregiver for her extended family. Now, as a divorced single mom, she wants to give her son the type of "normal" family and social life she missed out on. Austin, by contrast, wasn't around to help his mom during her illness. He vows to take care of his dad and grandmother on their Colorado ranch. The more family, the better— and he wants Vanessa and her son to be a part of it.

The closer they grow, the farther apart their visions for the future drift. The only hope must be somewhere in the middle, where the ground below is uncharted but holds the ultimate reward.

I hope you'll find a reward in their journey, as well.

Warmest wishes,

Susan Breeden

AND COWBOY MAKES THREE

SUSAN BREEDEN

Harlequin

HEARTWARMING

H Harlequin®
HEARTWARMING™

ISBN-13: 978-1-335-05148-6

And Cowboy Makes Three

Recycling programs for this product may not exist in your area.

Harlequin Enterprises ULC
22 Adelaide St. West, 41st Floor
Toronto, Ontario M5H 4E3, Canada
www.Harlequin.com

Printed in U.S.A.

Susan Breeden is a native Texan who currently lives in Houston, where she works as a technical writer/editor for the aerospace industry. In the wee hours of morning and again at night, you will find her playing matchmaker for the heroes and heroines in her novels. She also enjoys walks with her bossy German shepherd, decluttering and organizing her closet, and trying out new chili con queso recipes. For information on Susan's upcoming books, visit susanbreeden.com.

Books by Susan Breeden

Harlequin Heartwarming

Destiny Springs, Wyoming

The Bull Rider's Secret Son
Her Kind of Cowboy
The Cowboy's Rodeo Redemption

Visit the Author Profile page
at Harlequin.com for more titles.

For Daddy-O.

CHAPTER ONE

VANESSA FRASER HAD created a monster.

Furthermore, she wouldn't have it any other way. Her adorable six-year-old son PJ's blue eyes were crossed, and his right ear practically touched his shoulder as he exchanged goofy looks with his new best friend, Max, over video chat.

"This is how *you* look." PJ stuck his tongue out the side of his mouth and let it dangle.

"Oh, yeah? *You* look like this *all* the time," Max said.

Vanessa caught a glimpse of the little red-headed cutie on the computer screen, crossing his eyes and pushing up the tip of his nose while sneering.

Even though PJ had been spending a ton of time down the road at the local B and B owned by Max's parents, Becca and Cody Sayers, he seemed more attached to his friend than ever... thanks to their video chats.

PJ had become close friends with Max over the past few years during his and Vanessa's periodic two-week visits to Destiny Springs. But especially so over the last few days, when she and PJ returned to her grandfather Vern's ranch.

The back and forth from Cheyenne had been tiring, but necessary. She wanted to make sure that her oldest living relative didn't need help with anything around the house or ranch for a while.

Yet her main reason for taking this latest trip was so that she and PJ could spend a little more time with his pawpaw. In a few weeks, PJ would start school, and her new business would kick into high gear in Cheyenne. At that point, video chats would be the only way to "see" anyone in Destiny Springs for a while.

"Be careful, boys. Your faces might stick that way," she admonished, trying not to crack a smile.

PJ broke character, collapsed backward onto the area rug and rolled around as if being mercilessly tickled. From the sound of it, Max was doing the same thing.

Vanessa clasped her mug of hot green tea in both hands, shook her head and looked out the window, across the expanse of Fraser Ranch. In the distance, her grandfather appeared to be "horsing around" with his fiancée, Sylvie, as they exercised his two Appaloosas.

Vern's Wyoming ranch was about the same

size as the one she'd grown up on in Montana. If her dad were alive, he'd be in awe of how productive his father still was at the youthful age of eighty-four.

Not that her dad hadn't worked just as hard—if not harder—putting in overtime on their ranch while homeschooling his only child. Vanessa had worked as the unofficial resident caregiver for her terminally ill mom, although it hadn't felt like a job. By the time her maternal grandparents moved in with them, Vanessa was practically a professional, albeit an underage one. While other kids her age were going on field trips and to football games and dances, she was preparing meals and managing medications.

Her main regret was that her family didn't have the opportunity to "horse around." That was why she was determined to carve out at least a little one-on-one time with PJ each day of their remaining two weeks here.

No simple task. Even though her grandpa insisted he didn't need any more help, she still had a lengthy to-do list for the grand opening of Forever Home Caregiving and Recovery—her new business in Cheyenne. She was able to work remotely with her assistant to make sure the activity/recovery center and business offices were in tip-top shape for the open-house meet and greet as soon as she returned. Beth was a workhorse, albeit a panicky one. That made two of them. She was rather surprised she hadn't run the woman off yet. If anything, Beth seemed as caught up in the excitement of it as Vanessa was, and even eager for more responsibility.

Thankfully, the business had survived the rigors of licensing and accreditation, and her brigade was trained and bonded. The best part: her current private-care clients weren't abandoning her. They trusted her to assign loving and competent caregivers to meet their growing needs.

Vanessa considered each client family. But by switching from the trenches to ownership, she would have the flexibility and emotional bandwidth to give her most important family member a normal childhood. Just the two of them. In an actual city, with everything an urban lifestyle had to offer. Something she'd totally missed out on by living on a ranch with so many relatives around—most needing help in one way or another. In a way, she didn't even have a childhood.

She'd also be satisfying her inner geek by fulfilling her dream of running a business, complete with the joy of creating and maintaining spreadsheets. For Vanessa, this was one of the best parts, which she'd taught herself to do by watching online tutorials and reading technical manuals on the subject. As for the broader aspects of business ownership, her cousin Parker had given her invaluable guidance, having been a business consultant in Chicago for years before trading in his wingtips for cowboy boots and a home in the suburbs for a ranch in Wyoming.

Who needed a bachelor's degree from some fancy college, anyway?

"I get to eat ice cream for lunch," PJ explained to Max.

Vanessa didn't even have to correct him. Her number one priority for today was to make sure they got to have some fun together.

"Wow! Your mommy is cool," Max said.

"Yeah. I s'pose."

Mommy's just getting started. With a full tank of gas in the crossover, she was determined to treat them both to some fresh air this afternoon, even though the quantity would be limited. It would be worth staying up a couple of extra hours tonight after PJ went to sleep, if needed.

Vanessa couldn't help but smile as she took another long sip of tea, pretending not to overhear PJ bragging about the afternoon they had planned, exploring the nooks and crannies in town. Instead, she focused on the scene unfolding in the distance. Something was...*off*.

She nearly choked on her tea. Vern had dismounted his horse but lost his balance and was struggling to stay upright.

Sylvie jumped off her horse like some sort

of Olympian and caught him before he hit the ground.

If he'd gotten injured, Vanessa would've had to stay in Destiny Springs to look after him, and either postpone the grand opening or miss it altogether. She didn't know of any caregivers in the area besides herself. Folks here leaned on family and friends and neighbors more than professionals.

Then something beautiful happened. Vern stood up straight as if he'd never lost his balance, wrapped his arms around Sylvie's waist and engaged her in a dance.

"Arrrgghhhh!" PJ yelled out, shattering that peaceful feeling and causing Vanessa to practically jump out of her skin.

The boys were trying to out-zombie each other. PJ tilted his head to the side, extended his arms straight ahead and plodded across the rug in front of the computer.

Although it was all fun and games at the moment, monsters became real to him once the sun set. He'd run to her bedroom in the middle of the night, convinced that one was hiding in his closet or under the bed.

"PJ, was that an invitation to two-step?" she asked, knowing full well it wasn't, but she had to change the vibe in the room.

He'd shown some interest at the Sayers' wedding reception a few months ago. He and Max managed to get one clumsy dance out of the Buchanan twins until they all decided that the likelihood of getting cooties wasn't worth it.

Vanessa didn't have any better luck. PJ's zombie walk turned into a run when she tried to catch him. Then again, dancing with herself wasn't a problem. She'd become used to it since her divorce three years ago. Actually, during the marriage, as well.

As she pulled a random album from Vern's shelf and placed it on the old turntable, someone knocked at the side door.

"Don't open it, Mommy. It might be a zombie!" PJ yelled.

"If he'll dance with me, he's welcome here," she said in a not-so-subtle tease.

"Nooo!" PJ screamed.

Vanessa opened the door, despite PJ's protests. If the stranger standing on the other side of the threshold was a zombie...*then sign me up.*

The man was all Stetson and smiles, even though the far corners of his green eyes were a bit downturned, giving him a look that bordered on sadness. He removed his black cowboy hat, revealing thick, brownish-auburn hair.

PJ ran to her side and stared at the stranger. "Are you a zombie?"

"Not that I'm aware of," he said with a bit of a laugh. He looked at Vanessa. "These days, I feel like one, though. I'm Austin Cassidy. Vern's expecting me, but I'm a day early."

Her grandfather had mentioned hiring a part-time ranch hand to help mend a stretch of fencing and even make some repairs to the house. This guy certainly looked capable of it and was dressed for the part, from his well-worn denim jeans and soft flannel button-down shirt to his broken-in cowboy boots.

"I'm Vanessa. My grandfather is riding horses. Out there." She stuck her head around the door frame and pointed, but Vern and Sylvie had finished dancing and were back in their respective saddles, cantering in the opposite direction.

She and the cowboy looked at each other and shrugged in unison.

"Looks like he might be gone a while. I'd invite you to wait inside until he's back, but my son and I are heading out soon," she said.

She knew that Vern and Sylvie were going to exercise all four horses and could easily be out for at least another hour. Longer, if Vern insisted on another dance or two.

"Bad timing. Story of my life. I gotta get back to the house, anyway. Unless you could help me. Vern offered to loan my grandma Ellie one of those thingies with the tennis balls. Except fancier."

"Thingies?" Vanessa cocked her head.

Austin shook his head and looked down, clearly embarrassed.

"The contraption that older people use to help them walk. You know…" He took a step back from the threshold, stuck his arms out, clenched his fists as if gripping something and shuffled a couple of steps across the width of the patio.

"You *are* a zombie!" PJ shrieked.

To Vanessa, the guy looked more like Frankenstein's monster with that walk, albeit a handsome version. But what did she know?

Austin relaxed and threw his hands in the air. "You were right after all, young man."

"That's 'cause I'm one, too," PJ said, launching back into his own version.

She'd figured out that Austin was talking about a walker, even before his strange demonstration. But PJ was having too much fun, so she didn't fess up immediately.

Vern *had* been tinkering with that admittedly fancy walker of his, trying to fix the hydraulics for the hand brakes. Unfortunately, it was still a disassembled mess on the floor of his indoor workroom.

"I'll check with my grandfather when he comes back in. We'll bring it over whenever it's ready. Probably tomorrow," she offered.

We being the operative word. The only break she'd planned from remote work tomorrow was an outing to the farmers' market with PJ.

"I'm happy to swing back by. Save you the trouble," he said.

Odd, but his offer caught her off guard. As a single mom and professional caregiver, she was used to doing all the heavy lifting—both literally and figuratively—for little children as well as full-grown ones.

Hadn't been all that much different during her marriage, come to think of it.

"Vern might insist on bringing it, but we'll let you know," she said.

Austin nodded and put his hat back on. "Say, do you happen to know of any available caregivers in the area?"

Vanessa should have seen that question coming, considering his grandma was entering the walker stage.

"Afraid not, but I'll be happy to ask around." Hopefully that would put the topic to rest without requiring full disclosure.

"Just as well. Ellie probably won't consent to having a stranger in the house. Can't say I'm thrilled about it either, but..." He punctuated the sentiment with one of those sad-eyed smiles.

It didn't take a pro to see he was the one who could use some help. Caregiving wasn't for the faint of heart.

She wasn't sure whether her own heart was breaking over the sadness his eyes appeared to convey or whether it was aching to help if only to figure *him* out.

Austin tipped his Stetson, turned on his boot heels and headed toward his truck. He couldn't have been too far down the road when Vern ventured back inside and immediately removed his hat, unleashing his gray hair that was in serious need of a trim. As were his beard and mustache.

"Whew! Sylvie wanted to exercise the other horses, but I'm worn out," he said as he placed the hat on a hook, followed by his light jacket, revealing a cream-colored T-shirt and denim overalls.

"Maybe a nap is in order. I was watching from the window. You almost fell," she said.

"Nonsense!" Vern swatted away her summation. "I was pretending. Wanted to get Sylvie off that horse and into my arms. That was the fastest way I could think of to do it."

The whole scene did look a little dramatic. She'd never seen a man so much in love.

"A guy named Austin Cassidy just stopped by. He told me you offered to loan his grandmother a walker," she said.

Vern cocked his head. "Is it Friday already?"

"No. He said he was a day early."

"Good! I'm not losing my mind." He summoned her with his index finger to follow him down the hall to his tinkering room. Once there, he eased to the ground and knelt in front of the partially disassembled walker.

"Actually, I'm returning it. Ellie loaned it to me when I sprained my ankle real bad two years ago," Vern explained as he picked up a piece and snapped it back into place like it was nothing more complicated than a Lego.

"You never told me that happened," Vanessa said.

"That's because you would've dropped everything and driven all the way from Cheyenne to help. I could get along just fine, thanks to this beauty." Vern patted the side of the walker. "Ellie brought over homemade meals and lots of 'em. A hot dinner every night for over a week. Even stayed and visited sometimes. Least I can do is return this to her in even better condition. Another half hour, give or take."

"I hope she's okay," Vanessa said. Even though she'd never met the woman, what she'd done for Vern was really nice.

"Me too. Her husband passed a couple of weeks ago. That was the funeral Sylvie and I went to. I suspect her grandson is being overprotective, now that she'll be living alone, and wants her to have a walker on hand."

No wonder Austin's eyes seemed full of sadness. He'd recently lost his grandfather, and now he had to worry about his grandmother. It was too common a story.

"He's a zombie," PJ said.

Vern squinted and pursed his lips. "That's

strange. Ellie's talked about him, but she never mentioned that. She does brag about how handsome he is. Is that true, Angel?"

Ugh. That nickname she'd recently been given by a friend. *Earth Angel.* She didn't feel very angelic at the moment, having all but lied to Austin. And after everything he'd been going through. Not that she had much of a choice, with several to-dos remaining before the grand opening. And she most definitely planned to steal at least an hour each day to make sure the most important little man in her life had some fun, like children were supposed to have.

When she didn't concur, Vern continued. "Well?"

"PJ and I are leaving in two weeks. Sooner, if anyone insists on playing matchmaker. Besides, you must have seen him at the funeral," Vanessa said.

"I forgot already. We could deliver the walker together and get another look at him, since I can't remember and you don't seem sure."

Vanessa crossed her arms. "Grandpa…"

He pretended to zip his lips closed and lock them with an invisible key.

If Vern was the one to return the walker, that zipper would bust wide open, and he'd turn into a matchmaker. That seemed to be an epidemic in this town. No, she would deliver the walker. She didn't want Vern to throw out his back loading or unloading it.

"PJ and I will drop it off on the way to the drugstore for ice cream."

"I have Rocky Road in the freezer. He can stay with me," Vern offered.

"Nice try. I'll need protection from zombies," she insisted.

Specifically, a handsome one who happens to need a caregiver.

Although, with her son in tow as an adorable distraction, one more encounter with Austin shouldn't put her in any danger—specifically, in danger of acting from the heart again, instead of with her head. That was something she tended to do all too often, and not only when it came to business.

Also when it came to love.

Austin dumped the contents of the small shopping bag onto his bed and separated the cans of cat food from his toiletries.

Life would be a lot easier if he really were a zombie. Then he wouldn't have had to choose between purchasing a full tube of toothpaste or the travel size. Being the semi-optimist he was, he'd chosen the latter, only to second-guess himself now. Especially after his less-than-encouraging efforts to find a caregiver the last few days. Otherwise, his rule to travel light had served him well in the past.

Which reminded him of rule number two: don't get attached to this town or any of the people in it.

He had to laugh. Might be a little too late for that. Could PJ have been any cuter? Then there was the little boy's mom, Vanessa. Beautiful and charming. But a bit…guarded.

Austin had been too nervous to even look at her ring finger. Not that it would matter. The remainder of his time here belonged to Ellie, and his heart belonged to the Happy U ranch back in Colorado. This trip to Destiny Springs was supposed to be a travel-size-only journey. He'd planned to be here long enough to attend his grandfather's funeral and to persuade his grandmother to sell her property and move back with him.

But then his planned one-week trip turned into three and counting, with her needing emergency hip replacement surgery right before he'd been scheduled to return to Colorado. His dad really needed him back home, but his grandma needed him even more.

Austin looked up as the physical therapist was poised to knock on the door frame of his guest bedroom.

"We're all finished, Mr. Cassidy. She's doing very well and insisted on resting in that big, empty room. I pulled a supportive chair in there for her, but she's not happy with me since I won't let her see the cat without supervision."

"I understand."

Yet another thing he, or a future caregiver, would have to finagle. Tango—a long-haired orange tom who'd appeared on her doorstep after the funeral—had taken up permanent residence in his grandma's lap. Except that wouldn't be the case for the next couple of weeks, since her incision needed to heal without the possibility of infection. Plus, her lap didn't need the extra weight.

She'd joked that the cat was a feline version of her late husband, Shelton, with the ginger hair. Austin couldn't deny the possibility. The cat knew his way around the place from the moment he'd walked in the door and decided to make this name-less ranch his home.

Ellie and Tango had been inseparable until the surgery. Since then, the feline had been mostly missing in action. But he was somewhere in the house, because his food bowl was always licked clean and he cried on the other side of her bed-room door at night, wanting to sleep next to her.

Austin could tell the physical therapist was curi-ous as to why Ellie preferred the empty room when all the others were so warmly furnished. But he couldn't explain something he didn't understand.

"Thanks for your help. Will you be back at the same time tomorrow?" he asked.

"Every day, if that works for both of you. I'll evaluate her progress at the end of the week, and we'll go from there."

He'd last that long, but his new travel-sized

toothpaste wouldn't. He'd gladly give in and buy the regular-sized tube, but Ellie was already encouraging him to go back home to Colorado, insisting she didn't need help. His going back without her would be the worst-case scenario.

Scratch that. The worst would be if there was some kind of emergency at the Happy U. Due to a lifetime of ranch-related injuries, his cowboy-to-the-bone dad could no longer take care of their family's remote Colorado property and cutting-horse training business alone, even though he kept insisting on trying. The ranch hands could assist with a few things, which helped. At least the man had promised to pause the training sessions until Austin returned.

After the therapist left, Austin summoned his most optimistic smile and entered the big, empty room.

"Can I get you anything, Grandma? A blanket? Some hot chocolate?"

"You can get me Tango."

"You know I can't. I'm sorry," he said.

"Any idea where he is and if he's at least safe? I thought I heard him a few minutes ago."

"He's around here somewhere. If he runs outside, he won't go far. He knows a good home when he finds it."

At least, Austin hoped that would be the case.

"I know this is hard, but he'll be back in your lap soon," he continued. "By the way, I stopped by Fraser Ranch earlier to pick up your walker, but Vern wasn't there. Just his granddaughter and her son."

"Vanessa and PJ."

"You know them?"

Ellie shook her head and smiled. "No, but Vern's shown me pictures. Beautiful young woman. Looks more like a movie star than a caregiver. She reminds me of that pretty gal in *Love Story*. Ali MacGraw?"

"I guess I've never seen that one," he said, although he wasn't thinking entirely clearly. His mind was stuck on an earlier word. *Caregiver.*

Austin wanted to say that Vanessa was a bit of an actress herself, because when he'd asked if she knew of any caregivers, she'd said no without so much as blinking. Then again, she didn't know him from some random...zombie. Couldn't blame her for not spilling her life story to a total stranger. Plus, she wasn't exactly dressed for the part in that long skirt and stylish sweatshirt and boots.

"Let's move you into the den. You pick the movie, and I'll make a late lunch." He hadn't even been paying attention to the time.

"Popcorn, please. That's all I need."

"Done." He'd push for some veggies later, but he was trying to score points with her. After the movie, they had to have *the talk*.

He helped her stand. Didn't even bother trying to talk her into using the foldable walker that the doctors had told her to use. Together they made their way to the den, where she settled onto a firm ladder-back chair he'd robbed from the dining room set. In a show of solidarity, he retrieved the chair's equally uncomfortable mate but didn't sit. He positioned a small side table between them with room enough for the popcorn.

At least he didn't have to worry about the cat making an appearance. Not with him in the room.

"Sit on the sofa. It's much more comfortable," she insisted.

"Too soft for my back. I'll be in the kitchen for a few. Don't go anywhere," he said, which earned him a down-the-nose glance.

As if she would. At least, not safely. The walker that had been prescribed—and which they'd brought home—got the job done. However, it wasn't to her liking. She was all but holding out for the supposedly much nicer one forthcoming from Vern. At least she had the good sense to not try walking without it. In the meantime, Austin was having to be everywhere at once.

He figured he'd have to pick his battles with his strong-willed grandmother. Unfortunately, his picker was already exhausted and this journey had barely begun.

By the time the popcorn finished popping and he returned to the den, Tango had made an appearance and was poised to jump on Ellie's lap. His grandmother wasn't exactly discouraging it. Austin cleared his throat and the cat bolted.

"Do me a favor and get a box of tissues from the bathroom," Ellie said.

"You gettin' the sniffles?" he asked as he headed down the hall.

"No. But we're both going to need them," she said.

Odd. What movie did she have in mind?

By the time he returned, Ellie had already cued up the movie she wanted to watch. *Love Story.*

He remembered a little bit about it now. He'd seen it once. How could he forget? Girl and boy meet and fall in love. Girl gets sick and dies. Definitely not the kind of flick he'd prefer they watch so soon after his grandfather had passed.

"Sure you don't want to watch a comedy instead?" he asked.

"I'm positive." She delicately selected the most butter-soaked piece from the top of the bowl, popped it into her mouth and pressed Start on the remote.

Not even five minutes into it, she said, "I never noticed before, but you resemble Ryan O'Neal."

Austin laughed under his breath. He didn't see the resemblance himself, but he saw what Ellie had meant about Vanessa resembling Ali Mac-Graw. *The hair, the nose.*

Somehow, the comparisons failed to change the movie experience for him, and by the end, he was dabbing at the corners of his eyes with his sleeve and swallowing hard to head off a full-on weep fest.

When he looked over at Ellie, she wasn't even watching the television. She was watching him, but with tears in her own eyes.

"I knew this movie was a bad idea," he said. Mostly for her.

She shook her head and smiled, then reached over and squeezed his arm. "I had sixty beautiful years with Shelton. These kinds of stories only remind me of how lucky I was. You'll find the love of your life, too."

That was the last thing he needed to do right now. His love story sure wasn't going to happen in Destiny Springs. He was determined to help his dad with the Happy U and the business, whether the man thought he needed it or not. Although there was no substitute for family, at least the ranch hands they'd hired could handle the property-related ins and outs and keep an eye on his dad while Austin was taking care of Ellie.

His grandmother's bones might be healing, but his were aching to get back to training cutting horses since taking an unsuccessful six-year detour. He'd left his parents high and dry to pursue a woman all the way to Colorado Springs, get married and earn a real estate license at her request. A happy wife meant a happy life, right?

Wrong. She ultimately divorced him. How was that for a love story?

The worst part was, his mother had become ill during his absence. And Austin wasn't there to help. If he had been, she'd still be alive today—despite what his dad would say, though they'd never had a real conversation about it. But Austin made a new vow, and he was going to stick to it. This time to his father. And to himself.

He stood and collected the popcorn bowl that they'd depleted an hour ago. He'd barely made it to the kitchen when someone knocked on the front door.

"I'll get it," he called out, once again realizing too late that he was pretty much the only one who safely could. He set the bowl on the kitchen counter, then headed back into the den, toward the front door, past Ellie's down-the-nose glance and knowing smile.

"I'm sorry," he offered.

"Love means never—"

"*Don't* say it. You'll make me start crying again." In fact, his eyes were still a little damp.

He swung the door open, hoping for a respite from the movie images that lingered in his brain. Instead, he saw the other "actress" and her adorable son.

Vanessa smiled and said the three words he wanted to believe. But wasn't sure he could.

"Help has arrived."

CHAPTER TWO

"Is THIS A bad time?"

Vanessa really didn't have to ask. It looked like he'd been crying. The wounds from the loss of his grandfather must still be fresh. Her heart went out to him.

"No, not at all," Austin said as he straightened his posture. But his expression begged to differ.

To compensate for the guilt she'd felt over dodging the whole caregiver question, she'd hoped to surprise him with an early delivery. She even hid it behind her and PJ's backs. When he didn't invite them in, she stepped aside to reveal the walker.

"Voilà! Tennis balls not included," she said, which earned her one of those sad-eyed smiles. Only, a bigger one, complete with some soft wrinkles to cushion the edges.

He stepped outside and walked around it, giving it a thorough once-over. Did everything except kick the tires.

"That's one fancy machine. Does she need a license to drive it?" he asked.

"Hopefully she already has one. Grandpa said she's the one who originally loaned it to him and he's simply returning it. Although he did add this nifty cell phone holder."

Austin patted the seat. "Wanna go for a ride?" he asked PJ.

The little boy jumped aboard and served up a huge smile. Off they went for a test-drive to the end of the long porch and back.

"Please thank Vern for us. And thank y'all for bringing it over," Austin said.

PJ reluctantly jumped off and returned to Vanessa's side.

"Well, I guess we better get going," she said. That was an understatement. This detour meant she'd likely have to stay up an extra hour or so to follow up with the bingo supply company. Their tracking system said the cards, chips and daubers were delivered, but Beth insisted otherwise. No signature had been required, so it was their word against the bingo company's. She had already been advertising it as a grand-opening event at the center, so they had to figure something out.

"Can I pet the kitty before we go?" PJ asked, pointing at the blur that whisked past them, all the way to the end of the porch where the feline proceeded to bathe his paws.

Austin's eyes widened. "Don't move." He took a cautious step in the direction of the domestic feline as if he were approaching a dangerous mountain lion.

PJ obviously thought the request didn't apply to him. He ran to the end of the porch and plopped down beside the cat, who looked annoyed at first but then resumed bathing.

"Austin? I think Tango ran outside. Don't let him get away," a woman called out from inside the house.

"He's right here, Grandma," he said, but otherwise seemed paralyzed. He turned to Vanessa. "We need to get the cat inside. Somehow. But he hasn't warmed up to me yet."

PJ stood, picked up the cat and walked right past them and into the house. The feline wiggled in his grip for a moment but otherwise complied.

Vanessa hurried inside, and Austin closed the door behind them.

Across the room, an elderly woman was seated in a chair close to the fireplace but facing the television.

"Ellie, this is Vanessa."

The woman smiled and nodded. "I've seen your picture, but you're even lovelier in person. Austin and I were talking about how you look like that gal in the movie we just finished watching."

"Which movie?" Vanessa asked.

"*Love Story.* Hence the box of Kleenex." Ellie

pointed to the table between the two uncomfortable-looking ladder-back armchairs.

She'd heard of the movie and how sad it was, but she had never seen it for that reason.

"Also for my allergies," Austin said.

"Of course, dear," Ellie said, then smiled and winked at Vanessa.

So *that* was the reason for the damp eyes.

PJ certainly looked like he was comfortable. He was sprawled across the sofa, petting the cat, who seemed to be taking all the handling in stride. She retrieved her phone and snapped a photo of the adorable duo.

"Why does love hurt so bad you have to use Kleenex?" PJ asked.

Vanessa didn't think he was even paying attention, much less making those kinds of connections. At that age, children should know only of love and warmth. And fun, like the moments they'd be having if they could manage a quick but graceful exit.

"Not all tears are bad. Love offers lots of happy tears, too," Ellie said. "I tell you what *does* make me wanna cry is this hip of mine. Austin, is it time for another pain pill?"

He looked at Vanessa, then his watch. "Past time. I'll be right back."

After he was out of earshot, Ellie said, "He's usually the one to remind *me* about the medication. Now that I've got a decent walker, I won't have to bother him with such things. He needs to get on back to Colorado and take care of his ranch instead of fussing over me."

Vanessa wasn't about to take sides until she learned more. In fact, her policy was to not take sides at all. She certainly didn't want to influence any caregiver discussions that Ellie and Austin might be having. Although she may have her own personal opinions, the decisions regarding what was best for all parties in these situations were ultimately theirs to make, based on so many variables and family dynamics.

Perhaps Austin was being a little overprotective, however. Ellie seemed to be mentally sharp and capable, and probably just needed occasional help. The woman looked to be in her early eighties. Aches and pains went with the territory. It wasn't until Ellie removed the blanket from her lap that Vanessa began to realize that Austin hadn't told her the whole story.

"We're gonna get ice cream today. Will you go with us?" PJ asked Ellie, which Vanessa thought was supersweet.

"I'm afraid I can't today, PJ. But we could have ice cream here if you want to stay."

PJ looked to Vanessa. "Can we, Mommy?"

So this was how it felt to be stuck between a rock and a hard place.

"Of course. I'll get Austin to help me fix a bowl for each of us."

Vanessa made a quick and flustered exit, and located the kitchen easily enough. That was where she found him jotting something down on a notepad while reading a prescription label. He looked up, and then back down.

"I think I'm getting the hang of this," he said. "I double-check that I'm giving her the right pill, then I write down the time she takes it. Professionals probably recommend a better system, right? You didn't tell me you were a caregiver. Ellie outed you."

Her first thought was that she wasn't the only one who hadn't been transparent earlier today.

"You asked if there were any *available* caregivers. And my availability is limited. Besides, you didn't tell me you were a zombie. PJ had to out you."

"Then we're even," he said.

"Not quite. You didn't tell me Ellie had hip surgery, and that's why you needed the walker. And a caregiver."

Austin set the bottle back down on the counter and looked up. "I'm surprised she told you."

"She didn't," Vanessa said as she located some bowls, the ice cream and a scooper.

Austin cocked his head. "Then how did you know?"

"I'm a professional caregiver, remember? The

ladder-back chair, the top of a waterproof bandage peeking out from her warm-up pants, com-
pression socks."

"She doesn't want to inconvenience anyone.
Not even a stranger who's getting paid to care. I
jumped the gun in asking you about it. I intend
to respect her wishes and am handling all the
details, but…"

"You need help."

"She's getting physical therapy every day for at
least the rest of the week. Also, a nurse is dropping in to check on her every few days. And I'm
the chef, so she'll be assured of getting her rec-
ommended daily dose of sugar and carbs," he
said, adding a laugh.

But she saw right past the forced humor. The
internal *click* she felt made her stand up straighter
as her conscience implored her to act.

"No. *You* need help. With all of this," she said
as she plopped an oversize scoop in one of the
bowls. She'd seen it too many times with family
members trying to do it all and ending up getting sick themselves. She'd done it all for a long
time and knew the personal risks.

"I've survived worse," he said. Only, this time,
it didn't sound as though he was joking.

"How would Ellie feel about a professional
who's no longer a stranger and who does care stopping in to check on her every once in a while?"

Who really needs eight hours of sleep, anyway? There would be time for such structure once she and PJ were back in Cheyenne and she started working a regular schedule. It wasn't like their current schedule here had been normal.

Austin didn't answer. He just looked at her, but she understood. Even the small decisions could have huge consequences in such matters.

As much as she wanted to explore the sadness behind those eyes of his, she would keep this on a professional level. It was her policy to not get involved with clients or their family members. That was how her failed marriage had begun. And how it ended, with her a caregiver and him simply a taker. He needed her more than he loved her.

Why does love hurt so bad?

She knew the answer.

So you won't make the same mistake twice.

AUSTIN COULD LEARN a lesson or two from Tango when it came to taking advantage of an opportunity.

The feline had claimed ownership of PJ's bowl of ice cream while the little boy was in the throes of a brain freeze. After swallowing an extra-large spoonful of mint chocolate chip, PJ let out a painful *"Ooouuuch."* Then his little face scrunched up and he clenched his eyes tight.

"Press your tongue against the roof of your mouth, dear," Ellie instructed.

"I'll get a glass of warm water." Vanessa got up and rushed to the kitchen.

"We'll also get you your own bowl of ice cream," Austin added in lieu of any helpful advice.

Vanessa came back with the water and encouraged PJ to take a sip, although Ellie's suggestion seemed to have already helped.

"Huh. I didn't know that trick. Thanks, Ellie. All better now, sweetie?" she asked.

PJ opened his eyes and nodded.

Crisis averted. If only Vanessa could help with the conversation that Austin planned to have with Ellie later on. But he couldn't even bring himself to take advantage of her kind offer to help now.

Maybe he'd inherited his father's and Ellie's stubbornness when it came to accepting assistance, especially when the offer came from a woman who had her hands full raising a young son, possibly by herself. Or maybe because he couldn't take his eyes off her, which would make it next to impossible to get any repairs done around the ranch. Then there was the transparency issue. Vanessa hadn't revealed she was a caregiver when they first met, despite the perfect opportunity to do so. Now he kind of understood why. If they were to have any working relationship, they couldn't play hide-and-seek with the truth.

Except it wasn't going to go that far. He could do this by himself. Before he got into training cutting horses, he'd broken several wild stallions for their ranch. Gotten kicked in the gut and the shin as a farrier one summer just for the fun of learning the craft. How hard could it be to take care of an eighty-two-year-old woman who could barely walk?

Two text messages in a row helped lasso his resolve to stick to his original plan to talk with her about moving. Today, if he could summon the nerve.

The first text was from a couple who was interested in Ellie's property, even though he had yet to list it. Now, that was an opportunity he couldn't let slip by. At least those Realtor skills he'd reluctantly earned weren't going entirely to waste. Plus, if they made an offer, perhaps she would be willing to move sooner rather than later. Then he could give up his search for a long-term caregiver. Wouldn't want to hire someone, then pull the job out from under her or him.

The second text was from one of his ranch hands. The Happy U was receiving calls from their cutting-horse clients, asking when training would resume. Austin had shifted some sessions around to accommodate this trip so his father wouldn't attempt it alone, but he hadn't anticipated being gone this long. Even though his dad was the best trainer in River Rock—making Austin the son of the best—folks were only willing to wait so long.

That latter situation was a bit more of a problem since providing their clients with a firm answer was contingent upon how soon he could get Ellie to agree to move.

Working in his favor, Ellie seemed to have loved visiting the Happy U when Austin was much younger. The guest room she'd stayed in had a fireplace, and she would cover the floor in faux fur blankets and pillows and take naps in front of it while Shelton helped Austin's dad with some chores around the ranch. As Ellie enjoyed telling it, she'd wake up in her exhausted husband's loose embrace. Not wanting to deny him a well-earned nap, she'd remain still while the flames reduced to embers. At the end of each trip, Ellie would say, *I'm going to take that fireplace home with me someday.*

Now she wouldn't even have to try. It would already be home and full of warm memories.

After PJ finished his second bowl of ice cream, with Tango poised to jump in should the opportunity arise again, Vanessa took his dish to the kitchen and returned with a heavy smile, followed by a heavier sigh.

"We better get going, PJ."

"Can we come back later and play with Tango?" he asked.

"You come by anytime you want, PJ," Ellie chimed in. "Next time, I'll give you a ride on my cart."

Austin bit back his disapproval of the idea. That sounded like an accident waiting to happen.

"How about tomorrow? We can swing by here after we go to the farmers' market," Vanessa said.

"Okay," PJ said, after seeming to give it some serious thought.

Actually, it sounded like quite a good deal to Austin, too. He loved the energy a young child brought to the house. Although fatherhood might be years away, he was looking forward to that aspect of it.

PJ ran over to Ellie and gave her a big hug. Vanessa swooped in before he put too much pressure on her lap.

"Bye, Miss Ellie! Bye, kitty! Bye, Mr. Austin!" PJ waved as Vanessa set him down, took his hand and headed for the door.

Austin surged ahead of her and held it open, keeping his eyes trained on Tango. At least if the cat did get out again, PJ could probably catch him.

He escorted them to her truck and waited until she got PJ buckled in the back seat of the cab. She came around to the driver's side and paused before getting in.

"I guess we'll see you tomorrow," he said. "And I insist on paying you for your time."

She shook her head. "Absolutely not. I'm just

stopping in. I'll do it with a professional eye, of course. I'll let you know what level of caregiving she might need. Besides, PJ wants to visit the cat, so looks like we'll be coming over anyway. His happiness is the most important thing."

As it should be.

"Okay. This time," he said.

She climbed inside and drove away, leaving Austin in her dust. Not that his vision or common sense could be any more clouded.

Once inside, Ellie was nowhere to be seen. Panic struck, faster than the worst brain freeze.

"Grandma! Where are you?"

He checked the kitchen. Nothing. He knocked on the bathroom door, which was cracked open. She wasn't there either.

At least she'd taken the walker and she couldn't have gone far.

That was when he heard it. Music, coming from that empty room with the unique hardwoods. There he found her, sitting on the seat of the walker. He was too relieved to be angry. While he knew it was okay for her to walk, it was risky for her to try it alone when no one was around to help if she needed it. But he wasn't going to reprimand her. He'd just have to keep a closer eye on her.

He willed his heart to stop pounding, put on his cheeriest face and said, "There you are!"

She smiled and nodded but stopped short of apologizing for scaring him half to death.

"What did you think about Vanessa and PJ?" he asked.

"They were the bright spot in my day," she said. "Not that you aren't, too, dear."

"Don't worry. You won't hurt my feelings."

Unless you don't want to move to the Happy U.

"How about coming back out to the den? Not that the chair in there is more comfortable, but at least the room isn't so empty."

"This is the fullest room in the house. I need to be here. I'm waiting for Shelton to apologize."

Instead of seeming sad or angry about whatever his grandpa had been guilty of, Ellie placed her hands across her chest and smiled.

Now he was really confused. Hopefully this was part of the grieving process in losing a spouse, although he felt completely helpless in guiding her through it. If—when—Vanessa came back over tomorrow, he'd ask her about it.

So much for thinking that taking care of Ellie would be easier than shoeing or training a wild horse. Or getting that serious conversation about moving over with today.

There were two things he couldn't waver on, however. Number one: no more sad movies for Ellie.

And number two: no love stories for him.

CHAPTER THREE

"I WANNA BE a zombie," PJ said.

The face painter took the little boy's enthusiasm in stride, as if it were a common request. Most kids at the farmers' market children's corral wanted things like flowers or butterflies. Or even snakes.

Somehow, the subject of monsters hadn't come up during their visit with Ellie and Austin yesterday. Vanessa had hoped the phase had come and gone. No such luck. Her opposition to it wasn't because PJ might have nightmares—she was more worried about herself. This particular face painter took his craft to a whole nother level.

"How about a cat instead?" Vanessa pulled out her cell phone and showed PJ the photo she'd taken of him and Tango on the sofa.

The little boy practically jumped out of his seat. "I wanna look like that!"

She offered up the photo to the face painter.

He studied it a little too seriously. "By the time

I'm done, you'll look like the twin of that furry fella in the picture."

PJ grinned. Thank goodness for cell phone cameras.

"I'll be right back," she said, now that the direction was agreed upon and her little boy was in the care of a group of adults tasked for exactly that: looking after children while the adults got their shopping done.

Some juicy heirloom tomatoes had been calling out her name ever since she and PJ had walked past the stand. So were the fresh-baked whole grain bread, local mushrooms and variety of cheeses. Although she'd give Austin the benefit of the doubt that Ellie was surviving on more than popcorn and ice cream, she was happy to contribute a few things to the pantry and fridge for quick and easy salads, sandwiches or stand-alone snacks.

By the time she'd filled the recycled shopping tote that she kept folded in her oversize handbag, PJ had been transformed from her precious little boy to a more menacing version of Tango. Nightmares might be inevitable. PJ was happy, though, and ultimately that was all that mattered.

On the trek back to the truck, folks smiled and pointed as PJ pretended to extend his claws.

"You don't have to go to Ellie's with me. I can drop you off at Grandpa's for a nap. When I get home, I'll fix us a nice dinner. And tomorrow, you and I are going to the drugstore diner for steak fingers and fries," she said as she buckled him into the seat.

She was hoping to have some time alone with the woman today. See if she'd admit that she needed some help. Even though Austin no longer seemed open to having a caregiver, Vanessa would happily assist her with things such as changing the surgical dressing or dry washing and styling her hair until she was able to shower or bathe, every once in a while. It was the very least she could do after Ellie had been such a help to her grandpa.

"I wanna go! I want Tango to see me," he said.

"Then Miss Ellie's it is."

So much for having a deep conversation with the woman. At least with PJ along, their visit should be even shorter than the drive to get there. It took less than twenty minutes, but that was plenty of time for PJ to practice his cat cries along the way.

Maybe that idea wasn't her best. A zombie wouldn't have been so vocal.

It felt odd just showing up. A little too familiar, considering she and PJ had met both Austin and Ellie only yesterday. Maybe *familial* was an even better word, which was what she was determined to avoid most.

Perhaps she should have taken him up on his

offer to pay her. That would help her keep emotional distance, because this already wasn't feeling like a caregiver duty.

It took a few minutes for Austin to answer the door, but his reaction was worth the wait. The delight in his eyes buoyed her heart.

"You must be here to see Tango," he said.

PJ nodded. Then, in a true catlike maneuver, he brushed past Austin and into the house.

"If you can find him!" Austin called out, although it likely went unheard. He shrugged and turned to her. "And you're—"

"Vanessa. How quickly we forget."

Austin squinted and studied her. "No, that's not what I meant. I was going to say you were right."

Now she was the one to squint. "I don't understand."

"About my needing help."

Instead of inviting her in, he came outside and closed the door behind him. "Ellie said something yesterday that worried me."

"Oh, no. What?"

"She was waiting for my grandpa to apologize. Didn't want to leave her favorite room until he did. Oh, and she thinks Tango is my grandfather reincarnated."

Vanessa knew a little bit about the thoughts that the elderly had during such times, especially those who'd lost their spouse of decades. They didn't always make sense, even to family, but that didn't mean something was necessarily wrong.

"She's been through a lot in the past couple of weeks. Plus, she's on pain medication. I wouldn't worry just yet."

"Then there's the room."

The way he said it made it sound so ominous.

"She spends most of her time in it but won't say why," he continued. "The only thing in there is a love seat, which she can't currently sit on, and an old turntable with some records."

"Has it always been so bare?"

Austin put his hands on his hips and shook his head. "Funny, I don't remember. The door was always closed the few times I visited. She and Grandpa usually came to Colorado instead."

"Probably has a special meaning. Want me to talk to her?"

Austin exhaled. He looked relieved. "Yes. Please."

This was exactly what she'd hoped to accomplish in coming today but with an added twist. If there was one thing she'd learned from caregiving, it was that no two days were alike.

"Maybe you could keep PJ occupied. Give me some alone time with her."

He nodded, and together they went inside. "She's all the way at the end of the hall. Just follow the music."

That was a good sign. Music could be quite therapeutic, and what Ellie was playing sounded upbeat. It made Vanessa feel like dancing, in fact.

Austin hadn't exaggerated about the room. Must have been the largest in the house. And the emptiest. The door was open, but she knocked on the door frame anyway.

"Ellie? It's Vanessa. PJ and I stopped by to say hi."

The woman visibly perked up. Vanessa walked over and gave her a gentle upper-body hug.

Ellie pointed to the love seat. "Please, make yourself comfy."

Vanessa took a seat on a plush forest-green velvet love seat.

"Where's my favorite little boy?" Ellie asked.

"Playing with your favorite cat," she said.

"He's so adorable. And Tango is pretty cute, too," Ellie said.

A sense of humor. Another good sign.

"I'm crazy about that cat," Ellie continued. "He hasn't taken to Austin yet. Really no point since my grandson needs to get back to living his own life. But the kitty loves me and, obviously, PJ. He was a stray, you know. He was waiting on my doorstep when I returned from Shelton's funeral."

"I hear you suspect that Tango might be your husband."

Ellie laughed. "I wouldn't put it past him."

Vanessa had to laugh, too. This woman was beyond adorable.

"This is a lovely room, by the way." Empty as it was, it had a nice vibe.

"It is, isn't it?" Ellie inhaled for several seconds, as if breathing it in. "Shelton and I called it our apology room."

That made perfect sense, based on what Austin had told her and what she'd suspected. This room had a special meaning.

"Austin tells me you're waiting on an apology from your husband."

"I shouldn't have said anything. Now he's probably worried that I'm losing my mind," Ellie said.

"I think he's just worried in general. You've both been through a lot."

Ellie didn't offer any further explanation.

Vanessa's best guess would be that she wanted Shelton to apologize for leaving her alone. But she would rather know for sure, if only to help her with the emotional healing aspect. Get some closure on whatever happened. Then again, maybe the four-legged reincarnated version would cough up the apology Ellie needed.

They sat in silence and listened to music as Vanessa thought about ways to word the question she needed to ask, but there was something else competing with her thoughts. Another noise. Sounded like crying, and it was getting closer.

Vanessa looked at the doorway just as PJ ran through it and into her arms. Austin wasn't far behind.

"What happened?" Ellie asked Austin, then directed her attention to PJ. "And who are you, by the way?"

PJ was too upset to play along.

Austin put his hands on his hips. "We finally tracked down Tango, but when PJ sat on the ground next to him, the cat hissed at him and ran off."

Vanessa brushed back the hair from PJ's eyes. The face makeup was threatening to run down his cheeks but was holding so far.

"He didn't recognize you, that's all. Once this paint comes off, he'll be back in your lap," Vanessa said.

At that, the tears stopped flowing and PJ sat up straighter.

"I know what would make it all better. Steak fingers and french fries," she continued. Even though that had been her plan for tomorrow for the two of them, it seemed like a pick-me-up was needed now. "Which reminds me—I got some yummy things at the farmers' market, but I left them in my truck. Do you mind helping me with the bag, Austin?"

He locked eyes with her in an unspoken understanding that she had something to tell him. In private.

"Absolutely. We'll be right back," he said to Ellie and PJ.

Once they were out of the house, he asked, "So, what do you think? Did you have a chance to talk to her?"

"I did. I'm not a psychologist, but I think she's in the anger phase of grief. Upset with Shelton because he left her. Except she doesn't seem angry at all. Not even sad. I may be on the verge of getting an answer. How about I stop by tomorrow and try again?"

She hefted the reusable tote out of the car.

He eased it from her hand. "I have another idea. How about I take PJ out for steak fingers and fries? Maybe she'll open up to you without the threat of me barging in or the distraction of your adorable little boy."

That was a fabulous idea. Except this was definitely feeling too...*familial.*

"I don't think cats are allowed at the soda fountain counter. Or zombies," she teased.

"You'd be doing me a favor. I need to pick up a few things anyway."

A favor.

At that, her stomach dropped. Those had been her ex's favorite words, said so often he sounded like a broken record. Especially when he needed time to do "his thing" and put all the family care-taking responsibilities in her lap. The problem was, he never returned those favors.

"I insist on officially hiring you and paying. You're on the clock, as far as I'm concerned."

She breathed an inner sigh of relief. It wasn't because he offered to pay, yet again. Rather, be-cause he was looking at this as a business trans-action instead of a favor.

"I'll take the 'job,' but I'm not going to charge you for my time. Not after everything Ellie did for Grandpa when he hurt his ankle. I'll talk with her and give you my professional opinion. And I can probably come by every day or every other day to check on her and offer you some respite hours. Consider it a repayment for Ellie's care-giving help back when my grandpa needed it."

Austin cocked his head. "What exactly did she do for Vern? She never mentioned it."

"Brought him dinner every day for over a week and visited him almost on the daily."

Austin smiled. "Sounds like her. Still, if you end up spending too much time here, I'll pay you. So, can I take PJ out for steak fingers?" He added a warm smile, and once again, she got bogged down in the mystery of those downturned eyes.

She did feel as though she was on the cusp of getting something important from Ellie that could help. That was what she loved most about her job. And this was officially a job.

"Yes," she said.

Because *no* still wasn't in her caregiver vocabulary, despite her resolve to put it there.

"WHAT IS *THAT*?" PJ stopped swiveling on the diner bar stool long enough to stare at the saucer that the server had placed in front of him—at Austin's secret request, of course. The little boy's expression was priceless.

"It's milk. I figured since you're a cat, you'd prefer that over steak fingers and fries," he said. Also at his request, the server placed a huge plate, stacked extra tall with food, directly in front of Austin.

PJ's eyes widened. "Cats like steak fingers, too," the little boy said.

"They do? Well, that's a relief, because this is way more food than I can eat." Intentionally so—it was three orders combined into one. Vanessa would surely be hungry by the time they returned. He'd have to come up with something else for Ellie, because she wouldn't be interested in this. Her taste for fried foods was practically nonexistent.

Austin unwrapped his silverware and used his fork to transfer one steak finger and a single wedge fry onto the extra plate that the server had placed beneath the main one. Instead of giving PJ the miniature portion, he slid the full plate over, which made the little boy giggle.

Anything to make PJ happy after Tango's harsh rejection at the ranch, even though he couldn't blame the cat. PJ did look a bit scary.

The other customers obviously thought otherwise. They more than made up for the cat's reaction. As soon as Austin's mouth was full, someone would approach them to comment about how cute and realistic his *son* looked. Austin smiled at their assumption and continued to chew his food. PJ didn't correct them either. He would say "thank you," full mouth or not. That suggested that Vanessa was indeed not married, as her ringless finger seemed to suggest. Besides, if she was married, what kind of husband wouldn't be around to help?

He also hoped to win PJ over enough that the little boy would give Austin some insight into his mom. Specifically, whether she'd be open to being a more permanent *paid* caregiver for Ellie. Just long enough for him to get Ellie to agree to moving to the Happy U. He had to get back to Colorado, and soon, to handle a few things that were out of his ranch hands' pay range and ability. He also had to make sure his dad was sticking to their agreement to put a hold on the cutting-horse training until Austin could finish up in Destiny Springs. He was a lot better than his dad when it came to saying no.

Then there was the immediate issue of making sure Ellie's stubbornness didn't hinder her recovery. After her disappearing trick, he knew he'd have to keep a much closer eye on the situation. Besides, Ellie seemed awfully fond of Vanessa, so she couldn't use the excuse that a stranger would be in the house.

Austin was a bit fond of her himself. Miniature portion–sized, of course.

Who am I kidding?

PJ ate the steak fingers and fries with his hands, and Austin followed suit. After he'd finished his one and only piece, PJ grabbed a few more and put them on Austin's plate.

"Here. You can have some of mine," he said.

Austin wasn't sure whether it was unusual for a six-year-old to share, but he was proud of his "son."

"Should we take one back to Tango?" Austin asked.

Even bringing up the cat's name seemed to make the little boy sad.

"He doesn't like me."

"Oh, he more than likes you, PJ. Do you know that he won't even let me pet him? And then you walked through the door, and he won't leave your side. I'd go as far as to say Tango loves you. He just didn't recognize you, like your mom said."

PJ stopped chewing and looked up at him, as if wondering whether to take Austin seriously. Not that he could blame the little boy. Their whole father-"son" lunch date had started with a joke.

The little boy looked back down at his food. "So love does hurt."

Austin nearly fell off his bar stool. The six-year-old had not only processed everything the adults were talking about the other day regarding love, he'd now experienced it on a certain level. That was clear from the fact he'd started to take a bite of a fry, then set it down. What kid did that?

Time to do some damage control.

"It doesn't always hurt, but sometimes it does. The good news is, there's *always* a way to make it better again."

Okay, so maybe he'd overstepped a little. He'd had plenty of hurts that never completely healed, even though he'd tried. In fact, he'd even attempted to change his cowboy DNA to make his ex-wife happy. In PJ's case, the solution was much more likely to work, and it involved changing the little boy back into who he was in the first place.

It would have to work. If Austin could talk Vanessa into helping Ellie regularly, even in a limited capacity, perhaps having PJ around would draw his grandma out of that empty room. Sitting in there alone couldn't be good for her.

Austin swiveled to face the boy.

"Okay, here's the plan on winning Tango back. First, we take a steak finger and a fry to give to him. We'll also take that paint off your face so he won't be scared of you."

"'Cause he loves me for who I am and doesn't want me to be a cat, too?"

The little boy kept diving deeper into that ocean. Austin was beginning to wonder which one of them had the relationship experience.

"I couldn't have said it better myself, PJ."

The little boy picked up the fry he'd abandoned a few minutes ago and took a huge bite. "What if it doesn't work?" he asked, mouth still partially full.

Even though this outing had served up some lessons learned about love, he wasn't about to give PJ a lesson in etiquette. Wasn't his place. Besides, he knew plenty of adults who still talked with their mouths full. But just because he didn't want to *tell* PJ it wasn't a good thing to do, that didn't mean he couldn't *show* him.

Still facing PJ, Austin took a bite out of the biggest wedge fry on the plate and answered while chewing.

"I thought of that. We need a backup plan, and I know just where to look."

PJ giggled. "I see your food!"

Austin swallowed. "Oh, yeah. People shouldn't talk with their mouths full, should they? Thanks for reminding me. Cats, on the other hand, can do anything they want."

The server came back around just in time. Austin was eager to see if his theory about the steak finger was going to work.

"We're ready for our check and a to-go box," Austin said.

"Yes, sir."

Although the tab was swiftly settled, he still had a couple of things lingering on his shopping list. The convenience store section would hopefully have what he needed.

First, he located the cosmetics aisle and found some face wipes.

"Are those for Mommy?" PJ asked.

"No, they're for you. We're going to turn you back into a human as soon as we get out to the truck so Tango will recognize you again."

They then wandered over to the pet toy aisle. He picked up a stick with some yellow-and-green feathers tied to the end of it, as well as a pink-and-orange one.

"What are those?" PJ asked.

"Our backup plan for Tango. Since you're still a cat, too, which do you think he'd like best?"

PJ studied the options and selected the yellow-and-green one.

"Perfect! Looks like we're all done here," Austin said as he led them in the direction of the checkout.

"What if he still doesn't love me again?" PJ asked of the backup plan.

"Then we keep trying until he does. As many days or months or years as it takes."

"What if Tango doesn't want to go with me and Mommy back home to Cheyenne?"

Austin stopped in his tracks. So that was what she meant by limited availability. He'd assumed this whole time that she lived here with Vern, which he found beyond charming. Why else would she have offered to help at all?

Then again, he knew better than to assume anything. Life had already taught him that lesson. And he'd just set himself up to fail.

PJ was still looking up at him for an answer that was too hurtful to contemplate saying out loud. His heart ached even thinking about it. But that was nothing compared to the pain this little boy was going to feel over having to leave Tango behind. PJ was already almost as attached to that cat as Ellie was.

A certain big boy's heart wasn't going to fare much better. Austin had already been looking forward to the idea of seeing Vanessa more often, even though he had no plans of taking it beyond a working relationship. Hoped, perhaps, if he was honest about it. Now he didn't even have that much.

"Can you take a picture and send it to my friends Noah and Grayson in Cheyenne before I'm not a cat anymore?" PJ asked.

Austin smiled to himself. Hopefully taking the pictures would steer PJ's thoughts away from the kitty he'd have to leave behind and back to the friends who awaited him. He also wanted a photo of this moment for himself because this little boy was too cute for words.

"I bet you miss your friends, huh?" Austin asked.

PJ nodded and explained as Austin snapped a few pictures with his phone. "I miss them a *lot*. I like Noah best but don't tell Grayson. But Max is my best friend here. I wish I could take him back home, too, and then we could all go to the same school. But our mommies probably won't let us."

Austin had to bite his lip to keep from giggling. "Yeah, probably not. When are you and your mommy going back?"

"I dunno, but not too long 'cause she has to open her store."

Store? "Is she opening a business?"

PJ nodded.

Austin exhaled. His and PJ's vulnerable hearts

weren't the only problem. There were his own ranch issues to consider. And, most important, getting Ellie the care she needed.

There was only one thing he could do in the moment. And the solution was in aisle four.

"I need to get one more item. Wanna help me pick it out?"

The boy followed him until he reached the final destination for this little outing.

"Has to be a box from this row." Austin pointed to the full-size toothpastes.

PJ considered the options and picked out the minty fresh gel in the blue box.

"Better grab two," Austin said.

Looks like I'm gonna be here for a while.

CHAPTER FOUR

SO MUCH FOR finding out why Ellie's husband owed her an apology.

Instead, Vanessa and her new client spent nearly an hour listening to old records, on what looked to be the same kind of turntable that her grandpa Vern had.

It seemed to make the woman so happy. Vanessa didn't want to bring down the mood by asking anything about any fights the couple used to have. Or even a purpose this big, empty room may have served at some point. Such conversations would likely require a delicate touch.

Vanessa stared at the barely touched snack tray she had fixed for Ellie from the fresh items she'd brought from the farmers' market. Not a bad spread, if she did say so herself. Half a BLT sandwich using the fresh bread and heirloom tomatoes and a few leaves from the head of iceberg lettuce from the market and some bacon she'd found in the fridge. Plus, a charcuterie sampling of cheese squares and sausage medallions.

Ellie hadn't sampled anything except for a few of the cheese cubes. Another possible challenge Austin may be facing: getting her to eat enough. Very common and expected, yet concerning and frustrating for the caregiver.

As Andy Williams sang "Moon River," Vanessa searched for possible topics of discussion within the barren room. Although she didn't know much about architecture, this space must have been added on at some point. Such a large rectangular area tacked onto the back of the home. The wide-plank hardwoods were darker than their narrower counterparts throughout the rest of the house. The room may have been an outside deck or patio that was closed in. It even had a feel that it was here against its will. Yet the view from the floor-to-ceiling windows of the snowcaps in the distance was absolutely stunning.

Vanessa stood, took the finished album off the turntable and returned it to its sleeve. They needed to talk. Even though it threatened to bring up some painful memories, it might reveal something important.

"How long have you lived in this house, Ellie?"

Thankfully, the woman smiled as though the topic wasn't a painful one. "Ever since my wedding night. And it's the only place I'd ever want to live."

Okay, so no bad memories here. At least, nothing bad enough to make her want to leave. This was a good sign.

She sat back down on the love seat.

"I grew up in a house very much like this. Except ours didn't have an apology room. No empty ones either. Our rooms were full of people," she said, intentionally leaving out the part about not wanting to return to that lifestyle.

Vanessa looked to Ellie to gauge whether her prompt was going to work.

Nothing but a coy smile in return as she remained focused on some undetermined point, which made Vanessa even more curious.

"I cared for my sick mama and her parents—my grandparents—while my dad single-handedly took care of the ranch," she continued. Perhaps if she opened up, Ellie would do the same.

At that, Ellie looked at her full-on. "Oh, my. That's a lot of responsibility for a young lady."

"I'm glad I was there to help," Vanessa said.

It was true. She just wished she'd had more time with friends her own age. Then again, that still hadn't happened, had it? She'd been so busy getting her business going, she'd hardly had the time to nurture healthy friendships. And she wasn't about to sacrifice what precious little PJ time she could scrape together. Not for anyone.

But, hopefully, once the two of them got back

to Cheyenne and all the grand-opening kinks had been unkinked, there would be more time for all of that.

"I suspect that if things were different, Austin would insist on moving in here with me, judging by the way he coddles me. But I'll be my old self again very soon. I can feel it in these bones of mine."

It was still too soon for Vanessa to wholeheartedly agree, but she'd be willing to place a small bet on it being true, for now.

Ellie finally picked up the BLT and took a delicate bite. Then another.

Vanessa breathed a private sigh of relief that she had an appetite after all. At the same time, her own stomach growled.

The woman finished chewing, then swallowed. "I heard that, young lady. I'm gonna get out of this chair and make you a proper meal. What would you like?"

At least her hearing is intact.

Then the hunger pain tightened into a different kind of knot. Vanessa was beginning to *really like* this woman, which meant this was turning more personal than she'd intended. And so quickly.

At the same time, how long had it been since anyone cooked for her? The answer: too long ago to remember. But it was too soon for Ellie to do the kind of bending or twisting required to fix anything to eat. Opening the refrigerator and reaching for a prepared meal or snack was all Vanessa would feel comfortable encouraging.

With PJ's meal currently being taken care of, Vanessa could polish off whatever leftovers were in Vern's fridge when they got to the house. Then she would cook him a fresh dinner.

But Ellie's promise obviously wasn't an idle one. She rose from the chair. Vanessa stood and stretched, then held the walker in place, even though she'd noticed Ellie had been good about locking the brakes for stability. Vanessa carried the plate with the remaining food.

"You'll do no such thing. But a little walking will do us both some good," Vanessa said as they proceeded down the hall to the front of the house.

"What's your favorite food?" Ellie asked.

Vanessa was almost afraid to answer. The woman might take off for the kitchen.

"Cheese, which is sounding pretty good about now. I'll cut up some extra cubes of the sharp cheddar and add them to the plate for us to share once we sit back down," she said, to play it safe.

Ellie gave her a look that said Vanessa wasn't getting out of this without confessing.

"Okay. Chili con queso dip. With the works. Pico de gallo, fresh chopped jalapeños, ground beef, avocado slices. The chunkier and spicier, the better."

There. That was something Ellie couldn't try to cook for her because none of those ingredients were in the kitchen, that Vanessa could recall. And she knew the woman was much too smart to sneak out and try to drive to the market in her condition.

"I can manage that as soon as my caregiver gives me permission," Ellie said.

"Is that what Austin told you I'd be?" she asked. They'd only loosely defined her role between themselves before he left.

"No, but I know that's what you do as a career. And, I assume, as a passion. And I know he worries far too much about me being alone at the moment."

Vanessa had to smile. She'd actually forgotten she was there in a caregiving capacity. These types of moments were her favorite part of the job.

"Austin isn't paying me. I'm here because I want to be," she said. Unfortunately, it was the truth, even though there were other places she'd planned to be and would enjoy equally as much. Such as eating steak fingers with her son. Or at home, attending to all the finishing touches related to the grand opening of her business.

"I'll still wait until you give me permission to

make that queso. I may be stubborn most of the time, but I'm patient when it counts."

"That's good to hear. It's a deal," Vanessa said. She helped Ellie settle into the ladder-back chair. "How would you feel if Austin actually did want to move in?"

The woman looked surprised, but not necessarily in a good way.

"Why? Do you know something I don't know?" Ellie asked.

Vanessa blinked. She was reminded of an awkward position she'd been in before with her clients and their families. Being confided in by opposing sides and looked to for support by each of them. Thankfully, this was an easy one to answer because she didn't know anything. With any luck, it would stay that way.

"Not at all. Y'all seem so close, though. I can't imagine why he wouldn't want to live here," Vanessa said.

Ellie laughed. "Just between us, I'd rather not find out. I love my grandson more than anything, and he's gone above and beyond to help with the ranch. But I want him to live his own life. And find the kind of love I found with Shelton. That's hard to do when you're a little too worried about Grandma. I'll be just fine."

That's the spirit.

"I suspect you will. But until then, let us help.

The faster you heal, the faster Austin and I will be out of your hair."

It was a bold promise to make, but if Ellie did as the doctors instructed and let people assist her when necessary, Vanessa was reasonably sure it could happen. Especially after the woman didn't insist on getting up and fixing her something to eat.

She had no sooner draped a throw blanket over Ellie's lap when PJ burst through the front door. The little boy glanced around the room, then jetted down the hall as if he owned the place. He looked like his cute little human self again. Austin had done a commendable job removing the cat makeup. She knew from experience that removing face paint required patience and plenty of wipes or soap and water.

Austin wasn't far behind. He was carrying a to-go box, shaking his head and smiling as he closed the door behind him.

"I thought PJ was going to escape the car seat, jump out of the truck and outrun me to get here," he said.

"He's crazy about that cat," Vanessa said.

Although once she said it, she realized the long-term implications. They'd have to leave Tango behind, along with a little piece of PJ's heart. In the meantime, was it better to bring her son over here less often or more? Although she hadn't committed to coming over at any particular time or on any certain day, she still wanted to help. It might actually be good that they didn't have a formal paid arrangement right now. She and PJ could pop in but leave if everything was okay.

Austin handed the box to Vanessa. "I ordered a serving for you, plus we had leftovers. I figured you'd be hungry by now."

Her breath hitched at the kindness of the gesture. Sure, it wasn't quite the same as having someone cook for her, but it took a close second.

She lifted the lid. "Steak fingers and fries." As she'd suspected. And hoped for. Just as promptly, she closed the lid and tried to hand it back to him. "You keep this. It will be a convenient meal for you and Ellie to heat up."

When Austin refused to take it, she swiveled to face Ellie.

"You enjoy it. I'm still working on this delicious BLT," the woman insisted, picking up the remainder of the sandwich that Vanessa had brought back from the other room and finishing it off in a couple of big bites.

"The only fried food Grandma will eat is something I can't pronounce. And she won't tell me what it means either. Doesn't want me to go to the trouble of trying to make it," he said.

"Karaage," Ellie said, then served up that coy

smile Vanessa was beginning to recognize all too well.

Vanessa wasn't familiar with the dish, but anything would taste good to her right now. The aroma of steak fingers and fries was making her mouth water and her stomach turn cartwheels.

"Okay, then. I'll take this with me and share it with all the Fraser men. I'm pretty sure PJ won't turn down these particular leftovers," Vanessa said.

She set the box on a side table rather than taking it to the refrigerator. She needed to get back to the house and back to dealing with the bingo supply company and the missing delivery. She'd otherwise ask her assistant, Beth, to handle such a thing. But the woman was dealing with the painters and plumbers—the latter of which was the higher priority and required on-site supervision.

Luckily, there were still enough tasks Vanessa could handle remotely and she wouldn't have to make an emergency trip to Cheyenne.

They'd negotiated a great lease deal on the office space, but that was because it needed some work. Vanessa's fault. She was so focused on *location location location*—making sure it was situated in a central area that was convenient for all her clients—that she'd shortchanged her and Beth's time to make it functional and pretty.

PJ came back into the room with a reluctant cat in his arms, which was going to make this even harder.

"Tango loves me again," the little boy said.

"He never stopped," Austin said. "All you have to do is be yourself. Trying to be someone you're not never works."

Such wise words. Like something a good father would say.

Where did that come from?

Perhaps his words were too wise. He lowered his chin and seemed to study the floor. Vanessa suspected that last sentence had more to do with his own history than with trying to educate PJ on the ways of love. Or perhaps she was projecting.

In her experience, being something you actually *were* didn't always work out either.

Especially when that something was a caregiver.

"FIND OUT ANYTHING, Sherlock Holmes?" Austin asked as he rolled up the sleeves of his flannel work shirt and washed the nominal crumbs off the plate.

Although he couldn't speak for Vanessa, it seemed as though they were both pleased that Ellie had polished off whatever was on it.

One thing was for sure: neither Vanessa nor Ellie had any business doing the dishes or even helping him with the task. This was simply a natural way for him and Vanessa to have a few moments away from Ellie to discuss any findings, and they both seemed to realize it.

In the meantime, PJ and Tango were doing an excellent job of keeping his grandma entertained in the other room, and all it involved was the little boy and the feline being themselves, 100 percent, even though he was sure Ellie couldn't wait to have the cat back on her own lap.

Vanessa smiled and shook her head. "Not as much as I would have liked. Such as why she calls it the apology room. Although I didn't come right out and ask, I came up with an obvious opportunity for her to elaborate, which didn't work. She's being super coy about it."

Austin hadn't heard anything from Ellie about an apology room, but he had to laugh. "She does that a lot, even when you ask her outright about something."

Except his grandma usually didn't play coy with strangers. If anything, the woman didn't mince words. Which must have meant she liked and trusted Vanessa.

"Whatever that room means to her, I can tell she has no desire to abandon it. I'm not sure whether you'll think this is good news or bad, but she doesn't want you to move in with her," Vanessa said.

Austin nearly dropped the plate. Had he heard her correctly? Where had that even come from?

His discomfort must have been a little too obvious, because she eased the dish from his loose grip and proceeded to dry it while giving him a curious side glance. The stern yet gentle combination temporarily distracted him. It comforted him in one way but not in another. She wasn't his caregiver. But he couldn't say he minded that she'd insisted on helping him figure out some of the more cryptic things his grandma was saying or doing. This being the strangest.

Moving in with his grandma hadn't been a remote consideration. But it was similar enough to his own plan of having *her* move in with him and his dad to be a little unsettling. So much for thinking that convincing her to sell the ranch wasn't going to be difficult. If anything, it just got harder.

"Not that she doesn't appreciate you," Vanessa continued. "She talked about all the work you're doing around the ranch. I suspect she'd like to help you with it, but thankfully she seems to realize that isn't a good idea. At least, not for now."

"Ah, some good news," he couldn't help but say. No doubt she'd pick up on the sarcasm.

"Don't get too excited. If she's anything like my grandpa or any of my senior clients in Cheyenne, she'll probably try to do too much, too soon anyway. If only to keep from inconveniencing someone else. Especially a loved one. Don't be surprised if you find some burned cookware stashed away in a strange place."

Austin's anxiety level spiked at the thought. He drew in a deep breath, then exhaled. Couldn't help himself. Apparently, he'd been a little too audible about it, because Vanessa zeroed in on him as she handed back the dry plate. He opened the appropriate cabinet and tucked it away.

"Then I suppose the good news for Grandma is I have no intention of moving in with her. That's the last thing I intend to do," he said when he had no other choice than to meet her gaze.

It wasn't a lie, even though it wasn't the whole truth. He was privately hoping for an eventual ally in Vanessa. Someone to help Ellie realize that living alone at her age wasn't the best idea. But that was looking less promising by the minute.

"That's good to hear. It's important that she retain her independence but as safely as possible. Especially after everything that has happened the past couple of weeks. Getting back to normal and being able to control what she can is healthy, emotionally," Vanessa said, positioning the final nail of the proverbial coffin.

No use arguing with a professional caregiver who had been around the elderly a lot longer than he had. Didn't mean he was going to assist with hammering it home.

Austin smiled and shook his head. "I'm trying to make it fun and safe for her. But she *is* over eighty." *And fresh out of surgery.*

Vanessa's expression softened. She touched him on the arm, and his anxiety melted away.

"You're doing a wonderful job. But you do know that eighty is the new sixty, don't you? When I'm her age, I'll still want to make my own choices if I'm mentally capable of doing so, as I suspect Ellie is. And have my own life. No reason for you to feel like you carry the decision-making burden along with all the consequences." She added a comforting smile.

Was he being too overprotective? Reassuring touches and professional caregiving insight notwithstanding, he didn't think so. But there were things to consider. If not now—which he wasn't ready to concede, although her reassurances were working—then sometime in the near future.

"How do you know when it's time…?" Austin couldn't finish his own sentence.

"To make decisions *for* someone?" Vanessa asked.

He nodded.

Vanessa turned around, leaned against the counter and crossed her ankles. That was when a different kind of thought galloped across his mind. For some reason, those black boots of hers didn't look like something a caregiver would wear. Or a cowgirl. They were certainly a world away from the scrubs and nurse's shoes the therapist wore over there every day. Neither was the flowy skirt paired with a fitted long-sleeved basic T-shirt. Vanessa was understated, feminine and yet no-nonsense all rolled into one. Not that he thought he had her figured out, but all of a sudden, he was more intrigued than ever about who this woman really was.

"Every situation is unique. Sure, there are unmistakable signs. But short of that, on some level, you just know," she said.

He wanted to add, *Like you* just know *when you really like the caregiver who won't accept your money to take care of your grandma, even though you barely know each other?*

"How about I bring my laptop over tomorrow, get some work done here and keep an eye on Ellie while you do ranch stuff? She told me you need to get back to Colorado soon, and something tells me you aren't going to leave until all the loose ends are tied up here. PJ can play with Tango and keep Ellie company. It could be a win-win situation for all of us."

"That's an awful lot to ask."

"Just trying to pay off Grandpa's debt to Ellie before I leave," she said with a wink. Part of him loved that she wouldn't accept payment because of what his grandma had done. The other part of him insisted she totally deserved it.

"What about Vern?" he asked.

"Grandpa is doing great. His fiancée, Sylvie, makes sure of it. Plus, I think he's getting tired of my being around all the time."

Austin shook his head and smiled at the ridiculousness of what she'd said.

"How could anyone get tired of you?" As soon as the question escaped his lips, he realized how it sounded. He didn't even know her well enough to reach such a conclusion.

Yet on some level, he just knew.

CHAPTER FIVE

"BREAKFAST OF ANGELS," Vanessa said, then laughed under her breath as she took a big bite of a warmed-up steak finger and washed it down with a sip of hot green tea.

Although she'd fully intended to hang up her wings, which had taken her so many miles from client to client over her professional lifetime, she couldn't seem to help herself when it came to Ellie. It had been her plan to maintain proximity to the woman while keeping her own emotional distance miles away from the whole Cassidy clan. But Austin's comment—*How could anyone get tired of you?*—tugged at her heart. And it was still tugging. That, combined with witnessing the kind and effortless way he communicated with PJ, was making her whole plan weak at the pro-verbial knees.

Vern came inside carrying a large crate of eggs.

"I hope that isn't all you're having for breakfast," he said as he seemed to contemplate the best place to make the drop.

She was tempted to say that a steak finger was more than she usually ate, but that would only invite some unwanted advice from her grandfather.

"It's not. I'm going to have one of your pecan pralines, too," she said.

Vern looked at her sideways, then shook his head, set the crate on the kitchen counter and patted the side. "I've got plenty of these. You're welcome to have some."

"Thanks, Grandpa, but I'm fine. PJ had eggs this morning, though. He wanted hard-boiled but I managed to mess them up, so I ended up making him scrambled instead."

As I do every time.

"Well, if you're not gonna eat 'em, I need you to do me a huge favor," he said.

There was that word again. *Favor.* It always made her spine stiffen, except when it came from her grandpa. When he asked for one, he always repaid it tenfold.

"Anything for you," she said.

"I need you to take a dozen of these beauties over to Ellie's house this morning, if you don't mind making a trip. This back of mine is bothering me a little."

The way he rubbed it in such an exaggerated way while studying her expression suggested otherwise. She knew what he looked like when he was in pain, and this wasn't it. What was he up to?

"In that case, there's not a chance I'm leaving. I'm going to stay here and take care of you for as long as it takes," she said, calling his bluff.

He stopped rubbing, then stood up straighter. Even added a stretch.

"Oh, that's not necessary. That pain medicine is kickin' in as we speak. I can get around, but I don't wanna overdo it, is all. Sylvie will be over soon. She doesn't mind taking care of me."

Vern retrieved an empty egg carton from a stack inside one of the kitchen cabinets and loaded it up for her.

"If you say so. What's the occasion?" Ellie's ranch wasn't on his usual delivery route. He pretty much donated eggs to the Hideaway B and B and to Nash Buchanan over at Buck Stops Ranch, but that was it.

"I already eat too many myself. And with you and PJ leaving soon, I reckon I'll have extras. Don't want 'em to go to waste. I figure this could be a regular delivery."

Vanessa contemplated her response. She hadn't told him about her plans to spend a little extra time with Austin and Ellie anyway. She'd come straight home yesterday, followed up with the bingo supply distributor, secured a new delivery with extra layers of tracking and updated her expenditure spreadsheet. The latter was usually like candy for her inner nerd. Except this time it wasn't balancing. Hopefully she'd be able to figure that out today while at Ellie's since PJ would be occupied. But she could use Vern's request to her advantage.

"If I *do* take them, that means you'll owe me a favor in return," she said.

Vern cast her a perplexed look. Even put both hands on his hips.

"What? You don't think that's fair?" she asked.

"Oh, it's fair. It's just that I've never heard you ask anyone for a favor, much less demand one. Certainly never asked one of me."

Vanessa had to think about it, but he was right. Asking favors always felt selfish, especially when it was something she could handle herself. Maybe that halo of hers really was removable.

"But the answer is yes. Of course. What do *you* need?" he continued.

That was a good question. What she really needed, he couldn't give her: objectivity with this new caregiving arrangement. Today would be excellent practice for that, however. The weather outside was forecast to be perfect. Mild and sunny. Austin would be able to get some work done on the ranch, which would mean one less distraction for her.

"Nothing at the moment."

PJ ran down the stairs and into the kitchen, fully dressed. Usually, she'd help pick out his outfit and let him handle it from there. Today, he wanted to do it himself after cleaning his breakfast plate without even being prompted. He selected jeans, a little flannel button-down and his cowboy boots.

"Mommy! Can we go see Tango now?"

Right on time. She'd told Austin and Ellie that they'd be there around nine. Plus, it further confirmed that this offer of hers was time well spent because it put a smile on her little boy's face.

"Tango? Who might that be?" Vern asked.

"Miss Ellie's cat," PJ said, officially outing his mommy.

Vern squinted and looked at her. "So you're going back over there anyway, huh?"

"I am. I offered to work from there for a while and keep an eye on Ellie while Austin takes care of ranch stuff. Don't read anything into it, Grandpa." Might help if she told him the whole story—how she was doing this under the guise of working off Vern's debt—but she was quite sure her grandpa wouldn't approve of her working without pay.

"Who, me?" Vern smiled. "Why does Ellie need to be watched?"

"She's recovering from hip replacement surgery."

Vern rubbed his chin. "Well, I'll be. Surprised I hadn't heard about it."

Vanessa was a bit surprised that he was surprised. Nothing stayed a secret for very long in Destiny Springs.

"Sylvie and I will have to drop by for a visit sometime," he continued.

"I bet she'd enjoy that." The more friends who were around to check on Ellie, the safer she'd remain. It would definitely make Vanessa feel better, being so far away.

Vanessa polished off the remainder of the steak finger and finished her tea. She went to the bathroom and brushed her teeth, then retrieved her handbag and laptop from the bedroom. Once back in the kitchen, she handed PJ the carton of eggs that Vern had assembled.

"I know you'll be extra gentle with these, so I would like for you to carry them, if you don't mind. They're some eggs for Miss Ellie. From Grandpa," she said, stressing the last two words to let Vern know she was onto him.

PJ held the carton out and away from his body and took slow steps toward the door.

"We'll be back later. Call me if there's any emergency here," she said to Vern.

"Have fun today," Vern said, directing the comment to PJ first, then looking back at her without confirming.

Not that she expected him to. That was one thing about Vern. If he didn't intend on keeping a promise, he wouldn't make it in the first place.

"Okay?" she reiterated.

As soon as she said it, she realized she was practicing the opposite of what she tried to preach. To *not* micromanage loved ones of a certain age. Or worse, treat them like a child. In her experience, most of them didn't appreciate it. She didn't blame them one bit.

"I'll call if there's an emergency here that Sylvie and I can't handle."

"Fair enough." She gave Vern a kiss on the cheek.

PJ was a wiggle worm all the way to Ellie's house, and her previous concerns about his attachment to Tango rose to the surface.

"How would you feel about going to the B and B and playing with Max tomorrow?" she asked, hoping that spending time with his best friend would be the thing to divert some of his attention away from the cat.

The little boy seemed to think about it. "That would be fun. Can I take Tango? Max would like him, too, and he would probably like Max."

"True, but Max's dog would probably be jealous." She stopped short of suggesting that Max come to Ellie's. If that happened, she'd have two little ones to keep an eye on, because that particular duo always went looking for trouble. She'd even caught them investigating the barn where her grandpa kept his mechanical bull. Definitely not a toy.

"Plus, Miss Ellie really needs the company while she recovers from her surgery," she continued, even though the cat wasn't yet allowed on the woman's lap.

"Okay," he said, but not with the same enthusiasm as before.

She was sure that, once he and Max started playing, he'd forget about Tango as quickly as the cat had made him forget about zombies. It had been a nice reprieve for her. Except her little zombie might come back to life at the B and B.

Zombies, she could deal with. A broken heart from leaving a beloved animal behind, though…

Once they got parked, she helped PJ out of the car seat and handed him the egg carton. It would be better if he dropped those rather than her laptop. It would also prevent PJ from busting through the door without knocking.

The door swung wide open anyway as soon as they started up the porch steps.

"These are for you and Miss Ellie." PJ held out the carton, which Austin took off the little boy's hands. Austin's *thank you* got lost in the dust that PJ's cowboy boots kicked up as he disappeared inside.

"Need any help with that?" he asked, nodding to her laptop case as she walked past him and over the threshold.

"Only if you're good at finding missing numbers in my spreadsheet," she said.

"You're out of luck there. Grandma is good with 'em, though. Her checkbook is balanced to the penny. I paid a few bills for her right after the surgery and was pleasantly surprised. Now she says she's ready to pay them herself again."

"I consider that a good thing." It further confirmed what she suspected about Ellie's mental state. At least that didn't appear to be a concern when it came to her living independently.

She'd barely set down her laptop when PJ came running back down the hall.

"Tango is asleep with Miss Ellie."

Vanessa and Austin flashed each other the same look, then headed down the hall with PJ on their heels.

Fortunately, the cat was curled up on the plush velvet love seat instead of Ellie's lap, and the woman was safely situated in her chair, fully awake. No music this time, but they'd gone through all the albums yesterday, so maybe it was too soon to re-play them.

When Ellie realized she was being observed, she put an index finger to her lips and pointed to Tango.

Austin turned and headed back toward the den. Vanessa grabbed PJ's hand and they followed. So much for keeping her little boy occupied while she got some work done. She hadn't thought to bring any extra games or toys or books. But that gave her an idea.

"PJ, how would you feel about spending the time with Max this morning rather than tomorrow since Tango is sleeping? I'll have to check with Becca and Cody first, of course," she said.

The little boy shrugged.

Austin seemed to be evaluating the situation instead of doing whatever he needed to be doing outside.

Just as well that he was still there, since she might have to leave for a bit. Vanessa speed-dialed the B and B. Fortunately, Becca answered.

"PJ wants to know if Max is available for an early playdate today," Vanessa said.

"Oh, no! I'm sorry. He's at Hailey's, helping with a couple of trail rides. Might do the same tomorrow, but he's available the day after. Or maybe PJ could go on a ride today if there are any openings."

Vanessa had temporarily forgotten that Max helped colead the trail rides at Sunrise Stables. The little boy was only six years old. She had trouble wrapping her mind around the fact that he had a job. Yet she'd had one of those, as well, at a too-young-to-officially-work age, taking care of her mom and grandparents.

What was still fresh in her memory was PJ falling off his horse on one of the trail rides earlier in the year and breaking his arm. She wasn't going to let that happen again. Not now. She didn't need any more surprises or detours…at least, not until she was situated in her new office.

And in my new life.

She smiled at the thought. Even with all the frantic, last-minute details, her dream was finally taking its final shape.

All the more reason to plan at least a few more playdates for the boys, but in advance.

"Let's plan on later this week," she said, and Becca agreed.

Vanessa put away her phone and looked at Austin, who was strangely interested in this whole dilemma. She shrugged and sighed. It also made her think that she would be in this same type of scenario when PJ wasn't in school. That would require remote work rather than going into the office, unless she took him to the office or could find a good babysitter.

However, if she didn't get some work done here, and soon, there wouldn't be an office or business to go into. Perhaps an overstatement, but she wanted to get the stress over and done with so that she could enjoy the fruits of her labor at the grand opening.

"Looks like you'll have to see Max another day," she said to PJ. "But I'm sure Tango will wake up soon and y'all can play. Until then, I have some games on my computer. Or you can video chat with Noah or Grayson back home."

She could use the time to call her assistant and make sure they weren't dropping the ball on something important. Fortunately, Beth was an expert task juggler.

PJ nodded, and she proceeded to set up the laptop at the dining table. Austin, however, still hadn't budged.

"What about those numbers you mentioned?" he asked.

She shrugged. "It will get done. I'll figure it out."

Austin tapped his index finger against his lips as if evaluating the situation. If he didn't get moving, neither of them was going to get any work done today. Finally, he spoke. Only, he said the last thing she wanted to hear from him, of all people—much less at this moment. In fact, it made her spine stiffen and her heart tank.

"Vanessa, I need a favor."

AUSTIN RECOGNIZED VANESSA'S sharp inhalation as anxiety. Been there himself too many times over the past few weeks. So much for making this a playful way to win points with her. And just when he needed an ally in convincing Ellie to move to Colorado.

She exhaled, pushed her shoulders back and stood taller. "I need to hear what you have in mind before I commit."

"Understood. Some of the fence that surrounds the property needs mending. I could sure use a certain little cowboy's help. If you can spare him for a few hours, that is."

She cocked her head and stared as if trying to decide who was doing whom the favor. Little did she know, he'd benefit more than she would. He hoped to have a son of his own one day, and he could use the practice. A daughter, too. At least one of each, if only he had a say in it. The Happy U had too many bedrooms and not enough family.

"I don't know. That's a lot to ask. But whatever PJ wants," she said, without blinking or smiling.

Now he was the one who felt the need to cock his head.

"I realize that. I'd owe you one," he offered, just in case she really didn't want to let PJ help. "What do you think, PJ? Wanna help me out? It's a beautiful morning. We get to ride around on the Gator."

PJ's little jaw dropped. "Wow! An alligator? Will it bite me, though?"

"Not this kind of gator. This one has wheels instead of legs."

The little boy perked up instantly. He'd seemed a little down because his furry friend was too busy snoozing to play.

He looked to his mommy. "Can I?"

"As long as it isn't a horse, you may," she said.

That took Austin a bit by surprise. Although they hadn't really talked about their lifestyle and hobbies, he'd made some assumptions.

"Then it's settled. I'll have my phone with me, in case you need us back or want to check in. Follow me, young man."

PJ did one better than that. He slipped his little hand into Austin's, sending a jolt of warmth shooting up his arm and wrapping around his heart.

He glanced back at Vanessa.

Still no smile, but she mouthed, *Thank you.*

Austin tipped his hat and closed the door. Hand in hand, they walked around to the back of the house and opened one of the barn doors. Tucked inside was the utility vehicle. He grabbed all the tools they'd need while PJ looked on, then got the little boy belted in.

"So, what we're looking for is any break in the wire," Austin said as they slow-crawled as close to the fence line as possible. He spotted a place about a quarter of a mile down but wanted to see if PJ would notice.

The little boy didn't disappoint. He extended his arm and pointed his finger to the general area. "Is that one?"

"Good eye, PJ," he said, which made the little cowboy grin.

He put the Gator in Park, turned off the motor and helped PJ get out of the vehicle safely.

It was the perfect place to start, too. A simple break that wouldn't require a major rework. He knew of at least one of those much farther down. With this one, he could find out how good this idea of his was, and whether PJ would get too bored and restless to help with the others.

"If you don't have cows or horses, why do you have to have a fence?" PJ asked.

"That is an excellent observation." Austin retrieved his gloves, the fencing pliers and the roll of barbed wire, and set the items on the ground. He fished out a spare pair of gloves from the toolbox and handed them to PJ. "Here. Put these on."

PJ struggled with the gloves, which were much too large. Not that Austin intended to let the little guy do any work that would require them, but it was part of the whole experience he wanted to share.

"Wyoming is what's called a fence-out state, meaning if I don't want other people's livestock on the property, I have to fence them out," Austin explained.

"But won't they get hungry?"

"Definitely, but they can go back to their own ranch to eat."

"'Cause you have to adopt them as pets if you feed them."

Austin had to laugh. "Something like that."

He located one end of the broken wire. "Okay, PJ, I need for you to hand me the fencing pliers. Can you guess which tool that is?"

PJ took a long time deciding. The little boy was so serious. He finally pointed to one of the items.

"Good guess, but that's a fence stretcher. We'll use that to tighten some loose wires, if we come across any."

PJ then pointed to the correct tool.

"Perfect! Now, if you don't mind, please hand them to me and watch closely," Austin said.

The little boy couldn't seem to get close enough. Austin had no idea it would be this interesting for PJ. Austin made a loop with one of the broken ends, held it with the pliers, then twisted it back on itself, leaving a loop.

"Can you find the other broken end?" Austin asked.

PJ looked and looked, and finally found it.

"Excellent eye. Those can be hard to find. If

you don't mind, I'll trade you that loose end for the one I just worked with."

It took a few seconds, but PJ was able to grasp the piece of wire, despite the cumbersome gloves, and held on to it as if it were one of those eggs he'd helped carry this morning. Austin ran the end through the loop, then went through the same process of twisting the wire onto itself until the pieces were securely locked together.

"Okay, you can let go," Austin said.

"That's cool! It's like they're holding hands."

Austin hadn't thought of it that way, but it kind of did look like that. "We're all done here. Want to find some loose wire and I can show you how to use the fence stretcher?"

PJ nodded enthusiastically.

Yep. If he ever had a son, he wanted one just like this little dude.

He tried to swallow back an unexpected thought. Not "just like," because PJ was one of a kind. He'd want him to be *this* little guy. Austin had no business even imagining such a thing, but who could blame him?

Once back in the Gator, he tried to think of a way to approach the subject of horses, because Vanessa's warning about them was also a warning to his heart not to proceed down a certain path. He couldn't imagine a relationship with someone who didn't love horses. He'd tested that once with his first wife, and it didn't end well.

Not that his heart was inclined to listen to reason.

"How do you like riding in the Gator?" Austin asked.

"It's fun," PJ said.

"I think so, too. I like riding horses more, though. You ever been on one?"

"One time. I fell off and broke my arm in half. Mommy doesn't want me to ride anymore."

That explained Vanessa's comment. Then there was the tried-and-true saying about getting right back on, but he wasn't about to play devil's advocate.

"Does your mom ride horses?" he asked.

PJ shrugged. "I don't know. I think she might be scared, but I'm not anymore."

"How does your arm feel now?" Austin asked.

"Like a normal arm, but it felt like a zombie arm after I broke it."

At that, Austin had to laugh. "I know you're not scared of horses, but do you like them?"

"I liked that horse a lot. It just didn't like me."

"I seriously doubt that. I've fallen off a horse many times, but all of mine love me. You know who doesn't love me? Tango."

PJ seemed to study him.

"But I'm not giving up. I'll win him over eventually," Austin continued.

He came to a stop at the area of fence in need of repair.

"See how that wire droops?" he asked, pointing to the culprit.

"Pawpaw's fence looks kinda like that," PJ said as Austin helped him out of the Gator again.

"Your great-grandpa Vern?"

PJ nodded. "Maybe I can fix it for him."

"You sure could. And I could help."

"Mommy never lets me help with anything, except to help carry the eggs."

Now, *that* was an interesting observation from a child. Austin had been picking up on that himself. She was very protective of her son.

Then again, if PJ was his, he'd be the same way.

Unfortunately, PJ couldn't help with the tightening since it was on the top wire and too high to reach, but Austin went through the steps anyway with his captive audience. Once they finished and were back at the Gator, he noticed that someone had left a message on his cell phone. It was from the landline at his dad's house in Colorado.

He tried not to panic, especially since PJ was standing right there, looking at him. He got the little boy buckled back in and checked to see if his dad had left a message.

Nothing.

He dialed back, but his dad didn't answer. Instead, it was Randy, one of the ranch hands. That was odd.

"Someone tried to call. Everything okay?" Austin asked.

"Yes and no. Nothing I wanted to worry you about, but you did say to let you know if Wes started training again. He's out there right now. Asked me to look after the house for a while because he was expecting a delivery."

Austin squeezed his eyes shut and took a deep breath, then released it slowly. Not the worst news, but not the best. His dad had promised he'd wait for Austin before training again, and would let the ranch hands take care of exercising the horses. So much for that.

"Which client?" he asked. He didn't want to have to call all of them and try to delicately explain the situation.

"Ms. Harris. She's been calling a lot."

She was one of their newer clients whom Austin hadn't had a chance to meet before having to leave. She must've worn the man down. His dad was nice to a fault.

"I appreciate you letting me know. I'll give Dad a call tonight or tomorrow. And don't worry. I'll leave your name out of it," Austin said.

"Thanks, boss. If it's any consolation, looks like he's having a great time out there."

Now, *that* Austin could relate to. He himself

was still making up for lost time after his six-year detour. If Ellie had even one horse, he'd be out there riding it. He loved everything else about the ranch life, as well. Even the morning ritual of feeding and watering.

By contrast, he didn't know the first thing about the feeding and watering of children. But he really wanted to.

Now more than ever.

CHAPTER SIX

VANESSA THOUGHT THAT having Austin out of her line of vision would help her concentrate on work.

She thought wrong. The outfit PJ had picked out to wear this morning almost perfectly matched Austin's, right down to the navy-blue-and-baby-blue plaid flannel button-down. Not entirely unexpected. Seemed cowboys of all ages had a similar taste in clothing. They looked like father and son, especially when PJ reached up and took Austin's hand. The whole thing took her breath away, and she was still trying to get it back.

The way Austin had initially tricked her into accepting a favor from him was equally unexpected. And admittedly charming. Her grandpa was right about her not being good about asking for favors. But today, with Austin, she didn't even have to ask.

She hoped his morning with PJ was at least as productive as hers had been, and less disappointing. That accounting miscalculation had grown into a bigger problem, void of a solution. Thankfully, she thrived on such challenges.

Although she hadn't had the spreadsheet in front of her at all times, she'd gone over it in her mind at least a dozen, which paid off. She identified the error. Fixing it, however, created a whole new problem. She'd somehow ended up with too much office space and not enough activities. Although there was nothing she loved more than a challenge, she preferred one that didn't affect the bottom line as much as this one could.

One look at the business blueprint that she'd asked Beth to email to her, and it was so obvious. If she'd been there to walk through the reconfigured area, she would've noticed it sooner. Her only excuse was that she'd been more focused on the spreadsheet with its columns and rows, rather the aesthetics of actual space.

Vanessa leaned back and rested her eyes for a moment. The chair she was seated in wasn't all that comfortable. She was looking forward to the state-of-the-art ergonomic chair she'd splurged on for her office in Cheyenne. But this temporary one must be heaven compared to the ladder-back that Ellie had been sitting in for the last two hours while watching a movie, which was coming to an end.

Perfect time to take a break. She stood, stretched and walked over to Ellie.

"Good movie?"

Ellie sighed and nodded. "*Shall We Dance?* is one of my favorites. I love Richard Gere's character. He reminds me of my Shelton."

Vanessa glanced around, as she'd never done before, but didn't see any photos of the couple to verify the resemblance. While there, she retrieved Ellie's nearly empty glass of sweet tea.

"Another round?" she asked.

"Sure. But I can do that," the woman insisted.

"I know you can." Vanessa smiled and took the glass anyway, then retreated to the kitchen and retrieved the tea from the refrigerator and the sugar from the cabinet.

She'd noticed Ellie wasn't on any diabetes drugs, nor were there any lancets or test strips. But she'd ask Austin for a full dietary restriction rundown, just in case, as soon as he and PJ returned.

The tablespoon of sugar had barely dissolved when Ellie rolled into the kitchen. Austin was sure going to have his hands full with this one. Not that the woman couldn't manage to do a few things on her own, but no use taking unnecessary risks.

"I can bring this to you," she said.

"I know you can," Ellie said, parroting Vanessa's own words. "And I appreciate it, sweetheart. But I wanted to come in here anyway to make Austin's favorite snack, so he'll have something to eat when he returns. PJ, too, but I don't know what he likes."

"He isn't too picky. What were you thinking?"

Whatever it was, she'd find a way to make it, even though she didn't consider herself much of a cook. Her experience mostly included split pea soup and grilled cheese sandwiches, and even some Jell-O molds and pudding.

"Deviled eggs," Ellie said.

Oh, boy. Of all the things.

"I'm going to be honest with you, Ellie," Vanessa said.

"I expect nothing less."

"I'm so happy you want to cook, but I need to help you with anything that involves bending or stretching or heavy lifting. Only until you're ready, I promise. Unfortunately, you're not ready."

Ellie looked at her, then smiled. "As much as I don't want to hear it, I trust your judgment."

If only all of her clients would realize their limitations and accept help that easily. This woman was definitely unique.

"The only problem for me is going to be the hard-boiled-egg part. Specifically, peeling them without taking the whites with the shell. That's why I pretty much stick to scrambled or over easy."

"You just haven't found the right recipe," Ellie said.

"I gave up after about the tenth one I tried. Even those that other people swear by. I'll chalk it up to user error."

Ellie went to the refrigerator and retrieved the carton of eggs that Vanessa and PJ had brought over.

"Since you insist on helping, fill the Dutch oven about two-thirds full of water, then let it reach a boil," Ellie instructed.

"Before adding the eggs?" she asked.

"Yes, ma'am."

Vanessa did as told. Didn't take long to reach a boil. "How many should we make?"

"All of them," Ellie said.

"And if I mess these up and they fall apart?" Vanessa asked.

"Then we'll make egg salad sandwiches instead. I hate wasting anything," Ellie said, adding a smile.

Vanessa had to smile, as well. Turning ruined hard-boiled eggs into egg salad was so logical, yet it had never occurred to her. And she also despised wasting anything, so this was a welcome tip.

"After about thirty seconds, reduce the heat to a simmer and cover, then set the timer for thirteen minutes," Ellie said.

Vanessa counted silently, then did as instructed. Once the poor eggs' destiny for disaster was set into motion, Ellie took a seat on her walker. With a little time to spare, Vanessa took the opportunity to put away some dishes and wipe down the surfaces. Surprisingly, the woman let her. Once everything was spick-and-span, Vanessa leaned against the counter.

"You've witnessed me follow the instructions. You've also been warned, Ellie. Maybe we should go ahead and break out the mayo and mustard and bread, because these *never* work out for me. I suspect today won't be an exception."

"Not with that attitude, it won't," Ellie said with a tight-lipped smile and a confident lift of her chin.

Vanessa snickered. Was this precious little woman reprimanding her? All she knew was that time would reveal what she knew to be true.

"If you say so," Vanessa said. "But I'm willing to make a bet that they won't turn out."

"What's the wager?"

The woman was serious. This was getting interesting. And, quite honestly, more fun than she'd anticipated.

"If I win, you have to tell me everything about the apology room, including how it got its name." Vanessa looked to Ellie as the words hit, but the woman didn't so much as blink. She halfway hoped Ellie would say she had nothing to hide anyway, but she stayed mum.

Instead, Ellie countered with a wager of her own. "If I win, you and my grandson have to cook me *Karaage* together for dinner one night.

This week, preferably. But I'm not telling you what it is or how to cook it."

"I may not know what it is, but I know how to Google. Not that I'll have to, because these eggs will be, as they say, toast," Vanessa teased.

As if seconding her sentiment, the timer *dinged*.

"Oops! I got distracted by our delicious bet. We need to get these into an ice bath," Ellie said as she started to stand.

"You stay put. I'll do the heavy lifting and you can supervise," Vanessa said.

She hurried to put some ice and water in a deep bowl, then spooned out the eggs, one at a time. Only one had cracked, which surprised her. She'd always put the eggs in before bringing the water to a boil and avoiding cracking any. The sticky shells were another story.

"We'll let them chill for fifteen minutes," Ellie directed. "In the meantime, let's locate the salt, pepper, mayonnaise, mustard and white wine vinegar. And we'll make some extra-crispy bacon to crumble on top."

Vanessa set the timer again and scanned the pantry and refrigerator for the rest.

In those moments of banter, she'd almost forgotten that Ellie was recovering from surgery. The woman was definitely not a complainer, except for that first day when Austin was late giving her the pain pill. She made a mental note to get an update from him on her pill regimen, and not only any dietary restrictions. Depending on the medication, she might not be taking the pain pills much longer.

Not that Vanessa needed to know all the details. This working situation was temporary. But still, she could keep tabs on it to help Austin. Until then...

"The ice seems like unnecessary torture, considering the peels aren't going to come off without putting up an ugly fight," Vanessa said, if only to playfully bait her.

"You have to take the same approach with hard-boiled eggs as you do with love. If you're not patient and gentle, the outcome won't be pretty. And if you go into it thinking that it can never work out, then it won't," Ellie said.

Vanessa wanted to say that she'd entered her first marriage with the attitude that she could make it work out. As far as being patient and gentle, she'd been more than that, in her opinion. Yet it had turned out ugly anyway.

The timer *dinged*, saving her from entering into a discussion she didn't want to have.

Ellie wheeled herself to the counter, then stood. She looked so sweet and optimistic, Vanessa couldn't help but hope for the best outcome, even though it would mean making some weird-sounding dish.

Then again, the best outcome here would also

mean more time with Austin. The way he'd looked back at her while holding PJ's hand kept playing over and over in her head in a continuous loop. She couldn't seem to shake it.

After fifteen minutes, Vanessa removed the eggs from the ice bath and patted them dry with a paper towel, then tapped one on the counter just hard enough to crack the shell. Ellie looked on and smiled as Vanessa successfully peeled the first one, without any of the egg white sticking. Then the second. And third...

Vanessa was speechless. Such a small thing to accomplish, yet a huge boost to her ego. All thanks to Ellie. Although she swore she'd tried this version, to no avail.

Ellie wasted no time filling the silence.

"By the way, I like cabbage salad with my *Karaage*. If it's not too much trouble," she said with that adorable, coy smile of hers.

Oh, yeah. Their wager, which Vanessa would humbly honor, of course. Problem was, she'd committed to cooking with Austin without asking him first. She'd been so confident the hard-boiled-egg recipe wouldn't work, but Ellie had proved her wrong.

Now Vanessa was the one who had to ask for a favor.

AUSTIN LIFTED PJ from the Gator and carried him through the back door and into the den.

Vanessa looked up from her computer screen and gasped, then stood and rushed over.

"He's fine. All the excitement over repairing fences must have worn him out," Austin whispered.

She visibly softened.

He set PJ down on the oversize sofa. Vanessa fluffed a pillow and grabbed a throw blanket that was draped across the back. Together, they covered the little sleeping cowboy.

"Ellie lay down for a nap a few minutes ago," she said.

Truth be told, getting some shut-eye sounded pretty good right now to him, as well.

"Did you and PJ fix those fences?" she asked.

"Actually, we did. He had a blast, I'm pretty sure of it. You may have a budding rancher on your hands. My condolences," he said.

"That's what I'm afraid of," she said. "Not that there's anything wrong with it. I was kind of hoping to have an accountant or doctor or lawyer in the family someday, though."

Austin shook his head and laughed.

"Is that a bad thing to want?" she asked.

"Not at all," he said, but refrained from throwing ice water on her dreams. He could be totally mistaken, and he certainly was no expert when it came to six-year-olds, but he detected the makings of a future cowboy in PJ.

Austin's own mom had wanted him to go to law school instead of carrying on the family tradition of training cutting horses. She'd even mentioned it again after he got married and started studying for a Realtor license instead. But that would've taken more years and money than he could afford and would potentially end up being even more boring than selling houses. He'd wanted to start a family right away, but his now ex-wife had other plans.

Looking back, it was a blessing in disguise that their family goals didn't line up. He just wished he'd known that going in, because you couldn't change people. If they were going to change, it had to be their doing.

"Did you fix those numbers?" he asked instead of launching into his own sad story. Because, if she did, perhaps she'd be willing to come over again tomorrow.

"Yes! And, in the process, I came across two additional problems. As my grandpa likes to say, 'When you water your worries, expect some weeds to crop up.'"

If that wasn't preaching to the choir, he didn't know what was. While he and PJ were out, he noticed a rotting fence post and the condition of the old unoccupied stables, which added to the growing list of repairs that needed to be made, and a dwindling number of days to make them.

The couple who had texted him might lose interest if he didn't get on the ball, fix a few things and have that talk with Ellie. At least get her to agree to show the property as a first step.

"Speaking of fixing, Ellie fixed something special for you. They're in the refrigerator."

Austin looked at her with equal parts curiosity about what was awaiting him and how Ellie was in any shape to be cooking.

He headed to the kitchen with Vanessa on his heels. When he opened the fridge, it was like he'd died and gone to heaven. He immediately retrieved one of the deviled egg halves, popped it into his mouth and chewed. Just as he swallowed, an unfamiliar bell started *ring-a-linging*.

"Oh! That's Ellie. She must be awake," Vanessa said. This time, she took the lead and he followed.

"Then I wasn't hearing things," he said.

Vanessa laughed. "I brought a bell from Grandpa's house and admonished her to use it when she was ready to get up. She should be fine doing it herself, but if she's the least bit drowsy…"

"I'm surprised she complied. If you hadn't picked up on it yet, she can be hardheaded."

Vanessa cast him a look he couldn't quite define.

"Being—*ahem*—strong-willed is going to serve her well in the coming years, living here alone," she said. "Unless some lucky man whisks her away."

He knew it wasn't how she meant it, but whisking Ellie away was exactly what he intended to do. She wasn't the only strong-willed one in the family. Not the only hardheaded one either. Which reminded him—he needed to call his dad tonight and get the scoop on why he broke his promise not to do any training. Not that he'd forgotten, but there had been a few distractions. The feel of PJ's little hand taking his had been a big one. Everything about Vanessa had been the other.

And he still didn't know how he'd approach the subject. The man was his father, not a child.

They reached Ellie's room. She'd already sat up and was attempting to stand. Vanessa moved in to assist, which only further convinced Austin that she shouldn't be left alone. Not yet. *If ever again.*

Maybe he shouldn't call his dad. After all, the man wasn't hurt or anything. Perhaps Austin didn't want to know what was going on, because he couldn't so much as entertain even a quick trip back to Colorado at the moment, so why put any specifics into his head?

By the time they got Ellie situated in the ladder-back chair in the den, Tango had curled up beside PJ, and the two were sleeping peacefully. Vanessa retrieved her cell phone and took a picture of the duo. She then turned to Ellie and Austin and motioned for him to move in closer to his grandma. Although he felt a bit too grungy to be photographed after having worked on fences for a few hours, he complied and smiled when Ellie took his hand and pulled him even closer. He knelt and put his arm around the backside of the chair.

Come to think of it, he didn't even have a photo of the two of them together, except for a scattered few from when he was little. Then again, who needed lots of photos when you had loved ones nearby? No two-dimensional image could begin to compare. Except perhaps that adorable photo he'd taken of PJ with the painted face.

"Did Vanessa tell you she made you some deviled eggs?" Ellie asked.

"She told me that you made them," he said, looking directly at Vanessa instead. He was quite certain he hadn't misheard her.

"Your grandma provided the brains. I provided the brawn. I can't hard-boil a successful egg to save my life," she said.

"Not true. You can boil 'em now," Ellie insisted.

"Only because you were there, I'm convinced. We'll see how well I do in the real world," Vanessa countered.

Austin smiled and bit his lip. He wished he would have gotten a picture of that. Vanessa was the only person he'd met who could hold his grandma back from doing too much, too soon. *And* get her to ring a bell when she needed help.

"All this talk is making me hungry. I'm gonna grab a few more," he said as he headed back to the kitchen.

Vanessa followed, even though he hadn't asked her to, which hopefully meant she had some updates as to Ellie's mental state.

"Do you have any pictures of your grandma and grandpa when they were around our age?"

"I'm sure I do, but they're back at the Happy U."

Vanessa cocked her head. "What's that?"

Austin grabbed a small plate and loaded it up. PJ had to try these.

"It's my family's ranch. And the name pretty much says it all." Might as well start building it up and hopefully getting Vanessa on board with the idea of persuading Ellie to move.

Vanessa nodded, although she didn't seem entirely convinced.

"Why do you ask about the pictures? Curious?" he asked.

"Very. Ellie tells me that her husband looked like Richard Gere."

Thankfully, he'd already swallowed the deviled egg half. Otherwise, he would have choked. Not that his grandfather wasn't handsome, but he was never *that* brand of handsome. Distinguished, most definitely. A hard worker, a good husband and an excellent grandpa, although Austin didn't get to spend nearly enough time with the man.

He shook his head. "She also thinks I look like Ryan O'Neal. She can find a famous doppelgänger for anyone. Doesn't help that she's been watching lots of movies lately."

Too many, apparently.

Vanessa cocked her head. "Who's Ryan O'Neal?"

Austin had to laugh. He'd wondered the same thing. Instead of trying to explain, he motioned for her to follow him back to the den, where he offered PJ a deviled egg.

The little boy looked skeptical at first, but one bite sold him on it.

"Yum! You cooked these, Mommy?"

She brushed the hair out of the little boy's eyes.

"Your grandma—" Vanessa squeezed her eyes shut the same moment Austin realized her gaffe. "Ellie made them, but I helped."

That made Austin wonder, where were Vanessa's mom and dad? They hadn't really talked about such personal things. *Yet.* He definitely wanted to know more about her. At the same time, the reminder of his dad training again without him around kicked him in the conscience. As soon as Vanessa and PJ left, he'd make the call, which meant two heart-to-hearts on his plate tonight.

"We better get going. Give Miss Ellie a gentle hug," she said to PJ.

While she was collecting her laptop and purse, he patted his back pocket to make sure his wallet was there. He definitely owed her for spending, what, four hours over here? His grandma certainly didn't spend that much time "caregiving" Vern on any given day.

Once Ellie and Vanessa and PJ said their good-byes, Austin walked them to her truck and helped get PJ situated in the car seat before pulling out his wallet and filtering through the bills, removing only the large ones.

"I'm not sure what the going rate is for care-givers, but for now—"

Vanessa shook her head and pushed his hand away. "Like I said before, this is repayment for Ellie helping Grandpa. Besides, this worked out well for me, even though I did you the favor of letting PJ help you mend fences."

It was Austin's turn to shake his head. "You made deviled eggs. I'd say we're even as far as favors go."

Vanessa exhaled and looked away. Did he say something wrong?

"Actually, I have a favor to ask of you. I inadvertently got you into a huge mess."

Austin's stomach sank. "Should I be afraid?"

"I lost a wager with Ellie. I was so sure I'd

botch the hard-boiled eggs, and she was convinced I wouldn't. Ended up, I didn't. So now you and I have to make *Karaage* for her before I leave Destiny Springs. Sorry."

Not much of a favor to ask, in his opinion. The thought of spending time with her wasn't exactly torture. Far from it.

"I still don't know what that is," he said.

"No worries. I'll take care of the research. It's the least I can do."

Austin wasn't about to argue with her on that, because he couldn't even begin to guess how to spell it. "Before you leave, huh? That gives us how much time to pull it off?"

Vanessa had to stop and think. "A little over a week."

Not nearly enough time, in his opinion. And it had nothing to do with cooking a meal. There was so much more he wanted to know about her, along with getting to know PJ better.

"Regarding tomorrow, I should be able to come by again," she said.

"That would be appreciated. But I understand if you can't make it," he said. Since she wasn't even accepting cash for helping out, any time she could spare was truly a gift.

"Actually, my grandpa mentioned he and his fiancée would like to visit with Ellie, and I think it would do her a world of good to chat with some friends and get a change of scenery. How would you feel about bringing her to Fraser Ranch for a while tomorrow? You could get some more work done around here, and PJ would love having all of them together. I'd get some work done, as well. Maybe even make my life more complicated while I'm at it as I water my worries," she said.

"That's a great idea," he said without thinking it through. Sure, he did need to get more work done at Ellie's ranch. Plenty of it. But PJ had mentioned that Vern had some fences to mend. Austin could help.

Apparently, Vanessa wasn't the only one who was good at creating complications.

CHAPTER SEVEN

WHAT'S THAT NOISE?

Vanessa opened her eyes and squinted against the sunlight filtering in through the sheer curtains. She bolted upright, now fully awake. How late had she slept? Sure, she'd stayed up extra late working, but this never happened.

The more important question was: *Is PJ okay?* She almost always woke up before he did. Otherwise, she could count on him to come running into the room and jump up and down on the bed like it was a trampoline. No better way to wake up, in her opinion.

She grabbed her robe, put on her house slippers and headed to his guest room. The little boy wasn't there and—*gasp*—his bed was made.

Although he'd done it himself before, he hadn't mastered the concept of squaring the corners or fluffing and positioning the pillows, which had clearly been done by someone.

She hurried downstairs, where she found her precious little boy enjoying a plate of eggs that had been scrambled with bacon and cheese, while Vern vacuumed an area rug in the adjacent den. He was already decked out in a fresh pair of overalls and a red thermal shirt. Sylvie was busy dusting the top of the china cabinet, her hair in the usual long silver braid. She usually didn't come over this early.

When Vern noticed Vanessa, he switched off the machine.

"Did we wake you, Angel?"

Yes.

She had only herself to blame for giving him the heads-up about Ellie's visit in advance. Of course he would step in to help make the house look good. Vanessa wouldn't have been able to stop him.

And of course his fiancée would step in to help, even though Vanessa was quite certain her grandpa would have discouraged it. Felt good to know that she'd be leaving Destiny Springs with Vern under the caring eyes of such a strong woman.

"No. I should have gotten up a long time ago. I was planning to clean and straighten up down here, but you beat me to it." She tried to pry the vacuum handle from his grip, but he wouldn't allow it.

"There's a fresh pot of coffee in there. Just put it on a few minutes ago but it should be finished brewin'. Grab a couple of mugs for me and Sylvie, and some of that green tea for yourself while we finish up here. And don't even think about washing the pots and pans stacked in the sink."

Sylvie finally took notice of Vanessa.

"That's right, sweetheart. Vern will do the dishes," Sylvie teased.

Her grandpa passed the love of his life a stern look. "I was thinking we could do 'em together. But if you promise to dance with me later, I'll do the dishes *and* finish the dusting."

Now, that sounded like a good deal for her future grandma. At the same time, it left Vanessa without any chores.

"Is this my birthday or something?" she asked as she went to the kitchen, pausing for a moment to smother PJ with a kiss on the forehead. Vern had taken the time to set her favorite mug and a green tea bag on the counter, just for her. Who was supposed to be taking care of whom here?

"Mommy! Pawpaw cooked me breakfast, but he made me these eggs instead of the half ones at Miss Ellie's. And Miss Sylvie made me some raisin toast," PJ explained while Vanessa heated some water in the microwave.

Vern had resumed vacuuming and apparently didn't overhear the comment. Vanessa knew the eggs that PJ was talking about. She hadn't stopped thinking about how, after a lifetime of attempting the perfect hard-boiled egg, it came down to Ellie's magic touch.

If by some miracle she could be guaranteed the same success without her good-luck charm around, she'd gladly try again right now. But their guests would arrive in an hour, and she needed to help her grandpa and Sylvie finish cleaning the house, because that back of his didn't care much for twists and turns these days.

For now, she'd humor him, since she needed his help in convincing Austin that Ellie would have a strong support system here in Destiny Springs, and that he didn't need to feel guilty about returning to his own life in Colorado. Although Austin hadn't expressed it outright, she could tell he was worried, which was supersweet.

Vanessa refilled PJ's milk glass, then poured two mugs of coffee for Vern and Sylvie, leaving it black for both. She retrieved her mug from the microwave and left the tea bag in it to steep as she headed back to the den with the two coffee mugs. That was when she noticed two bowls on the ground. One was filled with water, and the other was empty, which meant only one thing: time to break a little boy's heart.

"Did you put those there?" she asked PJ, pointing to the bowls.

PJ nodded. "They're for Tango."

"Ellie isn't bringing him today, sweetheart. But

I'm sure you'll get to see him another day. And Austin will be going back to work on the ranch," she said. Although PJ hadn't asked about him, it was clear that the two had bonded, and so quickly. The image of the pair holding hands, once again, threatened to resume its continuous loop.

Vanessa headed to the den and presented one mug to Sylvie and the other to Vern, who had stopped vacuuming and was wrapping and securing the cord.

"PJ thought Tango was coming to visit today. Even put down food and water bowls," she said.

"Well, that little rascal. I s'pose we could have invited the furry little fella," Vern said.

Of course he would say that. His door was always open, even to people's pets.

But PJ was already way too attached to Tango. It was going to be painful for him when the time came to leave the feline behind. If she started putting some distance between them now, that might cushion the inevitable.

There was an upside, however. At least today she could be guaranteed that everyone would be busy and she could get a ton of work done.

Perhaps equally important, Austin wouldn't be around to distract her. Although he didn't really have to be, it seemed. She still had to smile at how he stepped in and enlisted PJ to help mend the fence while she worked. Very intuitive of him, although not necessary. Juggling tasks and people was her strong suit, even though she was actively working for a softer, more comfortable existence.

Vanessa sat on the sofa and patted the cushion next to her while Sylvie resumed dusting and straightening. Vern complied.

"I'm sure you have lots to talk about with Ellie. But in case you run out of topics, I know she loves music. Have you been to her house?" she asked.

"Sure have. I've probably been in and out of every home in Destiny Springs," he said.

That much, she believed. Everyone here seemed to love him. The place was like one big happy family sometimes. Too good to be true, if she thought about it hard enough.

"Ever been in that big, empty room in the back of the house?" she asked.

"Empty room…" Vern tapped his index finger against his lips. "I don't recall anything like that. Ellie and Shelton invited me over for dinner a handful of times, but I never got an official tour of the place. Why?"

Vanessa shrugged. "Just wondered. That's where she likes to listen to records on her turntable. There's a love seat in there, but otherwise it's bare." Vanessa stopped short of admitting that Ellie called it the apology room.

"Maybe she's turning into one of those minimalists," he said.

"I thought of that, except her house is otherwise very warm and cozy and full of memories, which you probably noticed. Except for photos. I haven't seen any of those. And I've been looking, ever since she told me her husband reminded her of Richard Gere."

The expression on Vern's face was priceless. She'd never seen his eyes open so wide.

"Maybe when he was younger, but not when I knew him."

Vanessa glanced at the clock. "Oh! I better get dressed."

She rose and checked on PJ. He'd pretty much cleaned his plate, which meant she wouldn't have to worry about meals for anyone until lunchtime. And he was already dressed for company. Had he done that himself, or had Vern helped him?

Time seemed to be escaping her. At this rate, she'd barely have time to blink before PJ would be off to college. Hopefully to earn either an accounting, law or medical degree.

She'd barely finished showering when she heard the knock, followed by some muffled pleasantries. She slipped on a pair of mom jeans, a white long-sleeved T-shirt and her favorite black boots, and paused at the top of the stairs. Ellie was already inside with her walker, with Austin and Grandpa and Sylvie all spotting her from a razor-thin distance.

Vanessa truly believed that Austin had nothing to worry about with her living alone, once she was fully healed. Hopefully seeing her in action outside of her home would put his mind at ease.

She descended the steps slowly so as not to interrupt their flow of conversation. Austin looked up anyway and smiled, those creases once again framing his eyes, making them look almost happy. As if he knew this suggestion of hers was a good one and that he didn't have to go it alone when it came to caring for Ellie.

Vanessa smiled in return, then picked up the pace and joined them.

Austin retrieved a dining room chair and brought it into the den for Ellie. This was the first time Vanessa felt as though she wasn't really needed. It was both a good feeling and an unsettling one.

When Austin smiled at her again, adding a wink this time, a feeling of a different kind overwhelmed her. One that was equally unsettling, but in a good way. Confirming what she was already starting to admit to herself. She wanted to know more.

About him.

Rejection never felt so sweet.

Austin didn't even get a smile or acknowledgment of his existence from his favorite little boy. PJ was on a mission to find the softest throw blanket to place over Ellie's lap, without anyone even asking him to do it. Austin had to smile at the similarities between the little boy and his mommy in the caregiving department.

If I ever have a son...

He did receive an arguably more important acknowledgment: Vanessa walked over and stood next to him. Hopefully he'd score some points with her today, because he couldn't put off the talk much longer with Ellie. Time to summon his courage. Since Vanessa would be stopping in again—at least, he hoped that would be the case—he wanted to make her aware of his intentions as far as Ellie's future.

He and Vanessa watched as Vern and Ellie sank deep into conversation.

"I guess I don't have to worry about entertaining anyone today," she said.

"You can get some work done. Glad I thought of this."

Vanessa looked at him. "Pardon me? I'm pretty sure this was my idea."

He bit back a huge grin. She was awfully cute when she was mad. Not that she was exactly that, but for some reason he couldn't resist teasing her, because of how she didn't let him get away with anything.

"I know it was, but I get credit for the idea I'm about to explain, even though I need your input. Maybe even your permission," he said.

"Sounds mysterious."

"I was planning to fix some of Vern's fencing while I'm here. I was gonna ask if PJ would help, because he really has a talent for it."

"He'd probably like that. Especially since Tango didn't come along, as he'd hoped. He's crazy about that cat. I'm thinking we might have to adopt one when we get back to Cheyenne," she said.

Austin nodded. He didn't even want to think about how much it was going to hurt PJ to leave that cat behind.

"Every child needs a pet," he said.

And a daddy. Austin blinked hard at the random thought. Yet it was true. He hadn't spent much time around kids at all, so hanging with PJ had been a treat. And it got him thinking about things he hadn't entertained much lately. Fatherhood, specifically. Why torture himself with daydreams when he wasn't even dating anyone?

"You don't have to fix the fence, even though it's a kind offer. You have a lot to do at Ellie's. Besides, Vern will insist PJ spend time with them inside," Vanessa said.

PJ seemed to finally find the perfect throw for Ellie and changed it out for the one he'd previously placed on her lap. She thanked him profusely, and the little boy lapped up the praise as sure as Tango would be lapping up all of PJ's attention if he were here.

In the meantime, Vern and Sylvie had selected a record album from his collection and powered up the turntable, which was connected to some amplifiers that were powerful enough to send the whole house rocking.

Vanessa covered her ears, then giggled. Austin did the same.

"So much for getting some work done here," she practically yelled. "I won't be able to hear myself think."

"How good are you at repairing fences?" he asked. Not that he expected her to help in any way.

She seemed to contemplate it. "Let's find out."

Before he could say he was just joking, she walked over to Vern and yelled something in his direction. He nodded, but who knew if he even heard. Ellie had a huge smile on her face, and her head was bobbing left and right to whatever song was playing. PJ was doing his teddy bear dance but paused when his mommy went over. After Vanessa gave whatever inaudible instructions she intended her son to follow, she walked past Austin and led the way.

"Grandpa doesn't have a Gator. We can take my crossover, but we may need to do some of it on foot if the ground is muddy. We don't want to get stuck way out there," she said, heading toward her own car.

"Tools are already in the truck bed, and my tires can handle anything. Let's take mine," he countered.

She seemed to contemplate it, then conceded and climbed in. They drove in silence down the road until Austin spotted one of the breaks.

Together, they got out of the truck and retrieved the fence pliers and the spool of barbed wire. Not exactly the romantic rendezvous he would imagine having with her. If he dared to imagine.

Actually, he'd been doing some imagining lately. Couldn't seem to help himself.

Vanessa slipped on the extra pair of gloves. They were too large for her, just as they had been for PJ.

Austin faced her, reached for her right hand first and rolled the opening of the glove down, creating some tension at her wrist, then adjusted the other glove. He then took both her hands in his. He could barely feel her delicate bones beneath the rough canvas and leather.

He released them but gave the fingertips of the fabric a gentle tug to make sure they wouldn't slip off. Instead of letting go once done, he enveloped her hands again and gave them a gentle squeeze.

"You've done this before," he said.

She seemed momentarily flustered. Not that he was thinking all that clearly himself.

"Done what?" she asked.

"Fixed fences. You knew to get gloves." He slowly

released her hands, even though part of him didn't want to.

"Actually, I haven't. I just figured I'd need some."

That was a good answer, because as much as he appreciated her help, he planned to do all the work. But there was something he did need her help with.

"I'm glad we have some alone time," he said as he located the loose end of the wire and began the process. "I wanted to talk with you about something that's been on my mind. Now that you've spent some time with my grandmother, I'd appreciate your professional input."

She gave him a look he couldn't quite define, then proceeded to locate the other end of the damaged wire. For someone who'd never repaired a fence, she had a solid grasp of what came next.

"Sure," she finally said.

"I want to bring her back to Colorado with me. Sell her ranch."

At that, Vanessa dropped her hand to her side but regrouped before she lost the wire. "How does Ellie feel about that?"

"I haven't asked. But after what you said about her not wanting *me* to move in with *her*, I don't expect a positive response to my suggestion that she live with me and my dad."

"What's your dad's name?" she asked.

"Wes."

"How does Wes feel about it?"

That was another person he needed to talk to, but not about Ellie. His dad was on board with whatever was best for her. However, what was "best" seemed to depend on who Austin asked. The person in front of him, however, could offer a professional and objective opinion.

"My dad wants what will be best for Ellie, as do I. And extended family is something we've always hoped to have at the Happy U. What do you think is best for her?"

At that, Vanessa straightened, and dropped the loose end of the wire long enough to retrieve the pliers that he had set down. Again, impressive that she'd watched what he had done—as was the time she was taking to form an answer.

He knew he was putting her on the spot, but it was going to come out anyway.

"I hesitate to offer an opinion because it's such a personal decision. Every family is different. But generally speaking, I'm in favor of allowing parents and grandparents to live out the rest of their lives on their terms, when at all possible."

"And if something happened to Vern?" he asked, knowing that he was crossing into personal territory.

"I'd always welcome relatives like Vern into my home, but it wouldn't be either of our preferences. If I somehow forced a move, he'd be kicking and screaming the whole way over. And rightly so."

Austin had to laugh. Having met Vern, he could visualize it. But the man seemed strong for his age. Ellie was much more fragile, which made his situation an orange to her apple. Really couldn't compare the two, and she said it herself: every family was different.

"If you were in my boots, what would you do, knowing Ellie needs help for at least a while longer?" he asked.

"You want my professional opinion? I don't give my personal opinion about other people's families, just my own."

"Then I suppose I want professional," he said, even though he wanted to know how she felt personally, as well. Because this whole thing was becoming personal.

She looked up from the wire and directly at him. "I live in your boots, in a way. I witness this type of situation almost every day. If I were you, I'd ask Ellie what she wants first. And take it from there."

Maybe he'd crossed a line in asking her opinion at all, but he wasn't going to apologize for not only wanting to keep his grandma safe, but also wanting her to be a bigger part of his life.

"I've based my whole life and career on keeping my clients as independent as possible and finding a way to let them stay in the homes they love, if that's what they want," she continued.

"I respect and admire that about you."

She shook her head and looked down, as if rejecting the compliment. What was that about?

"Not to change the subject, but I'd mentioned that she calls that empty room the apology room. Do you have any theories as to why?" Vanessa asked.

Austin shook his head. "Can't say that I do."

Sure, Vanessa had told him that Ellie gave it a label, but he hadn't imagined it could mean anything significant. Perhaps he was wrong.

They packed up the tools. He placed the toolbox in the truck bed and they headed back to the house.

"How did Ellie and her husband meet? Did she work, or was she a stay-at-ranch wife?"

More questions he couldn't answer. She'd always just been *Grandma*. That was who she was and what she did. Then it struck him that he didn't know that much about her at all, and a sense of shame washed over him. If that had been Vanessa's goal, she accomplished it beautifully.

"I'd rather she tell you her version. I might leave out something important," he said. As in, everything that mattered. "Or wait another year, after she moves to the Happy U," he continued. "Then I'll be able to tell you everything about her."

Vanessa nodded in a way that indicated she was onto him and his lack of knowledge. But that was going to change when Ellie moved to the Happy U. In fact, he couldn't wait.

By the time they opened the front door, the music had stopped. In its place was laughter. The kind that made the belly ache and the eyes water. Yet once they reached the back room, the laughter stopped. Ellie and Vern exchanged a smile that he could only describe as conspiratorial.

Without Vanessa as an ally—and with these two charming octogenarians seemingly becoming best friends—the road to the Happy U future he'd envisioned just got a lot longer.

Unless it was a matchmaking conspiracy he was witnessing.

After his and Vanessa's clash of opinions today, and even in spite of how her professional thoughts weren't what he needed to hear, he wanted all the help he could get with an equally important and heartfelt subject. At least for him.

Exploring a personal relationship with her.

CHAPTER EIGHT

"YOUR CORD IS SHOWING," Vanessa said.

Vern was trying to discreetly tuck the heating pad fully behind his lower back without her noticing but doing a poor job of it. What she really wanted to say was, *Your intentions are showing.* She knew her grandpa's Cheshire grin all too well. And Ellie's smile was the same one she'd cast her after their deviled-egg-making session. Whether Austin picked up on it, too, she wasn't sure. Vanessa wasn't about to call the little matchmakers out on it in case she was wrong.

No, she'd wait and confront Vern after Ellie and Austin left. And maybe even go ahead and confess that she was developing more of a personal interest in the handsome cowboy with the strong hands. If Austin had noticed her hands were trembling inside the gloves while he was adjusting them for her, he didn't let on. Sure, there was no denying he was cute. And charming. But she hadn't anticipated such a reaction from a simple touch.

She only hoped he would take the professional advice she'd given him to ask Ellie what she wanted to do about moving. Seemed like Austin had a different view on the subject than she did—personally, as well as professionally. Even though she was feeling closer to both of them than she'd ever intended on becoming, she didn't want to get in the middle of it. In fact, it was even more important now that she didn't.

Vanessa adjusted the heating pad for Vern, even though she risked embarrassing him in front of his new BFF, it seemed. "Care to share how this happened?"

"Zombies are what happened," Vern said.

They all looked to the little boy who was curled up in the recliner. He was fast asleep, despite the adult chatter.

"PJ showed Vern the right way to walk, which ended up being the wrong way for his back, I'm afraid. Those two were so adorable, though," Ellie said. "I've never laughed so hard. I may have even ripped a stitch."

Vanessa was tempted to reprimand all involved but resisted. Still, she would ask Austin to make sure the therapist checked the suture tomorrow, or have the nurse stop by to do it, although it should be closed by now.

"I need more practice, is all. This kink will work itself out before I have to exercise the horses tomorrow, when I'll get a whole new kink in my back." Vern cackled at his joke. At least one of them was laughing. Yet she knew she wouldn't be able to talk him out of it.

"I hope you didn't join 'em, Grandma," Austin said.

"I didn't turn into a zombie this time, but I've asked for a rain check," Ellie said.

"I'm happy to come over and exercise your horses for you tomorrow, Vern," Austin said. "How many you got?"

"Four at the moment. Two Appaloosas, two quarter horses."

And there he went again. Being a little too helpful and making it difficult for Vanessa to keep her emotional distance. She wanted to jump in and say he didn't have to do that, but the generosity of it warmed her heart. She fully expected Vern to scoff and swat away the offer with a brush of his hand.

"I appreciate that, Austin. I may take you up on it," Vern said.

Now Vanessa couldn't even swallow. He must be in worse pain than he was admitting to.

"Sylvie usually helps take care of that, right?" Vanessa looked to her grandpa. That was when she realized that Sylvie was nowhere around.

"When she isn't mad at me, she does," Vern said.

That was fast. Definitely a conversation for after Austin and his grandma left.

Vern and Ellie exchanged conspiratorial looks. Then he yawned. Ellie wasn't far behind.

Austin seemed to be trying to suppress one of his own. He rubbed his hands together. "We should get back to the ranch. I think we could all use a nap."

Ellie didn't put up an argument. Vanessa wasn't about to either.

"Can Tango come over and stay with us tonight?" PJ asked.

How long had he been awake? "Ellie might want the company, sweetheart," Vanessa said.

"That's true," the woman said. "Unfortunately, Austin still won't let Tango sleep with me. But we'll make up for lost time when he goes back to Colorado in a couple of weeks. Or sooner, if I have any say."

Vanessa's breath hitched. She shouldn't have felt any particular way about it. After all, she and PJ would already be back in Cheyenne by then.

"Where did you come up with that time line?" Austin asked.

"My therapist says all the tape and bandages will be off by then, and I'll be able to do a few more things on my own," she explained.

"Tango is more than welcome to come over

and stay here tonight. Angel and PJ can take him back tomorrow," Vern said.

Austin looked to Vanessa, as if it were somehow her decision. "What do *you* think, Angel?"

Wasn't anyone on her side? Yet that smile of his tested her resolve. The softness in his eyes wore it down even further. But it was the way his voice sounded when he called her "Angel" that threatened to completely do her in.

I think my hands are about to start trembling again.

She clasped them behind her back and focused. "It's Vern's house. He's a grown-up and can decide what's best," she said, even though her preference was for Tango to stay at Ellie's.

The implication was less than subtle, in her opinion.

"Then the decision is made. Tango will be our overnight guest," Vern said.

"Grandma and I will run back home, and we'll bring Tango and his litter box over," Austin said.

Vanessa sighed internally, then helped Ellie stand but insisted Vern stay on the heating pad. She caught them exchanging a conspiratorial look again. Her grandpa wasn't even trying to hide it.

She shook her head, and she and Austin helped Ellie to the truck. Once the woman was comfortable and secure in the seat, Austin turned to Vanessa.

"About tomorrow," he said.

"Yeah. We hadn't really talked about that. How about I come over in the morning and work from there. That seemed to be a good arrangement. Maybe even better than having those two entertain each other."

"They looked like they were up to no good," Austin said.

So the whole thing *wasn't* lost on him.

"They mean well, but they are victims of an epidemic that plagues this town."

"And turns people into zombies?"

At that, Vanessa had to laugh. "Even worse. Matchmakers."

"Ahh, I see." Austin held her gaze. Had he really not picked up on it?

"We might have to outwit them," she added. Might as well make it clear that she had no intention of being match-made. With the way things were going, she might be able to make the questionable decision to get further involved all by herself.

"You sure?" he asked.

Vanessa gulped. No, she wasn't sure. "What do you mean?"

"Well, they are adults and can make their own decisions." He added a smile, but she knew when someone was kicking a little sand in her face.

"Point taken. We won't interfere," she said.

At that, Austin got into the truck and he and Ellie both waved as they drove away. "See you in about twenty with Tango!" Austin yelled out the driver's-side window.

Vern was still on the heating pad when she got back into the house. She went to the kitchen and returned with a glass of orange juice.

"You don't have to do that," he said.

She settled onto the sofa next to him.

"I know. Taking care of people who don't want my help is a bad habit. I'm trying to break it."

"Glad to hear it," Vern teased.

"I'm sorry Sylvie is upset. Wanna talk about it?"

The two of them seemed more than okay when she'd left to help with the fence. But she knew her grandpa all too well, and that filter between his mind and his mouth sometimes malfunctioned.

Vern simply shook his head and wouldn't look at her, which was a clear sign that now wasn't the time.

"It sounds like you and Ellie had a great time, though," she said.

Vern took a huge gulp of juice and wiped his mouth on his sleeve. Vanessa resisted the urge to go get a napkin.

"She's a delightful woman. Told me I remind her of Anthony Hopkins."

Vanessa couldn't help but laugh, but now that

he mentioned it, there was a resemblance under all that white hair and beard.

"She used to be kind of famous, you know," Vern continued.

What? Austin had never mentioned such a thing.

"Really? How so?" Vanessa asked.

"She and her partner at the time won all sorts of awards for ballroom dancing."

"Why did she quit?"

"Said she fell in love."

"Makes sense to me." People gave up lifelong dreams and careers for love all the time. And many of them ended up regretting it.

"I hope she'll be able to dance again someday. Not professionally, of course, but for fun." A suspicious smile spread across her grandpa's face.

What? No, he couldn't be...

"I know Sylvie and you had a fight, but please tell me you're not thinking what I think you're thinking," she said.

Vern took a minute to think about it, then cackled. "Oh, I'm not letting Sylvie go, even if she is being unreasonable. I meant I hope Ellie will have *someone* to dance with again, too, someday. Apparently, Shelton had two left feet."

Vanessa breathed a sigh of relief. She wanted to say that she was sure Ellie would find someone, although there probably weren't a lot of men

around her age in Destiny Springs. Maybe not
even near the Happy U. Vanessa could think of
an eligible bachelor or two among her own clients
in Cheyenne. But that was a scenario she didn't
want to contemplate at the moment.

"Not that it's any of my business, but why is
Sylvie mad at you?" she asked.

Vern shook his head. "Seems I've been pressuring her to get married this year. I asked her
about it again while she was doing all that dusting, thinking that maybe she'd changed her mind.
But…"

"But what…?"

"She has her heart set on a Valentine's Day
wedding. I told her I didn't want to wait that long
to get our life together started. She took that to
mean I might look for someone else. I'm afraid
I'm making a mess out of this."

Vanessa reached out and squeezed his hand. "If
wanting to start your life with someone sooner
rather than later is unforgivable, then it would be
her loss. That said, Sylvie is too smart to let you
go, Grandpa."

"I apologized, but she isn't hearing of it. And
she made up an excuse to not see me tomorrow.
That's why I took Austin up on his offer."

"So it wasn't because you and Ellie are trying
to get our paths to cross as often as possible?"

Vern looked at her and smiled. "I plead the Fifth.

But Ellie had a suggestion for getting Sylvie to cross mine again."

Vanessa waited for an explanation. When Vern finally looked at her, she raised her brows.

"I'll tell you all about it if it works. Don't wanna jinx it by saying too much. I'm going to Ellie's tomorrow. Gonna take some of my records with me to play on her turntable. She and I thought that maybe you could stay here and get some work done. And don't you worry, because she says her physical therapist comes over around that time. Maybe she can recommend some exercises for my back."

She wanted to say he better be telling her the truth, but refrained. Clearly, he didn't want her there for some reason.

Vanessa thought about Austin's offer to help exercise the horses, and Vern's surprising openness to it. Even if Austin did do that for him, it would take a long time to finish without some help. He had other things to take care of at Ellie's ranch, and Vanessa would definitely feel better if someone else was on the property with Ellie and Vern. Just in case.

"I'll exercise the horses tomorrow," she said. She was going to take Becca up on the offer for a playdate at the B and B anyway, so PJ would be taken care of. She could get a ton of work done before and after in that big, quiet house with zero distractions or interruptions. No Vern, no PJ, no Ellie.

No handsome cowboy.

"I'd feel better if Austin helped you with it," Vern said.

"Because you and Ellie are plotting to get us together? Pleading the Fifth is almost the same as confessing, but I'd like to hear it anyway. I offered so you wouldn't have to plot."

Vern wagged a finger at her. "You're not gonna let me have fun with that, are ya? But that's not what I meant. I'm more worried that you haven't been on a horse since you were a little girl."

There was a reason for that. She'd left the ranch life—and horses—behind a long time ago. At least she wasn't disappointing PJ in that respect. Although the little boy liked the lifestyle more than she did, he expressed no interest in ever riding horses again after his fall.

She could make this one exception for herself, however.

"It's not something you forget how to do."

Like she'd told Vern, she had a bad habit of helping people who didn't want or need her help.

Austin, however, seemed to want her help. Question was, did he feel that way because he *needed* it even more?

AUSTIN HAD BEEN staring at the ceiling for at least an hour, and the answer still hadn't magically appeared as to why he kept chickening out and not talking with Ellie about moving. Even though Vanessa's suggestion was to ask his grandma what she wanted, it was almost like he already knew. So why bother?

Because this is important, and you'll regret it if something happens to her if she lives alone and you didn't at least try.

He'd had every opportunity after they'd gotten home from Vern's. But Ellie had seemed to have had such a good time, and talking about her moving would certainly have spoiled it.

Austin closed his eyes again, determined to get a few hours of sleep. But apparently Tango was on the kitchen counter, looking for crumbs. Or cooking up some mischief, because there was a noise coming from the kitchen. *Cats will be cats.*

He laughed at the thought, until he remembered that he and Ellie had retrieved Tango and his litter box, and the feline was spending the night with PJ at Fraser Ranch. Which meant Ellie possibly had rodents in her house.

Or worse.

He bolted upright and tiptoed down the hall, his heart thumping out of his chest. Hadn't even thought through what he would do if it was an intruder.

The kitchen light was on. Ellie was seated at the breakfast table, taking a bite out of a deviled egg. He eased into the chair across from her.

"I hope I didn't wake you up, dear," she said.

I wish you would have. Didn't Vanessa bring a bell for her to ring?

"Not at all. In fact, we had the same idea. You just beat me to it. Mind if I have one?"

"Of course not. They're yours, after all," she said, sliding the plate closer to him.

He took a half and pushed the plate back over. "You used to make these all the time at the Happy U, remember?"

"Yes. You were the only one who liked them."

Austin was about to take another bite but paused instead. "You mean no one else ate them? You made them just for me?"

"Oh, I had a few myself, as well, but mostly they were for you. I had to be quick if I wanted one, because once a certain adorable little boy discovered them, they'd disappear."

He reached across the table and squeezed Ellie's hand.

Oddly, his grandma's hands felt much stronger than Vanessa's, and the thought of when he'd taken Vanessa's hands in his came flooding back. He thought he'd felt her tremble underneath those way-too-big gloves, then realized that it was his hands doing the trembling.

"I never knew that you'd done that for me. Why didn't you say something?" he asked, getting back to the original subject.

Ellie squeezed his hand in return. "Why would I? You were my Little Buckaroo. Still are, even though you're not little anymore."

Austin shut his eyes and scrunched his nose. "Please don't tell anyone about that nickname. Especially Vanessa."

"You mean Angel?"

He couldn't help but smile at the thought of how perfectly the name suited her.

"Vern tells me that's her nickname around here," Ellie continued.

"She's lucky. It's better than Little Buckaroo. Promise you won't repeat it?"

"Because you like her?" Ellie asked.

"I can't deny it. But she'll be leaving soon. 'Liking' is all I can afford to do." But even he didn't believe she'd soon be gone. Or he simply didn't want to believe it.

"You can afford a lot more than you think. Sometimes you have to work a little harder for it, that's all," Ellie said.

That was all the permission he needed to fully own those feelings. Not that he could feel anything else, even if he'd wanted to.

There were a few other feelings he needed to own, and now was a good time for it. While he still had Ellie's hand, he took a deep breath and summoned his nerve.

"Grandma, how would you feel about living at the Happy U with me and Dad?"

She seemed to study his face as if she knew exactly where this was headed. "This is my home, dear. But I promise to come visit as often as I can."

"I worry about you being here, alone."

Her grip loosened ever so slightly.

"The last thing I want you to do is worry about me. Make that, next to last. The last thing I want is to leave Destiny Springs." With that, she reclaimed her hand, patted his gently and reached for another deviled egg.

He reached for one, too, and they chewed in an awkward silence.

"Well, I've had enough of these. Guess I'll head back to bed now," she said as she stood. Thankfully taking it nice and slow. He resisted the urge to jump in and help.

"One more question before you go," he dared to say. "If you don't come to Colorado, who's going to make deviled eggs for me?"

It was an impulsive attempt to at least get a smile out of her. Didn't work.

"The same person who made these. Vanessa," she said.

"I thought it was a joint effort," he countered.

"She simply didn't want to take full credit. But I'm making some tomorrow. You can compare, if you don't believe me. She added a dash of Tabasco sauce, which I'd never tried."

Come to think of it, they did taste a little different than he remembered. Not that it mattered. He'd never met a deviled egg he didn't like.

The bigger issue was, now he had to worry about her trying to cook, and so soon. He'd never force her to move to Colorado, but he had to put his foot down about this. Albeit gently. She didn't seem angry with him, but the temperature in the room had cooled several degrees.

"No need to cook anything. I don't want to get sick of 'em. But when you do, let me or Vanessa help you," he said, then added, "please."

Ellie finally smiled, although it seemed forced. "Actually, I was thinking about making some anyway. You may help if you insist. Or I might keep it simple and serve cheese and crackers instead. I'm having company tomorrow."

Who? And when was she going to let him know?

She gave him a look as if daring him to say something about it. All of a sudden, he was Little Buckaroo all over again.

And this little buckaroo needed help that no mere mortal could provide, in keeping his grandma from doing something that could hurt her.

He needed an angel.

CHAPTER NINE

VERN CLUTCHED THE album next to his chest for the entire drive to Ellie's, while PJ talked to Tango through his cat carrier in the back seat.

"I'll come back over tomorrow and we can play, okay?" PJ said to the cat, who meowed in return as if knowing exactly what was being asked. Maybe Tango really was Shelton.

Vanessa didn't bother correcting either of them, even though she'd hoped to spend some one-on-one time with Ellie in the morning before picking PJ up from his sleepover at the B and B.

"Which album did you decide to bring?" she asked Vern.

He loosened his grip and looked down at the sleeve. "'Mariage d'amour.'"

Vanessa nodded. "I'm not familiar with it, but I love the name."

"It's Sylvie's favorite. Thought I'd lost the album, but I found it way at the bottom of the last stack."

She gulped. She'd pretty much promised that everything would be okay with Sylvie, but if she turned out to be wrong, she'd be nursing more than Vern's overworked back. She'd be nursing his broken heart.

"I heard Ellie playing some terrific music. Maybe listen to that instead."

Vern didn't say anything. He simply clutched the album against his heart, once again.

This situation really was serious. They'd no sooner parked in front of Ellie's when Austin came out the front door. He insisted on helping with Tango's carrier and took PJ with him to see Ellie.

Vern eased out of the crossover and, within moments, Austin and PJ came back out.

"She isn't here yet, is she?" Vern asked. "I don't see her truck unless she's parked out back."

Vanessa was confused by the statement, but quickly realized it wasn't even directed at her. "Did I miss something? Who isn't here?" She looked back and forth from Vern to Austin, hoping one would fill her in.

"Sylvie," Vern said to Vanessa, then looked at Austin again. "Does she know I'm coming, too?"

"I don't think so. Go on inside," Austin said.

They watched as Vern made his way up the steps and disappeared through the front door.

"What's going on?" Vanessa asked.

"Honestly, I'm not quite sure. Ellie is barely speaking to me. So, should I follow you over to

the B and B, or would you like for me to drive?"
Austin asked.

Something was going on that she didn't know
about, and everyone seemed to be mad at someone. She was about to ask for clarification, but
PJ interrupted with a burning question.

"You're going with us, Mr. Austin?"

Vanessa closed her eyes and rubbed her temples.

"Uh-oh. Vern didn't tell you?" Austin said.

"I think Vern has been a little…distracted. He
and Sylvie got into a fight."

"Yeah. That much I know. Grandma's going
to try to straighten everything out."

"Did she say how?"

Austin shook his head. "Nope. In fact, she
asked me to leave for a few hours. More like
told me. Vern called over here this morning to
ask if Ellie had a specific album. I told him my
offer was still good to exercise the horses. Didn't
have anywhere else to go. He said you'd offered
to help me with it."

Vanessa rolled her eyes. So her grandfather
had gotten his way after all.

She wanted to suggest that he meet her at
Vern's ranch, but he was looking at her with those
eyes, which seemed more hopeful than sad at the
moment. Not to mention, her curiosity was kill-
ing her.

"Get in. I'll drive," she said. "I can bring you back over when I pick up Vern."

Together, they got PJ situated in the car seat. Austin was quiet on the way over. Sullen, like PJ had been at having to leave Tango behind.

"What's Ellie angry about?" she came right out and asked.

"I tried to persuade her to move to Colorado."

Vanessa wanted to tell him, *I told you so*, but refrained.

"You really want her there, don't you?" She'd heard every word he'd said about living with extended family at the ranch. And now she practically felt his disappointment.

Austin nodded and looked down to his fidgety hands, and Vanessa melted.

"She could change her mind," she continued. "That first mention is the toughest. I've seen it with my clients and their families. The grandmother or grandfather hates the idea at first. But sometimes they give it some thought and change their minds. The important thing is, Ellie has to want to go."

At that, Austin served up a warm smile. She didn't mean to give him false hope. She was simply telling him what she'd experienced.

By the time they got to the B and B, PJ had started getting wiggly. As soon as he saw Max outside, it seemed as though her own little boy had forgotten about the feline. At least, for now. Did he get that excited when seeing his friends back home? If so, she'd never noticed.

Becca and Cody, the owners of the B and B, waved from the porch as they all exited the crossover. Max practically flew down the steps and almost knocked Vanessa over getting to his best friend.

"Did you bring the kitty cat?" Max asked.

"My mom wouldn't let me," PJ said.

Vanessa wanted to say something in her defense, but there was nothing to say.

The two ran toward the house.

And to think she'd been such a cool mom a few days ago, letting PJ have ice cream for lunch.

"Let's go inside for a minute. I'll introduce you to the owners first," Vanessa said, leading the way to the top of the steps, where Austin received a hearty handshake from Cody and a hug from Becca.

Vanessa had a hidden agenda for going inside. Maybe Ellie had some sort of magic way to fix the argument between her grandpa and Sylvie, but Vanessa had an idea of her own as to how to mend the rift between Austin and his grandma. And she knew just who to ask: the best cook in Destiny Springs.

"Is Georgina around, and if so, can we all have

a girls' chat? Alone?" Vanessa asked Becca under her breath.

Her dear friend didn't miss a beat. "Cody, would you and Austin mind keeping an eye on the boys while I steal Vanessa away? I need her advice on something, and the boys can get into a lot of trouble together, unsupervised."

"Whatever you say, darlin'," Cody said.

Becca led the way to the kitchen, where Georgina Goodwin, the part-time helper at the B and B, was whipping up something delicious-looking.

"Vanessa needs us," Becca said.

Georgina stopped, midstir, and offered her full attention.

"Have either of you heard of *Karaage*?" Vanessa asked.

Becca's brows furrowed. Georgina, however, practically shrieked. "Of course! I love that dish."

"What, exactly, is it? I'd meant to do a Google search, but since I'm here..." Vanessa said.

"Japanese fried chicken, although it doesn't have to be chicken."

Now Vanessa was really confused. There went her big idea. She had a few tried-and-true recipes for fried chicken. She'd planned to have Austin make something a little more special for Ellie to make up for the indelicate way he must have brought up moving to Colorado.

She must have had a funny look on her face,

because Georgina added, "It's not just any old fried chicken, trust me."

All hope is not lost.

"Any chance I could get the recipe?" Vanessa asked.

Georgina started scouring the pantries, pulling out some items that Vanessa would never associate with fried chicken. Things like soy sauce, potato starch. Sake.

Becca lifted the sake bottle. "I didn't know we had this."

"You put me in charge of grocery shopping, remember? I believe in being ready for anything."

"Like a good Girl Scout," Becca added.

"I really can't take your condiments, if that's what you had in mind," Vanessa said.

Georgina stopped in her tracks. "Well, then, we'll just have to fix some while you're here, won't we? I hate to admit this, but I keep all my recipes in my head, and I have to walk through them each time."

Becca raised her brows and nodded. "Strange but true."

"I have to fix something for Becca and Cody for dinner later anyway, so I might as well pull the ingredients. We can do an imaginary walk-through for now, if you don't have time to actually make it. That'll trigger my memory, and I can write it down for you."

Now, that was a good idea. She could pull Austin in, as well. Then perhaps he could make it on his own, because the more she thought about it, the more she felt she shouldn't be involved, regardless of the wager. Any semblance of keeping this whole arrangement professional was already crumbling as easily as *Karaage* breading.

Vanessa held up one finger. "Give me one second." She scurried out of the kitchen.

After scouring the downstairs and not seeing any sign of Austin or Cody, or PJ or Max, she followed the sound of moaning and screaming to its source, only to find two full-grown zombies plodding toward two giggling little boys who would "escape" the zombie clutches in the nick of time.

She stood and watched for a few minutes, and it struck her that her ex-husband never played with PJ. And here PJ was, having the time of his life. With a man who was obviously working his way into both of their hearts. No way she was going to interrupt them. No way she was going to deny PJ these moments with a father figure, because she didn't know if he'd ever have a permanent one, at this rate.

But if he ever did... *I'd want it to be Austin.*

Vanessa's breath caught in her throat. It was way too soon to have anything close to those thoughts. They hadn't even kissed. Yet she felt like she knew him. *Really* knew him.

The least she could do was take the time for an imaginary walk-through of her own. And help him cook when the time came. Or she could stop these feelings in their tracks. Let him go it alone.

She willed her breathing to return to normal and went back to the kitchen, where Becca and Georgina appeared to be holding a collective breath.

"Let's do this," Vanessa said. And she wasn't entirely referring to the *Karaage*.

AUSTIN USED TO THINK that training cutting horses was physically demanding. Turned out, it paled in comparison to either being a zombie or being chased by one.

Yet he couldn't think of a better way to spend the day.

He did need to reserve some energy for exercising Vern's horses. With or without Vanessa. In fact, he was going to insist she get some work done. He could handle the rest. They'd only need about twenty to thirty minutes each. Add on time to tack and untack, and he'd still have a little time to work Ellie's ranch, whether she wanted him to or not.

The boys ran inside while he and Cody lagged far behind.

"You and Becca have an adorable son," Austin said.

"Yes, we do. How about you? Wife? Children?" Cody asked.

"Neither. I'd like to be a husband and dad someday. It would be nice to have a youngster around the house and a wife to pamper. Right now, it's just me and my dad. Hopefully my grandma will decide to move in with us, as well, but that's not looking too promising."

"You must have a big house," Cody said.

"We have a ranch in Colorado. The Happy U. Six bedrooms, not counting the two master suites. Not as many rooms as your B and B, but I'm hoping to fill 'em all someday."

"It's nice to have a house full of guests," Cody said. "But what I like even better are those rare weekends when none of the rooms are booked, and when any and all relatives are out of town. When me and Becca and Max have the whole house to ourselves."

"I'll bet," Austin said. He'd been trying to ignore the vision of being with Vanessa and PJ full-time, as part of his family, even though he'd yet to even kiss her. Having them both around at Ellie's was making what he was going through not only bearable, but enjoyable.

"I know my situation is unique, but consider that advice. I missed out on the first six years of

Max's life. I don't want to miss another minute or be away or distracted for any length of time. You can never get those father-son years back," Cody said.

"Mind if I ask?"

"Not at all. It's no secret. Not anymore. Becca and I divorced, but then she found out she was pregnant. She didn't want to hold me back from my dream of a bull-riding championship, so she decided to raise Max on her own. I found out, by chance. But now I'm where I should have been all along. No doubt about it."

"Max is a lucky little fella."

Cody nodded. "I'm the lucky one. I guess we better go check on 'em. I bet they're terrorizing Penny in the parlor."

Sure enough, the guy was right. The three-legged Labradoodle was barking and wagging her tail as the two little zombies trudged closer. The pup would then dodge their attempts to catch her at the last minute and reposition herself for another round.

The women exited the kitchen, single file. Austin watched as Cody gave his wife a tender, extended kiss, then pulled her back in for a quick peck when she started to walk away.

Georgina echoed what Austin was thinking. "Aww."

Vanessa looked away from the kiss, but he

could tell she was smiling. She walked over to Austin, then looked past him and into the parlor.

"I never knew zombies had so much energy and covered so much ground. First playing outside with some bigger zombies, now this," she said.

"You saw us?"

"Me, and probably all the guests with windows facing the back. Thank you for going along with it. It means a lot to him. And to me."

The last part got him right in the heart. No such sentiments ever crossed his ex-wife's lips. Seemed like he couldn't do enough, and what he did do was never the right thing.

"Anytime," he said. What he wanted to say was, *All the time, if there's any way...*

"I guess you and I better get back to the ranch and exercise those horses," she said.

"I was thinking about that. I can handle it alone. You have work to do."

"That's true. But you have work to do on Ellie's ranch."

"If she'll allow me back on the property."

"Oh, she will." Vanessa held up a piece of paper. He started to reach for it, but she pulled away.

"What is it?" he asked.

She smiled. "The perfect recipe for forgiveness."

CHAPTER TEN

NOTHING TO FEAR here except for getting my lucky boots dirty.

Vanessa tried to convince her racing heart of just that as she fastened the girth on the Appaloosa, then paused.

"Need any help?" Austin asked.

Yes. She needed help with a lot of things. But tacking a horse wasn't one of them.

For starters, her soon-to-be business in Cheyenne. She'd been doing a lot of work in the early morning and at night for the past few days and made exciting progress. But her assistant had left her three text messages while Vanessa was at the B and B this morning, chasing down a recipe, of all things. Now Beth was unreachable. With PJ sleeping over at Max's, she could hopefully get hold of her, resolve the issue and get a good night's sleep for a change.

She and Austin would only be out here for a couple of hours. Then she'd take Austin up on his offer to untack the last pair of horses and return them to their stalls while Vanessa did damage control. After that, she could take him back to Ellie's and exchange him for Vern, giving her another kind of closure.

She couldn't stop watching the way Austin communicated with the Appaloosa and how the animal responded. His confidence and comfort reminded her of her dad. Her hero.

In fact, something else about Austin had reminded her of her dad. The way he'd been playing with PJ.

Only a good man with a generous heart would willingly turn into a zombie, in front of possibly an entire B and B full of guests, to make a little boy happy. Her heart had felt so full she thought it would burst as she'd watched it unfold. Every time she replayed it in her mind, her heart somehow got even fuller.

And another good man—her dad—had carved out time, no matter what was going on, to play hide-and-seek with his little girl while his wife looked on and smiled. Sometimes Vanessa's mom would give her silent clues by pointing and nodding at where she needed to look when it was her turn to be the seeker.

In those moments, there was no illness in that house. No worries. Only love and support.

"I think I've got this. It has been a few years, though," Vanessa finally answered.

Austin gave her a thumbs-up, but she could feel him watching her. She must have gotten a passing grade, because he didn't say a word as they mounted their respective horses and headed out toward the open pasture.

"Vern says he doesn't have a specific routine, so I'll let you take the lead," Austin said.

She wasn't aware of a routine either. She did know that the horses were usually free in the pasture for a large portion of each day, so the exercise was more or less a bonus.

Vanessa launched into a trot, feeling the saddle beneath her seat and leather reins in her hands. As soon as Austin caught up, she transitioned into a canter, even though her feet weren't secure in the stirrups.

Definitely the wrong boots to wear for this, but it wasn't as though she had a choice. She didn't even own an appropriate riding pair these days.

Once they were back at a slow walk, he moved in closer beside her.

"You lied to me," he said.

Vanessa looked at him. That was out of the blue.

"About what?"

"About it having been a while since you rode a horse."

She looked straight ahead again. "Would you consider twenty years a while?"

He seemed to study her. "When it comes to being off a horse, I'd consider it a lifetime."

She couldn't have defined it any better. That was when her life had changed from being a typical little girl who loved horses to being a caregiver. From going to public school to being homeschooled.

"Longest I ever went without riding every day, or even every month, was six years," he continued. "I'm not going to make that mistake ever again."

She could hear the conviction in his voice and feel it in his determined expression. Although they were talking about horses, he could have also been talking about how different their ultimate goals were.

"I stopped riding when I was eleven. After my mother underwent her first surgery for her cancer, someone needed to be in the house with her at all times. I didn't have brothers or sisters, or even cousins who were close enough to help. And Daddy supported the family with the ranch, so..."

Even over the sound of hooves hitting the bluegrass, his sigh of compassion was audible.

She was starting a new life now. Or about to. A normal one for both her and PJ. Yet she wouldn't have done anything differently as far as her own childhood went, so no sigh of compassion was necessary. By being there for her mom, and doing everything she could do, she was able to get closure when her mom passed.

Vanessa had never gotten closure with horses. Today was an opportunity for that. It was her secondary goal behind the offer to exercise her grandpa's horses and save Austin from having to spend too much of his own time taking sole care of them.

Except riding this horse again was reminding her of so many things she'd once loved and had taken for granted. The peace and clarity that riding offered during a slow walk, the anticipation evoked during a trot, and the pure adrenaline pump of a gallop.

"Feels good, doesn't it?" Austin said, as if reading her mind.

He was smiling. She hadn't realized until this moment that she was smiling, too.

"Doesn't feel half-bad." A bit of an understatement, but the last thing she needed to do was to get swept away by riding again. Or swept away by anything, to be honest. No time for such things and no horses at their house in Cheyenne. Most of all, she didn't want to encourage it for PJ. Not after he broke his arm falling off a horse on a trail here in Destiny Springs not that long ago.

Thankfully, he hadn't asked to ride again. He'd be enrolled in public school and would have plenty of extracurricular activities to choose from. And friendships. Lots of them.

With that happy image in mind, she launched the horse into a final slow trot, transitioning back down to a walk once the barns were in view. Austin didn't miss a step and was by her side most of the way.

Austin was quick on the dismount. She took it a little slower, which must have caught his attention.

"Need any—"

"No. I'm fine," she said, picking up the pace. Except, in doing so, her boot slipped out of the stirrup. She managed to land on her feet, thankfully, but she wobbled anyway.

This time, Austin didn't ask. He stepped in to steady her.

How embarrassing.

Then she remembered what had happened with Vern and Sylvie, and she couldn't help but giggle.

"Riding accidents are no laughing matter, Miss Fraser."

"I know. It's just that this same thing happened with Grandpa and Sylvie. Except he was pretending to lose his balance on purpose so that he could get her into his arms."

A knowing smile crossed his lips, and he nodded slowly.

"But I wasn't faking it, I assure you. I was

simply…clumsy. The soles of my boots are too slippery for this," she clarified.

"I was actually kind of hoping you did that intentionally."

She wasn't quite sure how to interpret that statement. Did he hope she wasn't the clumsy type? Or was he looking for a sign of interest? If the latter was the case, she felt as though she was being pretty obvious that she liked him, with the way she hadn't eased out of his embrace. Regardless of his intentions, there was no misinterpreting the way he was looking into her eyes, and how he had yet to remove his arms from around her waist, even though she was clearly steady on her feet by now.

"Next time we go riding, you will wear appropriate boots," he said.

Next time. The thought barreled through that closure she thought she'd succeeded in achieving.

"In fact, I insist on exercising the quarter horses myself. I don't want to take a chance on you getting injured," he said.

She thought for a moment he might be implying that her getting injured would mean she couldn't help him with Ellie. But something else occurred to her. PJ depended on her, more than anyone. Perhaps he was thinking of that, as well.

Unless he really was thinking only of…*her.*

The glimmer in his eye as he held her gaze told her that it could very possibly be true.

It seemed that neither of them had planned what was obviously about to happen as they leaned toward each other at the same time, ever so slightly, inching closer and closer until their lips met halfway.

And just like that, she was swept away.

AUSTIN HAD DONE some impulsive things in his time, but this beat them all.

Maybe that was the key to happiness. To not overthink everything because...*whew!* His hands were definitely trembling.

The key to more happiness would be to never let go of this woman, which was beyond impulsive.

Although they both pulled away as if they'd accidentally slipped into this moment, he didn't see a trace of regret on her face. He didn't feel any either. Although now that he was regaining his own balance, perhaps he should.

Nah.

"I'd like to personally thank those boots of yours," he said.

Vanessa smiled and looked down at her feet. "I've had them resoled three times, including recently."

"Well, I'm glad you decided to wear them. Otherwise..."

He couldn't form the words to finish his own sentence.

"You might not have kissed me?" she asked.

"Oh, I would have kissed you." *Eventually, and as soon as I got the nerve.* "But you might not have kissed me back if I hadn't rescued you from a terrible fall."

She cocked her head and offered a sly smile. "Oh, I don't know about that."

He gulped. Hard. That told him what he wanted to know, more than anything: she felt something for him, as well. If she hadn't kissed him back, his injuries would have been far worse. He would have suffered a broken heart.

"But yes. I would have ended up with a horrible, life-altering bruise if it hadn't been for you," she continued.

"An awful bruise. Unsightly," he said, adding a playful shiver.

She dropped her head and laughed.

"You know, my policy has always been to not get involved with clients or relatives," she said, once she looked back up.

His heart sank. Not that he wasn't also wondering how this would affect the situation with Ellie, moving forward. A kiss definitely altered it.

"So it's a good thing I'm not technically on the payroll. Yet," she continued, giving him a bit of a smile.

He breathed a sigh of relief. "Good. Last thing I want is for you to compromise your policies."

She nodded, and they loosened their embrace and separated.

"So...did your grandpa steal a kiss from Sylvie, too?" he asked.

She seemed to think about it. "Not that I saw. But he did steal a dance."

It was his turn to look down.

"Good thing for you I went with the kiss instead. I would have stepped all over the toes of those pretty boots with these two left feet of mine."

Vanessa nodded but didn't laugh at his bad joke. "So you didn't inherit the dancing gene from Ellie?"

He shook his head. Not that he needed a reminder, but he did want his grandma to tell him all about her time as a ballroom dance champion, if she ever spoke to him again. Which reminded him of something Vanessa had said at the B and B.

"You mentioned a recipe for forgiveness. Care to share?"

"Sharing is exactly what I had in mind. Georgina knows how to make *Karaage*, and she walked me through the steps and wrote down everything we'll need."

Wait... *We'll?*

"You don't have to help," he said. "I'm the one seeking forgiveness. What is it, anyway?"

"I do have to help. It was part of the wager I lost, remember? And *Karaage* is fried chicken, basically. Specifically, Japanese style."

"Why didn't Grandma just say so?" he asked, even though it was more of a rhetorical question.

"Because Ellie is coy that way. Like the way she's being about explaining the story behind the apology room. But I don't have to tell you that."

No, she didn't. Ellie had always been one to tease by holding back information. He just hoped that fulfilling the wager counted as an apology, as well.

Vanessa started to remove the bridle from her horse, but he stepped in and stopped her. "I'll take care of all of this. Along with the other two horses, like I promised. You go do what you need to do for your business."

He could tell she was preoccupied. The fact that she didn't insist on helping confirmed it. In fact, they'd both been sidetracked today from work and had some catching up to do, although for him that work wouldn't mean anything without Ellie's cooperation.

"Thanks," she said. She walked to the house and turned around once to see if he was watching, then waved before turning back around and continuing.

He started to pick up where she'd left off with the bridle, but his phone vibrated in his back pocket. It was from Dad's landline again. Even though he wasn't yet grounded enough to have a serious talk after that kiss, he and his father had been playing phone tag. This was another opportunity he needed to take advantage of.

"Hey, Dad. Finally," Austin launched in.

"Sorry, not your dad. This is Randy again."

If Austin survived whatever news the ranch hand was about to tell him, he'd request that the guy call from his own cell from now on. His heart couldn't take this.

"Is everything okay?" he asked, even though this call couldn't be good.

The long pause didn't inspire confidence.

"I'm not sure how to tell you this, so I'll come right out and say it. Your dad is back at it again today. Same client."

"The pushy gal?" Austin asked.

"I'm afraid so," Randy said.

"Sorry I pulled you into this," Austin said. Randy wasn't family, and Austin didn't pay the ranch hand enough to get involved in someone else's family matters.

"No problem, boss."

It struck Austin that he'd been putting Vanessa in a similar position, trying to subtly convince her, by sharing his own heart and mind, that Ellie needed to move, in hopes of gaining an ally in his cause. To Vanessa's credit, she'd stood firm in her position.

"Thanks for letting me know, Randy. And thanks...for everything."

His ranch hand ended the call before Austin remembered to ask him not to use the landline anymore.

No matter. Getting an unexpected call from the guy's cell would make his heart sink just as deep because, so far, Randy had only reached out when he had concerns about Austin's dad. Either they didn't need him at the ranch as much as he'd thought, or he was going to have to clean up a mess when he got back to Colorado.

Austin tried to busy his mind as he exercised the quarter horses, but now two more dilemmas were added to his proverbial overstacked plate: his feelings being out in the open with Vanessa, and the training sessions his dad was trying to hide.

Then there was Ellie. He sure hoped that recipe for forgiveness worked, and fast, because this feeling of dread wasn't going away until he was back at the Happy U. For some reason, things never turned this complicated at his own ranch. Then again, Vanessa wouldn't be there. Or PJ.

Now that he and Vanessa had actually kissed, he, for one, didn't want it to end there. But they had barely over a week left to spend together, and she needed to spend a good chunk of that getting ready for her new business. Which, come to think of it, he knew so little about. And now she'd be taking time out to help him fry chicken, of all things.

All sorts of competing thoughts danced through his mind, but Vanessa kept reclaiming the lead. *That kiss.* It was so brief, but it lingered. He couldn't lie…he wanted another.

But his wish list didn't end there. He wanted them in his life—both Vanessa and her adorable son. Unfortunately, it wasn't something he could have by being impulsive.

This, he would have to earn.

CHAPTER ELEVEN

"LOOKING GOOD, MISS ELLIE," Vanessa said when the woman rolled down the waistband of her powder blue sweatsuit and showed off the fact that her bandage had officially been removed by a nurse who had been sent over early this morning for the task.

"Of course I look good. But how is the incision looking?" Ellie asked.

Vanessa laughed; the woman was beyond precious. It was true, though—Ellie always looked radiant. She was going to ask for Ellie's secret beauty recipe, but she suspected she already knew. The woman had experienced the kind of love and marriage that so many people only dreamed of.

She had allowed herself to dream it could happen to her, too, for several glorious minutes. Hours, actually. That was how long it took to return from being swept away by that kiss. Even with a full night's sleep under her belt and her boots now on somewhat solid ground, she still felt optimistic. The fact that Austin had "saved" her from falling because he was worried about her getting hurt—not how an injury would affect him or anyone else—made her feel all warm and fuzzy.

"Someone is in a good mood today," Ellie said.

"Seeing you healing so nicely is brightening my day. You'll be back on the dance floor in no time," Vanessa said with a wink.

"How did you— Did Austin give me away?"

"Vern is to blame. He's usually better about keeping secrets." Vanessa settled in on the love seat before Ellie had a chance to request some music. PJ was still at Max's, so she had decided to spend a bit of time with the older woman to see if she could get her to open up. More than that, Vanessa was truly interested in knowing more about this mysterious woman. And her handsome grandson. Especially after having shared that very special and unexpected kiss.

"Did you and your husband dance together a lot?" she asked.

Ellie nodded. "Yes. And I have the broken toes to prove it. It was never his strong suit, but he loved it. We had the best time!"

So what her grandpa had said was true. Ellie's husband did have two left feet.

"That's the way it should be. My ex-husband loved to dance, too. Just not with me," Vanessa said.

As soon as she said it, she regretted it. Ellie

probably didn't want to hear the details of her failed marriage. How her ex-husband would go out in the evening, claiming a flimsy excuse, while she stayed home and took care of his grandparents who lived with them. Vanessa had never told anyone any of this, ashamed that she'd let it go on even after learning the truth about him through a friend who had seen him at a bar. But it felt so right and natural confiding in Ellie.

The woman reached over and squeezed her hand.

"I shouldn't have burdened you with this. I've forgiven him and myself, and moved on. Even if it doesn't sound like it. The past is the past."

"That's a wonderful way to look at it. There are plenty of good men out there. I know of at least one," Ellie offered.

Vanessa knew exactly who she meant, and she couldn't disagree. She also wasn't going to dive into that subject.

"I know a few, too, and I'm lucky to be related to them. My dad was one. Vern's another."

"I'm surprised your grandpa heard anything I had to say about my dancing, what with the way his heart was beating so fast for Sylvie. They are so cute together."

"He looked so happy when I picked him up yesterday. In fact, I'm not sure I've ever seen one of his smiles last that long. Obviously he and Sylvie made up. Whatever you did worked."

It also worked to ease Vanessa's conscience a little. Not only for her sake, but for Austin's. They had been gone longer than expected while exercising the horses. Yet neither of them had been needed, fortunately. Hopefully, Austin would realize that Ellie staying in her own home, and in Destiny Springs, was best for her.

"Vern didn't tell you how he and Sylvie made up?" Ellie asked.

Vanessa shook her head. "He'll fill me in eventually. Like you pointed out, he probably wouldn't have even heard my question over his heartbeat."

Ellie nodded in agreement.

Vanessa couldn't have asked for a better segue into what she needed to know.

"Are you still mad at Austin?" she asked. Might as well cut to the chase.

Ellie offered up a reserved smile. "I suppose he told you that, which by the way isn't true, but did he tell you what he proposed?"

"Yes, although I have no intention of taking sides. I'm just helping out in a professional capacity," she said, offering up a smile of her own. She left out the part that the help had kissed her unofficial boss, and it had turned quite personal.

"I could never be mad at my grandson. I understand his concern, and I know his intentions are good. I simply need for him to understand me. I have a feeling that *you* do."

"If I tell you that I understand—without taking sides—will you tell me the story behind the apology room?"

Ellie squinted. "I'll consider it."

Vanessa matched the squint. "Maybe you don't have to. Is it a coincidence that Grandpa and Sylvie made up yesterday in *this* room?"

"You're on the right track," Ellie said.

"So if we get you and Austin in this room together, y'all can make up and everything will be fine again."

"And…off the track she goes. Doesn't *quite* work that way, I'm afraid," Ellie said playfully.

"What? I was so sure I was right," Vanessa said.

"Like you were so sure you were right about the eggs?" Ellie asked, offering up yet another perfect segue.

"Point taken. In fact, Austin and I owe you *Karaage*. Tomorrow night. He and I will do all the work."

Maybe a kiss to go with it while the two of us are cooking? Like with a chip loaded with chili con queso, she didn't want to stop at one. Her heart felt hungry just thinking about it, if that were even possible.

And there she went again. Off the track, as Ellie put it.

Not that she'd stopped thinking about it. So much so, she could barely focus on the grand opening. If—when—she came completely down from the cloud Austin had swept her off to after that kiss, she'd have to get back to reality. At least with her business, happiness was within her control and all but guaranteed. Not so with relationships.

In the meantime, Vanessa would be able to assure Austin that his grandma wasn't mad at him. Even though that would technically be considered getting involved with a client, it was the least she could do for all of them. Besides, she and Austin had already barreled through that line.

"So you found out what *Karaage* is," Ellie said.

Vanessa nodded. "Where did you first have it?"

"When my dance partner and I were in Japan. At a competition. I was craving American food, and that's what they served me."

So many things she didn't know about this woman but wanted to.

"May I ask what happened to your partner?"

At that, Ellie's smile deflated. "A prettier dancer. That's what happened."

It was Vanessa's turn to reach out and squeeze Ellie's hand.

"It didn't stop me, though. At least, not in a more important way. I was determined to find the perfect partner, and I did. I met Shelton, and I was never happier. Best thing that ever happened, although my toes may not agree."

"Funny how life can work that way."

The woman had a knack for turning a negative into a positive. Vanessa wasn't so sure she was capable of it.

Ellie turned quiet. Eerily so. Talking about her late husband must have brought up so many memories. Might be good for the woman to share more, however.

They sat together in silence for several minutes.

"A penny for your thoughts," Vanessa finally said.

"I was just thinking that maybe I'm looking in the wrong place for my future happiness," Ellie said. "Maybe Austin's proposal happened to force me to consider something that could end up being even better than what I think I want."

Vanessa had been thinking the same thing about her own life, but they were cloud-nine, lack-of-oxygen type thoughts that she quickly dismissed. Such major decisions needed to be made on solid ground, and Ellie's decision regarding where to live was no exception.

"Tell me about the Happy U," Vanessa said.

At that, Ellie truly lit up. "It is certainly a magical place, mainly because of the people who live there, because what is a home without its inhabitants, right? Shelton and I loved visiting. He'd help Austin's dad on the ranch all day while Lynette and I cooked."

"Austin's mom?"

"Yes. She was also my daughter."

Was. That one word, and the way Ellie said it, almost brought tears to Vanessa's eyes. While she was contemplating asking if Ellie wanted to talk about it, the woman changed the subject.

"The guest room with the fireplace was mine and Shelton's. And Austin was the happiest little boy I've ever known. Gosh, he loved those horses."

Although Vanessa wouldn't consider PJ the happiest little boy she'd ever known, she was working on it. Everything she was doing to get her business up and running was for him. To get him back to the life he knew and loved in Cheyenne, and to all the friendships he'd made there.

"Or, I should say, loves the horses," Ellie continued. "Thank goodness Austin is back to what he was born to do, and I couldn't be happier for him. Except he won't return to the Happy U until he knows I'm safe living alone. I can't say I haven't been giving some thought to moving because I'm not even sure I can convince myself I'll be okay here. Just don't tell *him* that."

The cloud beneath Vanessa felt a little thinner than before. It was ridiculous for her to even imagine a life with him after only one kiss, but she couldn't stand thinking that in less than two weeks, he might be out of her life completely. This was happening so fast. She needed more time. *They* needed more.

Vanessa stood, pulled an album out of its sleeve, then realized it was the one that her grandpa had brought over. "Mariage d'amour." She put it on the turntable and immediately understood why Sylvie loved it so much, as Vern had stated.

"Did you ever dance to this one?" Vanessa asked.

Ellie shook her head. "No. But I always wanted to. It was composed in the 1970s, as a tribute to Chopin, I believe. I'd already stopped dancing when this came out."

"You'll dance again. I'm sure of it. In fact, I'll dance with you, because I don't have a partner. And I'd love to give ballroom dancing a try after getting to know you."

"You've come to the right teacher."

No doubt about that. Vanessa smiled, closed her eyes and visualized her grandpa tricking Sylvie into a dance last week when they were riding the horses. And how lovely Ellie must have looked in a ballroom gown.

As much as she could imagine dancing with Austin—even with those two left feet of his—she was happy he chose the kiss instead when she'd nearly fallen during her dismount.

More than happy, actually.

FEELING UNWELCOME INSIDE Ellie's house turned out to be a good thing again today. Austin was able to evaluate the stables and put together a list of repairs and materials needed, and estimated costs. He got hold of his dad, who insisted he wasn't taking any risks. According to him, the student was more or less training her own horse, and he was instructing from the ground.

And Austin only thought about Vanessa every other minute, as opposed to nonstop.

He meandered around to the back of the house, where he could see Ellie and Vanessa through one of the large windows of the big, empty room and hear muted music through the walls.

Austin stood there long enough to see them smile and laugh. Long enough to visualize them both in front of the fireplace at the Happy U, listening to music on his dad's old turntable. At least, he was fairly certain the man still owned one.

Unfortunately, his spying backfired because Vanessa spotted him and waved before he could attempt to hide. Or at least hide the fact that he'd been admiring them from afar. Ellie waved, as well, which lifted his spirits a little. He took that to mean she wasn't upset with him anymore. Maybe he really did have an ally in Vanessa, whether she'd set out to help or not.

He wandered back to the front of the house, where he noticed a truck idling at the entrance.

Vern's truck. He waited what felt like a lifetime, but the vehicle didn't budge.

Was the man okay? Austin's chest constricted, but he managed to sprint to the end of the long drive. From a closer vantage point, he could clearly see Vern with his head tilted back.

Austin went into overdrive and tried the driver's-side door. It was locked. Vern didn't budge at the rattling sound. Austin sprinted around to the passenger's side, where he got a break. It was unlocked.

When he opened the door and climbed inside, it visibly startled the driver, who seemed otherwise okay.

"You scared the livin' daylights outta me," Vern said.

"I could say the same. You've been parked here for the longest time," Austin said, leaving out the part that he thought the eighty-four-year-old might be ill or hurt. Or worse.

Vern pointed to the entryway arc. "I've been here a number of times over the years, and I just now noticed this ranch doesn't have a name. Unless you know of one."

At least he could answer that question, because he seemed to otherwise be all out of answers when it came to his grandma. "It doesn't have one. But don't ask me why."

Vern shifted the truck into gear and they rolled down the dirt road toward the house.

"My grandson Parker and his wife, Hailey, run the ranch she inherited. The place didn't have a sign for the longest time, but it does now. Sunrise Stables. Original sign, original name. Home to the legendary Destiny Springs trail rides."

"I've seen the place. Even noticed the sign."

"Maybe Ellie and Shelton never got around to putting one up," Vern said.

Austin certainly didn't want to suggest opening that door to Ellie. Not that she was so much as entertaining the possibility of moving, but putting up a sign at the ranch would be like the way she'd given Tango a name that day he showed up on her doorstep. It would signal a long-term commitment.

Vern put the truck in Park, then reached into the back seat, grabbed a couple of albums and climbed out.

When Austin didn't immediately get out, Vern climbed back in. "Now I'm the worried one. Everything okay with you?"

"Not entirely. You go on inside. I'll wait here."

Vern shook his head, stayed inside the truck and closed the door. "Wanna talk about it? I'm a good listener when I'm wearing my hearing aids. And when I'm not, I'm arguably an even better listener." Vern cackled at his own joke.

"It's no big deal, but you may want to take out your hearing aids for this. Ellie isn't too happy with me right now."

"Nah. I heard you just fine, and I don't believe that."

Austin wasn't all that sure anymore either, but just because she waved didn't mean he was forgiven.

"I told her I wanted her to move to Colorado. To the Happy U. Move in with Dad and me."

"She told me and Sylvie about that. But she's not mad at you."

All of a sudden, Austin felt like he was six years old, worried about someone being angry with him and having to be talked out of it by an adult. Except Ellie wasn't just "someone." Her opinion and feelings toward him mattered.

"You really want her to live with you and your dad, or are you just worried that something will happen if she stays here alone?"

Austin didn't have to think twice. "Both. Always loved the idea of an extended family. Being able to help care for her is a bonus."

Vern seemed to think about it. "I can't help with the moving part. That's up to her. But she has plenty of people here who love her. We're all a phone call away. No need for you to worry. I tell Vanessa the same thing all the time, and I think she finally started to listen. She needs to focus on that little boy of hers. And on her new business. Hard to do that when you have to worry about someone else."

Austin hadn't thought of it that way. A child would need the parents' focus, especially one as young as PJ. Being a single parent, she had to play both roles.

"In any event, I'm not leaving you outside alone in this truck, and definitely not alone with those thoughts you're having." Vern opened the door again and stepped down onto the ground but winced and wobbled on the landing.

Austin thought about the story Vanessa told about how Vern had tricked Sylvie into dancing with him. Was Vern trying to trick him now into getting out of the truck? The man certainly wasn't looking for a dance partner in Austin. No one should be. But Vern clearly wasn't faking the pain.

Austin got out and speed-walked around the back to the driver's side.

"Everything okay?" Austin asked.

Vern rubbed his back. "I'll be fine. Tweaked it while I was dancing with my fiancée yesterday. Totally worth it."

Austin eased the albums from Vern's grip. The man could gripe that he didn't need the help if he wanted to. Even if Vanessa came out and took Vern's side, it wasn't going to change anything. Vern finally seemed to realize it and shrugged. Together they walked up the steps and inside.

"Vanessa tells me you've gone to some great lengths to get a dance out of Sylvie."

Vern cackled again, which made Austin smile. "Yep, that pretending-I'm-gonna-fall ruse works every time. I'm just afraid that one day I'll really be falling, and that's when she'll refuse to catch me."

It was Austin's turn to laugh. That was one thing he could say about Ellie. She didn't ask for help unless she really needed it. Even then, it took a lot for her to take that step. No chance she'd cry wolf too many times. In an odd way, and thanks to Vern, he could now see that her stubborn independence wasn't necessarily a bad thing.

Vanessa was coming out of the kitchen, carrying a plate and a glass of water, when Austin and Vern entered. If her hands weren't full, Austin would be inclined to test Vern's ruse and pretend to lose his balance. Then claim another kiss.

Instead, he waved for Vanessa to walk ahead of him as they followed Vern to the big, empty room down the hall.

"I found it! And a few others you may like," Vern said to Ellie as he reclaimed the albums from Austin and set them down beside her.

"That's wonderful. And I want you to take your record back and select something from my collection."

"I'll take you up on that." While Vern flipped through her stack of albums, Austin went to his grandma's side and leaned in for a hug. "I'm sorry about—"

"No apology necessary," Ellie whispered back.

"This is the apology room, isn't it?" Austin asked. Ever since Vanessa had told him of Ellie's name for the room, he couldn't shake his curiosity. But, like Vanessa had pointed out, his grandma liked to wear a shroud of mystery.

"It is. But any apologies to me aren't accepted here."

Great. Another layer of mystery he'd have to unpeel without making an even bigger mess. Which reminded him of those deviled eggs that his two favorite women made for him. And the fact that he and Vanessa were going to cook for Ellie.

He wished it would happen tonight. Sure, Ellie claimed she didn't require an apology this time. But if he did a good job on the *Karaage*, maybe it would serve as an apology in advance, because he wasn't finished trying to persuade her to move to the Happy U.

And he was just getting started in finding a way to keep Vanessa in his life.

CHAPTER TWELVE

BEING AWAY FROM PJ was almost worth the reward of having his little arms wrapped around her neck so tightly and enthusiastically.

"I missed you, Mommy," he said.

"Aww, I missed you more." She gave him an extra-tight squeeze right back. The one-night sleepover at the B and B had turned into two. Seemed that Becca also wasn't immune to the little zombies' charms when they begged to let PJ stay an extra day. And since she was insistent, Vanessa had agreed. After all, she wanted PJ to spend as much time as possible with his friend before they went back to Cheyenne, after which video chats would take the place of playdates entirely. Of course, she hoped to make the three-plus-hour drive to Destiny Springs as often as she could on weekends, or Max and his parents could visit them in Cheyenne.

However, it would be a while before either scenario would be possible. Normalcy wasn't a clean and simple process. Or a quick one.

Becca and Max stood nearby, with Max clinging to his own mommy's legs and looking so sad that his best friend couldn't sleep over forever.

"Did y'all have a good time?" she asked her own little one, if only to have PJ reassure Max that he wouldn't be forgotten once they went out the front door.

PJ nodded and smiled so big. That was one thing about him. He was easy to read. She rarely had to guess how he felt. Hopefully, that would never change.

She felt pretty sure she could guess how Austin felt. She'd tried not to hide her feelings around him either.

"Our B and B guests here had a blast, too. All but a couple of them turned into zombies," Becca said.

At least the game was still alive and well, so to speak.

Something else good came out of PJ's extra sleepover night. Vanessa was able to make progress on a few of the outstanding items needed for the rest-and-recovery room at the center. The sofas she originally ordered were much too hard. But when she had the cushions restuffed, they were too soft. Not good for anyone's back. Then she realized it was best to have an assortment of firmness to choose from and instructed the business to add the stuffing back in increments.

The most stubborn problem remained, however: how to make use of that empty office space. She was still kicking herself for overlooking something that was right there in front of her eyes. The money she would've saved could have been spent on additional caregivers and therapists, even though it wasn't an immediate need. But if her client list expanded, it could quickly become an issue.

Since she'd overestimated the lease space needed, she'd have to spend even more money she didn't have to fill the room with something useful, because the thought of the space being wasted made her feel even worse.

"Let's get going, shall we?" she said to PJ.

The little boy nodded but looked at his feet. He really didn't want to leave his friend, even though this wasn't the last time they'd get to play before she and PJ left.

Becca made a move to block the door. "You can't leave just yet."

"Why not?"

"Because there are zombies all around us, and y'all are safer here," Max chimed in. "PJ can sleep in my room again with me, and you can sleep in another room or on the couch."

Vanessa thought it was adorable how Max would go to any lengths to keep PJ around. But she'd already suffered through two nights without her little boy. She'd fight zombies before she'd leave him behind for another.

"I'm afraid he's right," Becca said, not budging from her post. The woman then looked past her, toward the kitchen. "Georgina! Hurry up. They're trying to escape."

"You sure all the zombies are outside of the house?" Vanessa teased.

"No. They're inside, too. Mommy is one of them," Max said, followed by a full-blown giggle, which proved to be contagious, because it tickled her throat until she giggled, too.

"That's right, cowboy. And when I'm done here, I'm coming for you!" Becca said.

Max shrieked and wiggled as if he were being tickled.

"Don't let her leave. I'm almost done," Georgina called back.

"Now I'm getting scared. What's going on, exactly?" Vanessa asked Becca.

No explanation was forthcoming. Just a shrug of Becca's shoulders.

Finally, Georgina emerged from the kitchen with a large picnic basket. She set it on an entry table next to Vanessa, opened the lid and pointed to its contents.

"You'll need to get these chicken thighs in the refrigerator, but they're sitting on an ice pack, so don't get a speeding ticket on the way home. Everything else should be fine to store in the pantry for now. Some may need refrigerating after opening, but all that's on the label."

Vanessa peered into the basket. Soy sauce, ginger root, potato starch...

"How did you know that Austin and I are making this tonight?"

Becca and Georgina looked at each other.

"We didn't. Y'all are cooking together?" Becca asked.

"That's so romantic!" Georgina added. "I did not know. I just wanted you to have all the ingredients on hand and not have to hunt them down at the market."

Vanessa was speechless. This was probably the only time anyone had ever done the grocery shopping for her. And cooking with Austin was kind of romantic, wasn't it? Except Ellie and PJ would be in the next room.

"We better leave now before you two spoil me any further. Thank you so much! You have no idea how extremely helpful this is to me. I'll return the unused condiments."

"You don't need to do that. You're like family to us, Vanessa. What's ours is yours," Becca said. "In case you don't believe it, Max calls PJ his brother all the time. I'm pretty sure he believes it."

"He is my brother, and I'm his brother," Max confirmed.

This whole town felt like one big extended family.

She got PJ buckled into the car seat and looked at him in the rearview mirror. Now that she didn't have to go grocery shopping, that freed up a little time before she had to be at Ellie's. That also meant they could stop by the house and check on Vern. Unless there was something specific PJ wanted to do.

"So, sweetheart, is there anywhere you want to go? Maybe a quick walk around the square?" They couldn't do much more than that in the spare time they had, plus she had the raw chicken thighs to consider.

The suggestion didn't seem to thrill PJ.

"Or we could stop by the house and give Grandpa a big hug before we go over to Ellie's."

That did the trick.

"Can Pawpaw go with us?" PJ asked.

Now, there was an idea. Georgina had certainly provided enough food. Vanessa could barely lift the basket.

"I'll ask Austin and Ellie to see if they're okay with it. If so, you can invite Pawpaw."

That perked PJ up a little after having to leave Max behind just now.

Vanessa texted Austin. By the time she got to Fraser Ranch, he had responded:

Of course! The more family, the merrier.

Right. She could have written that answer for him.

Vern was sitting on the heating pad when she came home. Before she could ask, he explained.

"I tweaked it while I was dancing with Sylvie. I'll be fine. You go on to dinner."

"Speaking of Sylvie, is she around?"

"Not at the moment, but soon. I lured her into coming over by offering to play the album that Ellie loaned me. I'm pretty sure she'll like it."

"Come to Miss Ellie's with us, Pawpaw. Miss Sylvie can come, too," PJ piped up.

That would require another text to Austin, which would give him an opportunity to drive home the *merrier* fact.

Vern shifted and tried unsuccessfully to suppress a grimace.

"How about tomorrow?" he asked.

That was when Vanessa knew he really was in some pain. He wouldn't have otherwise turned down the invitation.

PJ looked crestfallen. "Okay."

"That will probably work." She'd figure out *tomorrow* when it arrived, because all she could think of right now was that raw chicken sitting in the picnic basket in the crossover.

"I'll have my cell phone out at all times. Please call if you need help with anything," she said, at the risk of being too bossy.

He gave her a captain's salute as she took PJ's hand and headed toward the door. But PJ stopped and dug in his heels before they even reached the door.

"What's the matter?" she asked.

"Can I stay with Pawpaw? I can help him if he needs help, so you don't have to."

She didn't see *that* coming. Yet PJ was picking up on everything these days. She needed to be extra careful with her words around him.

"He'll be fine, sweetheart. Just an achy back. You can take care of yourself until Sylvie gets here, can't you, Grandpa?" She turned and looked at him, hoping he'd play along.

"Believe you can and you're halfway there. Pretty sure Teddy Roosevelt said that. I'd add that halfway is good enough at my age."

Not the resounding support she was looking for.

"But I *want* to stay with Pawpaw," PJ said.

Vanessa gulped. Sounded similar to something Austin might say. After all, he not only felt that Ellie needed to move in with him, he actually wanted her to.

Like father, like…

She shook her head to dislodge the totally inaccurate connection, then looked to Vern, who seemed equally surprised at PJ's choice.

"Tango will miss you, but I suppose you can see him tomorrow," she said.

That prompted him to look at his feet again. She wasn't playing fair, making him choose, and she knew it.

She was feeling a little unhappy, as well, at the thought of leaving PJ and Vern behind. Maybe Austin's preference for having family together under one roof was getting through to her. There were definite benefits that offset the responsibilities. Learning how to finally make hard-boiled eggs came to mind, or finding out a better way to stop an ice-cream brain freeze. Both thanks to Ellie. But Vanessa wasn't quite yet swept away by the idea.

Problem was, she no longer felt any solid ground beneath her boots either.

THE OVERSIZE PICNIC basket that Georgina had packed seemed bottomless. Then again, she'd not only packed the food items but also the utensils. And even a mini deep fryer. No wonder the basket was so heavy.

I bet Georgina could fill that extra office space.

Vanessa smiled at the thought while cringing inside. She still hadn't come up with a halfway decent idea, although she could blame Austin for that. For choosing to kiss her instead of dance.

Beth, her assistant, hadn't thought of anything either. The woman seemed distracted but was denying it. She did have lots of balls in the air with Vanessa not being there, but thankfully there hadn't been too many dropped ones. That she was aware of, at least.

Austin came into the kitchen and slowly surveyed the counter. No doubt he didn't recognize the place.

"You forgot the most important thing," he said.

She looked over the multitude of items and pulled out the recipe to check everything off again, one by one.

Austin eased the piece of paper from her hands. "I was talking about PJ."

Oh, yeah. When she'd first walked in, she came directly to the kitchen to put the chicken in the fridge. And to set the basket down, empty the thing and take a full inventory before she started. Nothing was worse than being in the middle of cooking and discovering an ingredient was missing. She vaguely remembered Ellie calling out something as she whisked by but had said she'd be right back. That was at least ten minutes ago.

"He wanted to stay home with Grandpa," she said.

When her words landed, Austin's smile flatlined and his eyes turned sad again. That made her realize she hadn't seen that version of them lately.

"Vern didn't feel up to joining us, huh? Is his back gonna be okay? I knew it was bothering him," he said.

She was beginning to wonder about that herself. He was having more and more incidents lately. More than usual. At least he wasn't falling yet. Not that he'd admitted.

"When I left, he was sitting on a heating pad. Said he tweaked his back while dancing with Sylvie. Then he said it was worth it. I get that," she said.

Austin shuffled his self-described two left feet. That was when Vanessa made the connection to what he'd said about not being a good dancer.

"So PJ was worried about his grandpa and picked family over fried chicken? The kid has his priorities straight."

It was her turn to feel the sting of words, even though she wasn't sure whether his were intentional. Was she being selfish by being over here, rather than taking care of ailing family? Or perhaps by going back to Cheyenne and leaving her eighty-four-year-old grandpa to fend for himself? Maybe cooking together wasn't going to be so romantic after all. Maybe she should simply get down to the business of fulfilling the wager instead of thinking this evening could end up being anything more.

She chose to ignore the remark. Instead, she said, "Georgina packed everything we need except for a mixing bowl. I'm sure Ellie has one somewhere…" Vanessa began opening cabinets, working around Austin rather than asking him to move.

He opened a cabinet and pulled a bowl from a high shelf. When she tried to take it from him, he wouldn't let go until she looked him in the eye.

"Hey, I didn't mean that the way it sounded," he said. "Your priorities are right where they should be. On PJ's happiness. I'll try not to be too envious that he picked Vern over me."

"Oh, I'm pretty sure he adores you. If he had it his way, we'd all be together tonight."

Austin would surely like hearing that. Perhaps even gloat a little.

Still, his words made her think. Her whole life had been about making such decisions when caring for others. Caregiver burnout was real. It was important to set realistic goals and take time for self-care. For the first time in her life, she'd begun that process with the opening of her business. And with being here tonight and daring to hope for a relationship that wasn't based on someone needing what she had to offer professionally but, instead, needing *her*.

But it was too easy for doubt and guilt to seep in. Even when unintentional words didn't open the door and usher them in as they could so easily do.

Austin unpeeled her fingers from the bowl, set it down on the counter and wrapped his arms around her, pulling her in and holding her tight. All doubt and guilt dissolved, to be replaced with warmth and assurance.

He loosened his hold and looked into her eyes again.

"You're the strongest woman I know. The most giving. But Vanessa needs to take care of Vanessa. And if there's anything I can do to help…"

There was one thing she could think of. He seemed to have the same thought as he leaned in for a kiss. This one lasted more than a heartbeat, and when they pushed away from each other, it was as if a force beyond them pulled them back together for seconds.

No telling how long that one would have lasted, because it was interrupted by the sound of wheels on linoleum. There was Ellie, driving the walker and wearing a big smile that didn't register any degree of surprise.

"Don't let me interrupt. I'm just going to grab some iced tea. I'll be out of your way in a second, and you can continue…you know…"

Vanessa felt her face turn red. There was no question that Ellie had walked in on them in the middle of the kiss.

Austin started to help Ellie with the tea, but Vanessa squeezed his arm and stopped him.

"She's got this. As long as she doesn't have to reach or bend," Vanessa whispered. But, of course, they both watched her every move, ready to step in. And Vanessa wouldn't have it any other way.

"Carry on," Ellie said with a smile that hadn't shifted for one second that Vanessa could tell. She set her glass on the seat of the walker to transport. The woman had filled it so full, Vanessa was afraid it would tip over.

At least that would be a mess that could easily be cleaned up.

The one she and Austin might be creating? Not so much.

They watched Ellie until she was out of their line of vision before daring to look at each other again. It seemed to be understood that they needed to get back to the reason—or one of the reasons—Vanessa had come over in the first place. *Karaage*.

She picked up the recipe and struggled to focus.

"We'll need to do the marinade first. I'll grate the garlic and ginger, you measure out the sake and soy sauce. We'll add the pepper and cayenne last. Oh, and a pinch of sugar."

"Yes, ma'am," Austin said.

After they finished mixing the ingredients and saturating the chicken, getting the marinade into all the nooks and crannies of the boneless thighs, Vanessa read the recipe again. She'd all but forgotten one important step. One that might require a little dancing around.

"O-kay. So, this has to sit in the fridge for at least an hour," she said. They looked at each other with the same thought in mind. How would they pass the time?

There was only one answer: visit with Ellie in the den—while knowing that the woman knew that she and Austin more than "liked" each other. Vanessa felt like a naughty child who had promised to "be good" and keep this relationship completely professional, then spectacularly broke that promise.

Austin's situation was even less comfortable. At least she'd be going back to her grandpa's house at the end of the evening, and the man didn't know anything about the kiss. No doubt Ellie would eventually tell Vern, but at least Vanessa would have a little time to enjoy their secret.

"Looks like we'll be talking with Ellie for the next hour. Gosh, I wonder what subjects will come up?" Vanessa teased.

"My thoughts exactly. But I have a suggestion."

"Do tell," she said.

He smiled. "Shall we dance?"

Her breath hitched. "What about your two left feet?"

Austin looked confused for a moment, then

laughed. "I mean the movie. It's one of her favorites."

Vanessa hoped the disappointment didn't show on her face. Even though she'd love to dance with him, she was a bit surprised at how much the thought had thrilled her. But his actual idea to watch a movie was the next best thing. At least any conversation or additional matchmaking on Ellie's part could be dodged. There was only one problem.

"She watched that movie a couple of days ago."

"And the week before that. And when I first got to Destiny Springs. I suspect she can't watch it enough."

"Y'all also watched *Love Story*, if I remember correctly. But we won't suggest that one."

Austin nodded. "Agreed."

Vanessa covered the chicken with clear plastic wrap and placed it in the refrigerator. Together, they would brave this new situation: the one they had created with Ellie by letting her catch them in the act.

More importantly, the situation that the two of them had just begun to navigate.

AUSTIN WASN'T SURE whether the smile on Ellie's face for the past hour had been because she was watching her favorite movie, or because she'd walked in on him and Vanessa kissing.

Either way, he was thankful to be back in the kitchen, cooking up some *Karaage*. And perhaps a little bit of trouble, if he were to be honest. His grandma would be occupied for a little while longer. Although he wanted another kiss, he didn't want to disrupt Vanessa's focus on the task at hand.

She'd set up a pan with aluminum foil but was looking for something else in the cabinets.

"I need a baking and cooling grid," she said before he had a chance to ask. "We're going to dredge the marinated chicken in potato starch, then deep-fry. Fill the fryer with oil up to the mark on the inside, if you don't mind."

Vanessa handed him a bottle and pointed to an extruded mark inside the fryer, then resumed her search.

"Ah! Here's one," she said. She placed the piece over the pan with aluminum foil.

Yeah, he would have never guessed what she was looking for. He did as he was told. She poured something into a bowl and coated each piece, then spaced them out on top of the grid.

"You're really good at this," he said. "You sure you haven't made it before?"

She looked up long enough to smile. "I've probably made everything except this. But I got an earlier start than most. My mom loved to cook, but after she got sick, I took over."

He remembered how much time and love his mom would put into meals. And how many times he'd grab a fried chicken drumstick and run out the door, rather than sitting down with his family and having a proper meal.

Austin regretted those moments now. Whenever he had a family, eating dinner together would be a requirement. But to be in the role of meal preparer growing up? He couldn't begin to imagine.

"When did you start cooking?" he asked.

"Eleven."

His jaw could have hit the floor. He was thinking she'd been a teenager or young adult when all that happened.

She dropped a couple of pieces into the fryer. He leaned over to observe.

"That must have been so difficult," he said.

Vanessa set a timer, then turned sideways and leaned against the counter, facing him as the chicken sizzled.

"It wasn't as hard for me as it was for my mom to go through chemo. The worst part about the whole thing was, she lost her independence. Even though I was young, I saw the importance of that through her eyes. Even more so as I got older."

His own father sprang to mind. Maybe these behind-his-son's-back training sessions had something to do with Austin's need to control the situation. His intentions were good, but that didn't mean they were right or fair to his dad.

All of a sudden, he felt a bit embarrassed that he'd been making such a big deal of it, and having the ranch hands essentially spy on the man and report back.

But Vanessa's situation had been much different, and worse. Her mom didn't have a choice but to depend on others.

"She was so lucky to have such a wonderful daughter and support system," he said.

"Being able to take care of her was a privilege I wouldn't trade for anything. Wouldn't even trade it for all the football games and school dances I missed. At the same time, I wish I hadn't had to, if that makes sense. I sure don't want PJ to miss out on such things."

The timer *dinged*, and she took the lead in flipping the chicken.

"This is looking so good," she said.

He couldn't agree more.

"Let me know when they're done, and I'll fish them out with that thingy," he said, pointing to some sort of slotted spoon. "Can't let you do all the work when it's supposed to be a team effort."

"The thingy is called a spider. And you're a terrific team member," she said, setting the timer once again.

"Well, I think you're lucky to have been able to

help your mom. Mine passed while I was off living a life that I didn't even enjoy. And I still didn't make it to football games. Professional ones, that is, like a lot of guys I worked with. But I'd rather go to the rodeo anyway."

Vanessa smiled. "I can totally see that."

Austin peered into the fryer, then looked at the timer. He did have something else he wanted to share while they were on the subject.

"I'm pretty sure I could have saved my mom if I'd been there to care for her," he said without embellishment.

Vanessa unfolded her arms and rested her hands on her hips, looking as though she might reprimand him for the thought.

"No," she said, shaking her head. "I don't know the specifics, but do *not* blame yourself."

He willed the tears not to well up in his eyes. Vanessa had already seen him cry once. Over a movie, of all silly things. Wasn't going to let it happen again.

"If I don't blame myself, then who? Not my dad. He did everything he could. And not the caregivers he hired."

He fully expected a genuine reprimand now, because on some level even he knew how unrealistic that sounded. But he'd held these feelings in for so long, he couldn't stop the spill.

Instead, she gave him the fiercest hug he'd ever

received from anyone. She really *was* the strongest woman he'd ever known. Literally. But in a very warm and loving way.

Not to mention, just the Angel this Little Buckaroo needed in the moment.

The timer *dinged* once again. Thank goodness they had set it, because both of them were reluctant to let go.

He grabbed the spider before she could intervene and fished out the pieces of fried chicken. If it tasted as good as it smelled, then it could make Ellie forget the kiss she'd witnessed.

But he would always remember it.

"If you don't mind, slice these lemons into halves. We're supposed to squeeze lemon juice over the chicken as we eat. I'll fix the cabbage salad," she said.

He did as instructed, admiring the way she could focus during such moments. But that was likely the mark of an excellent caregiver. To be able to separate her personal feelings from her professional duties. Not that what they were doing right now was a duty. Not in his eyes. In fact, it was a pleasure.

"My father died in a ranching accident after I got married and moved away. Initially I thought that if I had been there, I could've prevented it. But I quickly concluded I was wrong. It would've happened anyway. Besides, he was doing what he loved, and on his own terms," she said, without a trace of regret in her voice. In fact, she continued to prepare the cabbage salad without even pausing.

It took a moment for that to sink in, but he knew what she was trying to tell him. And even *show* him by not letting it hurt her now.

Not that he totally embraced it. He still felt as though he could have made a difference in the outcome. At the very least, he wouldn't have lost that time with his mom.

He grabbed some dinner plates as she arranged the food on a tray, and together they went into the den, where Ellie was still immersed in the movie that, if he remembered correctly, would sum up in another ten minutes.

Much to his amazement, Ellie stopped the movie and surveyed the feast that Vanessa had laid out on the coffee table in front of them.

Vanessa fixed Ellie a plate, then prepared a generous serving for him. One bite into the *Karaage* and he understood why this was his grandma's favorite dish.

Ellie closed her eyes as she savored the chicken. "This is even better than I remember. And I must have tried every recipe."

"Meals made with love are always the best," Vanessa said. "Austin wanted this to be special for you. So did I."

Austin took another bite of the extra-crispy but extraordinarily juicy chicken. He'd already been digesting everything that Vanessa said and realized that perhaps he was trying too hard to control his grandma. And to control every outcome in regard to his own father's safety.

In fact, if Ellie wanted to stay here at her ranch in Destiny Springs, he would support it. With a little more thought, he might even encourage it.

They savored the meal in silence until the tray was all but licked clean. He helped collect the plates and take them to the kitchen. Once he set them in the sink and was reaching for the faucet, Vanessa said, "I've got this. You go find out if we got a passing grade from Ellie."

He didn't argue, nor would he complain. It would give him and Ellie a few moments alone.

His grandma still had a satisfied look on her face when he returned to the den. Hopefully from the chicken, but more likely from the kiss she'd witnessed.

"Thank you, Austin. This was the most wonderful meal," she said.

"I'll cook it for you anytime. And if you change your mind and move to the Happy U, we can have this as often as you want," he said, half teasing.

She'd clearly forgiven him for the first time he'd brought it up. There was no easy way to keep the topic alive, however.

Instead of laughing or agreeing, she folded her hands in her lap.

"I've been thinking a lot about that, Austin," she said.

He wanted to tell her to stop thinking so much. No need to do anything rash because the door would always be open for her at the Happy U.

"I can't help but think about it, Grandma. Mainly, about how I was wrong to bring it up," he said.

She reached over, patted his hands and looked him in the eye. "Not at all. I can see your side of it. I want to see your side of it. If *Karaage* is always on the menu at the Happy U, then I will consider it."

The air left his lungs.

What? Just when he thought he had it all figured out. This was what he had wanted all along.

Yet having her willing to move to Colorado may have changed everything about a future he was just now daring to envision. One that included a level of happiness he'd stopped believing in long ago. Specifically, a future that included Vanessa.

If he could somehow make that happen, he really would "have it all."

CHAPTER THIRTEEN

PJ RAN INTO the den and wrapped his arms around Ellie's legs before Vanessa could warn him not to.

"I missed you, Miss Ellie."

The woman visibly winced and clung to her walker.

"Not too tight, PJ. Miss Ellie's still healing from her surgery."

PJ dropped his head and loosened his grip on the woman, which broke Vanessa's heart. She hadn't meant to break his enthusiasm.

With one arm, Ellie managed to pull him back in for a hug.

"I missed you, too," she said. "But I'm glad you wanted to stay with your pawpaw instead last night. I know he loved and appreciated it."

Vanessa set down her laptop and ran over to assess the damage and unpeel her son.

"Are you okay?" she whispered to Ellie.

"Yes, dear. No harm done."

"Did Tango miss me, too?" PJ asked.

"Absolutely! I saw him wandering down the

hall, looking for his best friend," Ellie said, which sent PJ running to find the feline.

Vanessa helped Ellie get situated in the ladder-back chair, hoping that PJ truly hadn't caused her any pain. Young children and the elderly didn't always mix, like certain chemicals. Individually? No problem. But when together, potential trouble.

She'd never had to worry about PJ giving too-tight hugs to her other clients, even though a couple of them had grown close to her little boy, and he'd grown close to them. One in particular—Mr. Lake—who was staying on as her client and promised to be at the grand opening. But PJ seemed to have a special fondness for Ellie.

It only took him a few minutes to locate Tango. The feline was quite wiggly as the little boy returned to the den with him.

"Would you like to watch another movie or maybe listen to some records?" she asked Ellie.

"I know you have to concentrate, so I thought I'd read a book." Ellie pointed to a hardcover novel on a side table, just out of reach.

PJ set the kitty on the sofa and retrieved the book for her. "I'm sorry I hurt you, Miss Ellie. I love you and Tango and Mr. Austin."

"We love you, too, PJ. And didn't we all agree that love hurts sometimes? But not always in a bad way?" Ellie said.

"I didn't mean to hurt *you*, sweetheart," Vanessa swiftly confessed to PJ.

"I'm sorry, as well," Austin chimed in from somewhere in her periphery.

Vanessa had assumed he was outside on the property. Instead, he emerged from the kitchen wearing rubber cleaning gloves and holding a sponge.

"For what?" Vanessa asked.

He shrugged. "I don't know, but everyone was apologizing, and I felt left out."

Vanessa couldn't help but laugh at the lovefest vibe in the room. She was rather grateful that someone had lightened the mood.

Austin shifted his focus to Ellie. "Almost done, Grandma. The couple will be here in about an hour, so if you can't think of anything else inside the house, I'll sweep the front porch."

Vanessa hadn't really thought about it, but the house did look particularly tidy. And it smelled of lemon oil. The wood furniture looked freshly dusted, and the area rug had vacuum cleaner tracks.

"I didn't know y'all were having company. I can always come back later or tomorrow if you need me to."

Although they didn't have a set schedule, coming over had worked out so well for everyone. She could get work done while Austin was outside. Besides, their visits had become the high-light of PJ's day.

Ellie shook her head. "You're welcome to stay. Austin, tell Vanessa what's going on."

Austin set the sponge down and removed the rubber gloves. "Some folks expressed interest in the ranch and house. They're coming over to look at the property."

Vanessa searched Ellie's face for some kind of clue as to whether this was what she wanted, even though she had mentioned that she might con-sider it. But the woman's resting expression was always a warm smile, so it was difficult to tell.

"That sounds promising," she said, for lack of a better response.

"Ellie is still undecided," he said to Vanessa, then turned to Ellie. "Your happiness is the most important thing, Grandma, although, in my opin-ion, it's tied with your safety."

"You and Tango can move in with me and Mommy if you don't have a house to live in," PJ said to Ellie.

Vanessa's stomach seized. Although it would be fun to have Ellie living under the same roof, it wasn't part of her plan. Besides, she still be-lieved that the woman would eventually be per-fectly fine living alone for a while longer. She'd tried so hard to remain neutral when it came to this situation.

Tried, and failed.

"That's such a sweet offer, PJ, but Tango and I might be moving to Colorado. You and your mom are welcome to visit anytime. Right, Austin?"

"I insist. We have plenty of room for guests. And family," he said without losing eye contact.

All of a sudden, everything seemed to be moving too fast.

PJ wasn't taking the news so well. He held Tango even closer and looked as though he was about to cry.

Vanessa walked over and brushed the hair out of his eyes to make sure he was okay. "Everyone is welcome to visit us in Cheyenne, too. We have a couple of spare guest rooms."

What else could she say?

"Tango can sleep in my room when you come visit," PJ said.

"I'm pretty sure he'd insist," Austin said.

"That is a splendid idea, PJ," Ellie added.

Austin was still looking at her, but with a different kind of expression that went farther south than those naturally downturned eyes could convey. He didn't have to say a word. She felt it, too.

What she hoped her own eyes didn't convey was her desire that Ellie would choose to stay in her own home. Not that that would change anything between her and Austin. Even though they were growing closer, certain facts remained. He shared a ranch and business with his father, who Austin claimed needed assistance at times. And she had worked so hard to get to the point that she was opening her own business. Her life, for the next while at least, was in Cheyenne. Maybe this was the wake-up call she needed, because she had lots of work to do before the grand opening in a week. She'd been swept away too many times now.

"Take your laptop, Vanessa, and let's head to the back room," Ellie said. "I'm sure the folks will want to look at the space, but no doubt they'll be more interested in the rest of the house. PJ and Tango can hang out with us, too. We'll keep the door closed so the kitty doesn't run out."

Sounded like a good plan to Vanessa. She needed a quiet place away from Austin to collect her thoughts and process this new development.

She grabbed her laptop while Austin spotted Ellie as she stood and took command of the walker. PJ picked up the reluctant cat, once again, and took the lead down the hallway.

Ellie got comfortable in her chair, book in hand, while PJ and Tango claimed the larger portion of the love seat. Vanessa stayed in the hallway with Austin and closed the door behind her.

"So this is really happening," she said.

"I don't know what's going to happen, to be

honest. It's Ellie's decision. I think I convinced her of that."

Vanessa didn't say what she was thinking: that his desire for her to move factored into that decision. How much remained to be seen.

"You don't seem convinced," he said.

"It doesn't matter what I think, Austin. This is a decision for your family. Personally, I think she'll find happiness in either place, so I'm not worried about her."

"Then who are you worried about? Me? You don't have to be. You know how much I'd like this to work out, but if she doesn't want to go, I can't force her."

She shook her head. "I'm worried about *us*."

There. She'd said it, even though she hadn't planned to. She had no idea whether there was even an "us" to be worried about. Or whether he felt the same way. Or whether the kisses they'd now shared happened out of weakness or opportunity…or something more. For her, it was the latter. It was…*falling in love*.

Austin rested his hands on his hips. "I am, too, Vanessa." The way he looked at her was convincing enough. But it would take more than that for them to take moving forward literally.

She hadn't come here expecting such a heavy conversation. She was sure he hadn't either. It was the last thing either of them needed. Thankfully, a knock on the door saved her from saying even more, because she hadn't put too many words to her feelings just yet.

"They must be early," Austin said.

"Well, we'll be in here," Vanessa said, her mind reeling after what she'd just confessed. She tried for some humor. "Hey, with any luck, Ellie will finally tell someone the history behind the apology room, and then that mystery will be solved." Might as well hope for clarity on something.

That made him smile. She certainly didn't intend on leaving Destiny Springs without knowing the full story.

Austin turned and headed down the hall.

"Good luck!" she called out. And she meant it. She hadn't intended to bring up their relationship—or whatever it was, although it was definitely something more than friendship—and put that into his head before having to do a real estate pitch. In fact, she needed to wrap her mind around her own business problems. One in particular—what to do with that extra room at the center.

He gave her a thumbs-up.

She went back inside the room and closed the door. Ellie was a few pages into her book, and PJ was fast asleep, with a relaxed and purring Tango tucked beneath his arm. It was the only sound in the room, next to the turning of pages.

She settled onto the love seat and turned on

her computer, resting it in her lap. Maybe not the best way to work, but it certainly was comfortable. And the view was spectacular from here.

As she responded to the emails that had piled up in her inbox, she kept getting distracted by Ellie, who was setting down her book, then picking it up again, then huffing and practically slamming it down on the side table.

"Not a good story, huh?" she asked.

"I'm afraid not. It's science fiction. I don't even know where this came from, except it was on my bookshelf and it was the only one I was pretty sure I hadn't read."

"Did Shelton like the genre?"

"I didn't think so. He liked romances, if you can believe it. Personally, I never did care for them. Maybe because my personal story was so much better than anything a writer could come up with."

Precious.

"Even with the fights and apologies y'all had?" Vanessa dared to ask. The woman was captive in this room. If Vanessa was going to take advantage of a situation, this was her opportunity.

"Possibly because of them. In fact, Shelton would intentionally pick fights with me."

Now, *this* was getting interesting. Ellie didn't seem like the type of woman to put up with such things.

"For example…?" Vanessa prompted.

"He'd accuse me of being too good of a cook, and that I was making him fat."

Vanessa couldn't help but laugh. Those kinds of fights, she could handle.

"And he'd tell me I was too pretty, and that's why he forgot to do this or that task that I'd asked him to do around the house. Too distracted by my beauty, he'd say, and therefore it was all my fault. But it always ended up that he'd done the chores anyway. Like I said, he enjoyed picking fights. I actually got mad at first, until I figured out he was doing it for fun."

"Aww. He sounds like quite a character."

"He was one of a kind." At that, Ellie turned quiet and reflective.

After a moment of silence, Vanessa resumed working. Or tried to. She wanted to close down her computer just as Ellie had closed that book, but there was so much to do and she was running out of time.

She blew out an audible sigh. Couldn't hold in her frustration any longer.

"Sounds like you've got some interesting reading there," Ellie said.

Vanessa reached up and rubbed her temples. She felt a migraine coming on.

"I've been struggling with an issue for my grand opening. I leased too much space and have an empty room. I'm stuck with a space I won't even be using. It's not the end of the world, I suppose, but I hate wasting things. And I mean *hate*. I know you understand the feeling."

Ellie raised her brows and nodded. "What kind of building is it?"

"Commercial. It's for my offices, as well as an activity center for my senior clients. We have a large space that we're using as a relaxation room and we've filled it with comfortable chairs and sofas for reading or chatting and drinking coffee. We added a large-screen television and are planning to have a movie matinee once a week. We also have a gym with treadmills and light arm weights. Our licensed trainers and physical therapists are there to supervise and get necessary permissions from doctors. And there's another room filled with tables for board games and painting and puzzles, and bingo on Sunday afternoon. But this empty space is wasted. I don't need the storage, and I don't have the budget to add anything else."

"I have a spare turntable you can put in there. That's all you really need," Ellie said.

The comparison to the big, empty room they were currently in wasn't lost on Vanessa. Yet the suggestion got her thinking.

"I like it. Maybe it could be a music room. Except we'd need for someone to donate instruments. At least a piano. Otherwise, it would cost too much. So I guess that idea is out."

Ellie shook her head. "All you need is a turntable and some records, which I could donate. And maybe a dance instructor at certain times."

The woman was beyond brilliant. Dance lessons would be perfect. Even without an instructor, her clients could come in, put on a record, dance alone or together, or simply listen. Either alone or with each other. Fast or slow or whatever. She made a mental note to check on some sort of seating. Wouldn't have to be anything expensive, but she'd need to have someplace for them to sit and rest. And a light dimmer, which wouldn't be a huge expense. She could wrap it into the other work the electrician was supposed to address before the grand opening.

"How much would an instructor cost?" Vanessa asked, not really expecting an answer.

"Depends on their experience, I suppose. As an example, a previous international ballroom dancing champion might cost you a *Karaage* dinner."

If only she could take Ellie up on the offer. Not only was the woman currently not in any condition to teach dance—although Vanessa wouldn't make any assumptions about the future—she would be too far away for such a thing, whether she stayed in Destiny Springs or moved to the Happy U.

"Aren't you moving to Colorado? Or are you going to take PJ up on his offer to move in with us?" Vanessa looked to her little boy, who was still fast asleep, which was a good thing. She didn't want to get his hopes up. He might not know she was only teasing.

Yet living with Ellie would be...*fun*.

Ellie deployed that coy smile again. "I'll let you know."

Before Vanessa could press for any other information, there was a tap on the door. Austin peeked in. "May I show the room?"

Ellie motioned for him to bring in the guests. They looked around with muted enthusiasm. Vanessa wasn't an expert, but she suspected they were interested but didn't want to seem *too* interested, for negotiation purposes.

"Was this room added on?" the woman asked.

"Yes. Sixty years ago. Stays warm in the winter. On a clear night, it feels like the stars are in the room with you," Ellie said.

"This would make a great playroom for the kids," the man said.

The woman with him nodded in agreement. "It's awfully big. We could add a partition and divide it into a playroom and study. We'd have to tear out that side wall and add a door and more windows, though."

Judging from Ellie's expression, they might as well have torn out her heart.

No doubt about it: this room had special meaning. Something that Austin's Happy U ranch and Vanessa's three-bedroom subdivision home would never be able to offer this sweet woman who'd found, and lost, the love of a lifetime.

At the thought of possibly never having that for herself, it felt as though her heart was being torn out, as well.

"WHAT'S THAT?" PJ WIGGLED off the love seat and ran to the window, leaving a rudely awakened Tango in his wake.

Austin walked over to the window and looked in the direction PJ was pointing. "That's an elk and her calf."

"We've seen elk near Grandpa's house, sweetheart, except I'm pretty sure it was a male, based on its size," Vanessa said.

Austin didn't even think she was paying attention, the way her head was practically buried in her laptop the same way his grandma's was buried in that book. Neither had said a word or asked any questions about the couple who'd looked at the house. Not that he could get a firm read on them, but there would be others. Word was already getting around that the property was likely being put up for sale soon. No advertising expense required in this town.

"That one is little, like me. Can I pet it?" he asked, directing his question to Austin instead of his mother.

Thankfully, there was only one answer to this question, because he didn't want to get on the wrong side of the protective mother sitting on the love seat.

"I'm afraid not. The mothers can be very protective when it comes to their young," Austin said.

"Just like humans," Vanessa said, proving his initial instinct correct. He dared to look at her, and the serious expression struck fear in him.

Vanessa didn't have to tell him what she thought of the idea of Ellie moving. She'd done nothing but stress how important it was for the elderly to maintain their independence. How could he convince her that he had no intention of taking that away from her? He just wanted to stay nearby in case something happened.

"Humans are protective of their older members, too," he shot back, except he added a smile and a wink.

"Yes. They certainly are." She seemed to force a similar smile-and-wink combo in return, although hers wasn't the least bit reassuring.

No doubt she was feeling a bit protective of Ellie in this moment. He just wasn't sure at what point she'd take sides and try to talk his grandma out of moving, because he had a bad feeling Ellie wouldn't choose his side.

But if it came down to it, would Vanessa choose him? The "us" part of their brief conversation in the hallway was dominating his thoughts.

Now that Vanessa seemed to be thinking in those terms, he dared to envision Vanessa and PJ in Colorado. *All of us.* It was obvious that Ellie adored Vanessa. And the way Vanessa seemed to enjoy riding the horses and her comfort level around them suggested it was possible. Then there was the relationship that she and PJ had forged with Ellie. It was enough to make him think that maybe he really could have it all.

"How about we move to the den? I'll make lemonade for everyone, and I can tell you about the couple that was just here."

Ellie shut her book. "I'm going to stay right here and listen to some music."

"Then I'll bring the lemonade to you."

She nodded but didn't say anything else.

At least she didn't refuse the drink, but he was picking up on a distinct vibe that she wasn't too happy. It was almost as if Vanessa and Ellie had talked about this while he was busy. Or talked about him. And what they said wasn't good.

"I wanna stay here, too, but can I have some lemonade?" PJ asked.

"Of course you can," Austin said, then looked at Vanessa. "May I bring you a glass, as well?"

She closed her laptop and stood. "I need to stretch. I'll help you carry the glasses."

Austin led the way to the kitchen. "You didn't have to stop working. I could've brought everyone a drink. I have four hands, after all."

He thought it was funny, but it didn't even earn him a smile. Definitely something going on here.

"Actually, Ellie helped me come up with a solution for a major problem with my office space, so I was at a stopping point. I'll finish up tonight. I thought we could talk."

"I'm listening," he said as he poured the lemonade.

She lifted two glasses and he grabbed the other two.

"Away from Ellie and PJ," she said. "Let's do this first."

He set the glasses down but followed her to the back room anyway. Before they got there, music started blaring across the threshold, where he stopped. He watched as Vanessa handed PJ a glass and set the other down on the small table next to Ellie. She squeezed the woman's shoulder and said something into her ear, then brushed past Austin toward the hallway again.

Once back in the kitchen, they each took a lemonade. He grabbed her free hand and led her out the front door to the porch swing, leaving the front door open in case Ellie or PJ needed anything. Not that he or Vanessa would be able to hear any voices calling out over the music.

For someone who needed to talk, Vanessa was being awfully quiet. They sipped on lemonade, stared into the distance and swayed gently to the music.

"You wanted to talk about something," he said.

So did he, but he wanted to hear what she had to say first. And also to find out if she was trying to influence Ellie's decision in any way.

Vanessa set her glass on the ground, dried her hand on her dress and released a heavy sigh. "I'm concerned that Ellie's only considering the move to make you happy."

That thought had occurred to him, but Ellie had assured him that wasn't the case. They'd agreed to be open and honest about their feelings, so he had to trust that she had been, as well.

"You two have talked about it," he said. It wasn't a question, because there was no question in his own mind.

"No, we haven't."

"I'm confused, then. Is it that you *just know*?" They'd had that discussion about her caregiving experience and skills. He would never discount them, but he was pretty sure he knew his grandma better than Vanessa did.

"I know that room has a special meaning for her. I know that her expression changed when the prospective buyers talked about adding a partition and tearing out a wall. What I saw broke my heart."

Austin hadn't even picked up on that. No wonder Ellie was acting strange. This was becoming too real. He'd felt the same way when his dad mentioned the possibility of selling the Happy U, and even had a few interested parties over to look at it. The thought of the home belonging to someone else, and all the changes they would certainly make, was upsetting.

He dared to look at Vanessa, and her expression was a mix of disappointment and concern.

"I'll have another talk with her tonight. Confirm those feelings and see if she still wants to go through with selling it. And find out, once and for all, what's so important about that room."

That brought out a little smile. At least they shared that common frustration. As much as he wanted to have his way on this, it wasn't worth the possibility that Ellie would resent him. He'd been on the receiving end of that kind of pressure in his marriage. Nothing good could come of it.

He wasn't sure whether it was the particular song that was in the air, or the wide-open Wyoming landscape ahead of them, but he could imagine being in Ellie's shoes. And they were a lot more comfortable than his in the moment.

Maybe it was time for him and Vanessa to get in lockstep about the future, because that two-letter word she seemed to accidentally utter—*us*—was lodged in his thoughts.

"How would Vern feel about babysitting PJ and Ellie at his house for a while tonight?" he asked. He could drop Ellie off and help get her situated.

"I don't know. He'd probably be thrilled. Why?"

"I want to take you out, to someplace I've never been."

"Okay. Where?"

"Someplace I'd be too afraid to go alone."

She squinted. "You're being very cryptic. Not even a hint?"

He thought hard about it. "Only this. Wear your favorite black boots. Otherwise, I'll just need you to trust me."

After a long pause, she said two words that sounded like music to his ears. Even more so than the record that Ellie was playing.

"I do."

CHAPTER FOURTEEN

RENEGADE WAS THE last place Vanessa expected Austin to take her tonight. But it was the first she would have chosen, if asked.

The country-western bar was packed, it being the only dance hall within a hundred miles of Destiny Springs. She and Austin managed to snag two open bar stools at the far end of the horseshoe when a couple got up to dance.

The band was in full swing, and the dance floor was a blur of smiling two-steppers. Just looking at them made her a little dizzy and a little giddy. She hadn't two-stepped in years, and even then, not much.

Austin rested his arm across the low back of her bar stool and gave her a self-satisfied look as if he knew he'd nailed it.

He had.

Except...they hadn't danced yet, and she wasn't so sure he would even ask after his confession about not being able to. Not that she needed to dance.

No, simply getting out of the house like a normal person and going on an actual date was more than enough.

Austin rolled up his flannel sleeves and proceeded to flag down the bartender.

"We'll have two lemonades, please," he said.

The bartender's expression was priceless. "Is that so? Pink or yellow?"

Austin turned to Vanessa. "Any preference?"

The bartender smiled and winked at her.

"No. But I think he's playing with you," she said.

"Sorry, I couldn't resist. No one's ever asked for lemonade before, although it's not a bad idea. Folks work up quite a thirst out on the floor," the bartender said.

"There's nothing like lemonade to cool you down," Austin said.

He sure was being a good sport about being teased. That was one of the things she loved about him.

Loved? The ease at which she now thought about it wasn't surprising, although she wasn't ready to say it out loud.

"Unfortunately, we don't offer that drink here. I'd be happy to give you some ice water, lemon wedges and sugar. You could make your own."

Austin leaned toward the bartender while still looking at her and said loudly enough for Vanessa to hear, "I'm trying to impress my date. Do you have any other nonalcoholic drink recommendations?"

"We serve a mean Virgin Mary," the bartender said.

He looked to Vanessa, who nodded her approval.

"We'll take two," he said, tipping his Stetson to the guy.

At that, the bartender finished serving a couple of other patrons, then started on their order.

Austin turned to her. "So, come here often?" he asked, then dropped his chin as if realizing how corny it sounded. Maybe that meant he was out of practice, which would be a good thing. Not that he needed a line, of course.

"Actually, I've never been," she said.

Austin leaned back and blinked hard, as if in disbelief. "Really? I thought I was the only one in town who hasn't. My grandma has even been here."

Wow. I really don't have a social life.

"Don't get me wrong. I've always wanted to. I've just been so busy taking care of one person or another..." Vanessa started to say, then pulled herself off that negative path. This was supposed to be a night of fun and self-care.

"That you don't have time to take care of yourself," he said, finishing her sentence and holding her hand down that path anyway.

She shrugged.

"Tonight, I'm doing all the caregiving," he said.

Her heart could have melted right then and there.

The bartender placed the two drinks in front of them. "Here ya go. Two Virgin Marys. Fully loaded."

They were a work of art, with celery and green beans and olives. At this rate, they may not even need to order any food.

The bartender printed out the ticket and placed it in a cup. "No hurry on this. And ignore it if you decide to order more rounds. I'll print out a fresh one."

The fact that Austin didn't pay the tab suggested they might be there a while. It felt good to not be in a hurry for a change.

At least her grandpa and Ellie and PJ were taken care of for dinner. Vanessa had cooked *Karaage* out of the remainder of the chicken at Vern's house while Austin was bringing Ellie and Tango over. Sylvie was coming over later with dessert for all of them. And the whole empty office space situation was no longer weighing her down. For the first time in a very long time, Vanessa didn't have a worry in the world.

Or at least not one that would make her feel guilty for taking an evening to enjoy herself.

Austin lifted his drink to obviously make a toast, and she followed suit.

"Here's to taking chances," he said.

There were a million ways she could interpret that, but she didn't want to assume anything. Now, if he'd said, *Here's to us*, she'd know for sure. Yet he'd given her some hope when she'd let that word slip.

"What chance are you taking tonight?" she asked.

"That I don't break all your toes or mess up your favorite boots when I get the nerve to take you out on the dance floor."

"Your two left feet don't scare me." She wasn't exactly a professional dancer herself. Just the fact that he was open to it earned him major points. "But I'm not exactly dressed for the two-step. My boots might get all caught up in my maxi skirt, and we'll both end up on the ground."

He studied her face. "Then I'll have to insist on a rain check."

It was a thoughtful offer, and if the stars aligned within the next few days, she'd take him up on it.

"I should probably keep my phone handy, in case Vern calls," she said, fishing the phone out of her purse and placing it on the bar. No missed calls so far. "Do you think they're behaving?" She took a sip of her Virgin Mary. Even better than lemonade, although she'd now associate the latter with Ellie's porch swing.

"I'm sure PJ is. The other two, we need to keep an eye on," Austin said.

That was enough to make her nearly spit out the sip she just took. He spoke the truth. Vern could be a handful, and so could Ellie. By putting those two stubborn seniors together, no telling what kind of trouble she and Austin would come home to. Hopefully Sylvie would keep them somewhat in line.

Then again, what fun would that be? She and Austin were crossing some lines themselves, first with the kisses and now with an official date.

"May I ask you something kinda personal?" he asked.

"You can. I may or may not answer."

"Fair enough. Is your ex-husband in PJ's life?"

Vanessa shook her head. "He didn't even challenge me for custody."

Austin cocked his head and squinted. He actually looked…angry.

"He didn't want children, but I got pregnant," Vanessa continued. "I'm sure he thought he'd have to pitch in and help take care of his grandparents and his own son. But I handled all of that just fine. Until I couldn't anymore."

"They lived with y'all?"

Vanessa nodded.

"I guess you never went out dancing. Didn't have the time."

"Bingo. I didn't…but he did." She took a long sip of her drink. She'd said enough already. To Austin, and to Ellie. Apparently, the woman hadn't spilled Vanessa's full confession to Austin, and she hoped it would stay that way.

Last thing she wanted to be was the person who complained about things. Her ex had some good qualities, too. Even shared some with the man she was on a date with tonight. Specifically, loving his grandparents and wanting them under one roof. Except it became obvious that her ex wanted more support than he was willing to give in return.

She wasn't putting Austin in that category, but whether a person intended to reciprocate when it came to support was impossible to know, up front. Action over words was the only way to find out for sure.

Austin looked at her for the longest time. Searching her face for something. But what?

Yep, I said too much.

She'd started to put away her phone when it vibrated in her hand, which made her breath hitch. It wasn't Vern but possibly something worse. Her assistant in Cheyenne.

"Hey, Beth. Everything okay?" Vanessa asked.

"Yes. And no," her assistant said. "My grandparents' sixtieth wedding anniversary is tomorrow. My family is putting together an impromptu surprise all-day party. Don't worry—I'm not helping with it or anything. But I'd really like to be there and spend a little time with them, because they're going to Paris for a whole month after that. There's just so much going on here, I'm trying to figure out a way to do both."

Vanessa's shoulders relaxed. She hadn't even been aware that she was tensing them. This was an easy one.

"You can't miss that. Go! I'll take care of whatever I can from here. We'll figure out the rest," she said, even though she wasn't sure how. They were down to the wire, and a successful opening depended on both of them at this juncture. But what was one day?

The woman breathed a sigh of relief. "Thank you, Vanessa. I can catch a flight out first thing in the morning and will finish up as much as I can before then. I'll sleep on the plane."

Plane? "Where do they live?"

"Dallas. I shouldn't be gone more than a couple of days, depending on return flight availability."

Vanessa's heart sank. Might as well be Australia. She swore the woman's family lived in Cheyenne, which would've made it more likely that they wouldn't lose too much time. One day, tops. But Dallas?

"Just have fun and keep me posted on when you expect to return. And, if you haven't already, cc me on any emails and give me a list of what you don't get done before you leave," Vanessa said.

She ended the call, put her phone in her purse and shook her head.

"This was a mistake," she said.

"Being here tonight?" he asked.

That snapped her back to the present location.

"No! Not at all. I meant I'm beginning to regret starting my own business." *And thinking I could also take yet another trip out here to see Grandpa before it opens.* Turned out, the timing was not exactly ideal.

Austin retrieved the tab from the cup, replaced it with some cash and returned his arm to the back of the stool and gave her a look of concern she had yet to see from him.

"Want to talk about it?"

"No. I refuse to bore you with the details. I already said more than anyone should have to hear about my failed marriage. I'd rather you not hear about my other failures, too."

"I want to know everything about you, Vanessa. The good and the bad."

She gulped. "The short version is, my assistant has to go out of town for a few days. She's the only point person on-site."

"Do you need to get back to Cheyenne?"

Vanessa shook her head. "No. I'd wanted everything to be perfect, but that isn't going to happen anyway. Most things I can handle from here. But I shouldn't have left Cheyenne with only one person in place to take care of everything else. As a business owner, that's a big fail."

Instead of disagreeing, he stood and extended his hand. "Let's get out of here where we can talk. I'll tell you a story about failure."

AUSTIN TOOK VANESSA'S hand and led her out the door. He found an open area on the extended front deck away from the tables and benches, and the cowboys and cowgirls who occupied them.

They found a quiet spot and leaned against the patio railing. He hoped the song that the house band had just launched into wasn't a sign: "A Good Run of Bad Luck."

Was it wrong of him to look for a silver lining in a dark cloud? If Vanessa was serious about re-gretting opening a business in Cheyenne, could that be a possible opening for them to have a life together at the Happy U? He wanted better for her than to be halfway happy. Same went for himself. But that meant putting the past behind him, once and for all.

"You mentioned a story," she said, breaking the silence.

"Yeah. You mentioned failing at business. I not only failed, I lost myself in the process. Traded in my jeans and spurs for a suit and tie when I got married. Worked odd hours as a Realtor in Denver."

At that, she looked at him. "Suit and tie? I can't picture it, but I'm sure you looked great."

He couldn't argue with that. His ex-wife made sure of it, because his image was a reflection on her.

"I looked the part but didn't feel great about it. I'd show you photos, but I threw away every last one of 'em. Just like I threw away everything and everyone I loved to make my ex happy. You could say I changed my DNA, but even that wasn't enough. After all that, she threw our marriage away. Failure accomplished."

"You should never have to change who you are for anyone. Unless *you* want to," she said. "But I disagree that you were a failure."

Last thing he wanted to do was provide more examples, but he did want to find out how she'd justify that opinion. "How so?"

"We usually have to fail in order to succeed. Finding out the hard way what we don't want before we discover what truly makes us happy."

He had little doubt what would make him happy. In fact, he was looking right into her eyes.

"What if we know what would make us happy, but we're not sure we could ever have it?" he asked.

"Then find a way to be halfway happy, I suppose," she said.

"Halfway isn't good enough."

She visibly gulped. People were coming and

going, but no one looked twice as he faced Vanessa and slipped his arms around her waist.

"What are we doing?" she asked, adding a smile and tilt of her head.

"I'm cashing in my rain check."

"Here?"

"Why not?"

"I wasn't joking about tripping and falling." She pointed at the bottom of her skirt where the hem brushed the tops of her black boots.

"We're not doing the two-step, and I'm not going to let you fall." He pulled her even closer.

She paused, then draped her arms around his neck. They naturally fell into a slow dance. The music wasn't perfect for it, but this moment certainly was.

The voices of the other patrons faded into the background as they swayed without talking for a good long minute in silence. The band must've been between songs, because there seemed to be no sound. Only the beating of their hearts as she pressed closer and rested her head on his shoulder. At that moment, there was no distance between them.

The crowd inside erupted in cheering when the band launched into "The Devil Went Down to Georgia," jolting them both out of the moment.

She removed her arms from his shoulders, and he reluctantly released her.

"I guess we should check on the 'kids,' huh?" she said.

Even though he knew she was talking about Vern and Ellie, another scenario came to mind. One that included PJ, and maybe a little sister or two. He tried to push the image out of his mind because it was way too soon to think about it.

"I suppose you're right." Once they reached the truck and climbed inside, they both checked their phones. He was pretty sure he'd heard his ring while they were outside, but he hadn't been about to answer it. Once they'd started slow dancing, he'd pretty much forgotten about everything and everyone else.

"No more calls for me, thankfully," she said.

"One voicemail for me. Guess I'm more popular," he said with a smile and a wink. But there wasn't anything funny about getting a call from ranch hand Randy's cell. Why did seeing that number strike more fear in him than his dad's landline? And why did he always assume the worst?

That was easy. Bad things happened when he stayed away from the Happy U too long.

He slipped the phone back in his pocket.

"Not going to listen to it?" she asked.

"I will when we get back," he said. And he only felt a little bit of anxiety about it.

Maybe he'd been creating his own good run of

bad luck by assuming the worst, and that needed to stop. Tonight, he had everything to be positive about. He was on a proper date with the sweetest, prettiest woman he'd ever known, his grandma was all but sold on moving to Colorado, and the family cutting-horse training business was almost back to where it was before he'd made the mistake of moving to Denver in the first place.

They rode back to the house in silence. Once inside, he was privately relieved to find Ellie and Vern laughing and safely seated. Vern had turned off and unplugged the heating pad, which was a good sign. There was a snack tray in front of them, and it looked as though they'd almost polished off whatever had been prepared. Apparently, Sylvie had already come and gone.

PJ stopped watching some cartoon-looking show, then got up off the floor and ran to his mommy first for a hug. Then to Austin. Now, *that* was something to be positive about. His heart concurred, and a warmth engulfed him.

"Did y'all have fun?" he asked PJ.

"Uh-huh. 'Cept no one would play zombie with me, so they let me watch whatever I wanted on the television, except anything with zombies."

Austin didn't say a word. He simply opened his eyes as wide as possible, raised his arms in front of him and took one clumsy step forward. That sent the little boy into a wild, excited frenzy.

Vanessa probably wasn't going to thank him for that, it being close to the little boy's bedtime. Perhaps even past it.

That was another thing he was looking forward to. Being a dad. Tucking his children in at night. Spoiling them rotten, like his own folks had done for him.

Vanessa had sat down next to Vern, and the adults were talking about something, but they stopped to watch.

PJ ran up the stairs, shrieking and giggling. Austin plodded past his grandma but broke character as soon as the little boy was safely out of sight. Judging from their "living dead" game at the B and B the other day, he knew he'd have at least a few minutes before PJ would reappear to find out how close Austin was to finding him.

Vern and Ellie were both wearing that same familiar conspiratorial smile again. What had Vanessa told them, if anything?

"Dancing, huh?" Vern said.

Mystery solved.

Then something pinged his conscience. He still hadn't played Randy's message. Maybe the pessimist within him was backing off.

Exactly the opposite. *Like a stubborn zombie, it's getting closer and closer.*

Austin willed himself to think positive. Randy would have been lighting up his phone if it was urgent. The tension immediately eased up at the thought.

That wasn't so hard, was it?

"I guess I better turn back into a zombie now before someone comes looking for me," he said.

Austin clomped up the stairs, being intentionally loud, and started opening doors. He came across what looked to be PJ's room first, judging by the stuffed animals scattered about. He plodded over to the side of the bed, looked beneath it, then opened the closet. No PJ.

He went down the hall to another bedroom that looked like it hadn't been slept in. Ever. Way too neat. But he didn't find PJ there either.

All of a sudden, he started to worry, which was ridiculous. PJ wouldn't have gone far.

He finally located the little boy in what had to be Vanessa's room. There he found PJ on the side of the bed, giggling and clutching a huge teddy bear for protection. No doubt this also felt like the safest room in the house since a zombie had been hot on his heels.

He sat on the end of the bed, rather than going in for "the kill."

"Who's your friend?" he asked, pointing to the stuffed animal.

"Big Bear. 'Cause when Mommy bought it for me it was bigger than me. But now I'm bigger," PJ explained, then let out a yawn.

At this moment, this room was the sweetest one in the house. He was overcome by a desire to protect this innocent little boy, whom he'd grown to love. Yet that even failed to describe the extent of it. How much was he going to miss PJ after the little boy moved back to Cheyenne?

No. *If.* After tonight, he was optimistic enough to believe anything was possible.

He patted the bed. "Big Bear looks sleepy. Maybe you two could rest here for a while."

PJ didn't put up any argument. Instead, he crawled onto the bed and put Big Bear's head on the pillow next to him.

"Will you stay here with me in case there are any zombies?"

Austin smiled. There was no place he'd rather be in this moment. Well, maybe one place: back in Vanessa's arms, dancing.

He retrieved a blanket that was draped over the foot of the bed and covered them both, and stayed there until the little boy fell asleep. He then tiptoed out of the room and headed back downstairs.

"Found him. He's now asleep in your room, Vanessa. At least, I think it's your room."

Actually, he knew it was. It even smelled like the fresh, citrusy perfume he'd noticed her wearing as they danced. Uncomplicated, like her— unlike their situation.

"It's close to our bedtime, too, Grandma," he said.

Vanessa and Vern stood and moved closer to

Ellie, making sure she had her footing and a solid grip on the walker.

Austin swept in and collected the tray and empty glasses, and washed them in the kitchen sink. The song from tonight, "A Good Run of Bad Luck," had been just a song after all, because he felt he'd had some awfully good luck tonight.

The tune was quickly turning into an earworm, and he couldn't stop himself from humming the song under his breath. And smiling. Until he was rudely interrupted.

Austin pulled the ringing phone from his pocket. *Randy.*

The warm and fuzzies he was feeling were replaced by pure dread. He immediately answered. "I saw you called and was about to play your message. What's going on?"

"I'm in the truck. Following the ambulance to the nearest hospital. Got you on Bluetooth," Randy said, clearly winded.

Austin's heart leaped into his throat. He could barely speak, but managed to ask, "What happened?"

"Your dad had an accident. Didn't think the man was capable of falling off a horse and breaking an ankle. At least, that's what the paramedics say. He didn't think he needed to go. Refused to call 9-1-1 or let me do it. He thought an ice pack would do the trick."

Sounded like his dad.

"That's why I called you earlier," Randy continued. "To see if you could talk some sense into him. Then he finally realized it was worse than a sprain, and he better do somethin'."

"Was he with that same client?" Austin asked. Not that there was anything he would do if that was the case, but he wanted to know.

"Not when he fell, but she was here earlier," Randy said.

So the man was riding alone, which was even worse than being with a client. If he was with a client, at least someone else would be there if something like this happened.

"Let me know where they take him, and I'll talk to him as soon as they let me. And, trust me, I'll answer the first time from now on. Thanks for doing this, Randy. I'll get there as soon as I can make arrangements here."

"Will do, boss. And don't worry. I'm sure he's gonna be just fine."

At that, Austin hung up and inhaled a deep breath, then closed his eyes and slowly exhaled.

As calmly as he could muster, he returned to the den. To that scene in front of him that had kept the pessimist at arm's length. It was fully embracing him now.

Vern and Vanessa walked him and Ellie to the truck and Austin helped her in. He closed the door after Vern said his goodbyes. The man promptly returned to the house, but not without first giving Austin a knowing smile.

If only Vern *did* know everything Austin was going through, maybe he'd have a solution. The experience and wisdom of that generation was something Austin couldn't get enough of. But he wasn't going to burden any of them with this.

Austin attempted a smile for Vanessa, who looked as happy and content as he'd felt less than ten minutes ago. Then her lovely open-mouthed smile turned into a pleasant but cautiously concerned line.

"Is something wrong?" she asked.

He looked up at the clear Wyoming sky and what should've been a perfect ending to a perfect night.

"You've been in the caregiving business all your life. How long does it take a broken ankle to heal?"

Her smile faded completely. "Is that what the call was about? The message you didn't want to play?"

He nodded. "My dad fell off his horse."

"And broke his ankle? Any other injuries?"

"I'd say his pride, but apparently he was alone when it happened."

Austin crossed his arms, but Vanessa gently nudged them apart and wrapped herself around him.

"I bet I know what you're thinking. But even

if you'd been there, you couldn't have prevented it from happening. To answer your question, it will probably depend on how much damage was done and whether he'll need surgery. My guess is a minimum of four weeks."

He simply nodded. Not much else he could do. His whole body was going numb, and his mind wasn't far behind. River Rock wasn't Destiny Springs, and the Happy U wasn't Fraser Ranch. Or even Ellie's. No neighbors around for miles. And no one currently living with his dad. His ranch hands would only be able to do so much.

Then there was the family business, which he could carry on for a while. But not from nearly three hundred miles away.

He squeezed his eyes shut and searched for a solution. But then his own personal angel offered a temporary respite.

"We'll work something out. Go check on your dad."

CHAPTER FIFTEEN

WE'LL WORK SOMETHING OUT.

Austin knew Vanessa had meant they'd work something out for Ellie's care while Austin went back and forth between River Rock and Destiny Springs. Not simply while Austin left town to assess the situation. It was all so overwhelming. But there was one thing he was getting clearer about. He was in love with Vanessa.

There was something else they needed to work out: whether there was an *us*.

Yes, she was the one who'd said the word. Make that, had said it first, because he'd already been thinking about it. But did those two letters mean the same to her as they did to him? Because if they didn't, and if she ended up moving back to Cheyenne for good, his heart would be torn in two—one half for her, the other for PJ.

Austin stared at the toiletry bag filled with everything he'd need for a quick trip. At least he assumed that much. The past hour or so was a blur.

He couldn't be gone for long, because Vanessa had her crisis to deal with and needed to get back to Cheyenne, as planned, by the end of the week. She also had an adorable son to take care of. The crisis with Ellie and his dad was his to figure out.

Ellie wheeled to the doorway of his room but no farther.

"Any word on your dad?" she asked.

Austin nodded. "It wasn't a clean break. The surgery is scheduled for tomorrow morning. He's been sleeping, so I haven't talked with him directly."

She moved in closer. "I don't like the idea of you driving this late, and for four hours or more. Your father wouldn't want you to do that either. Why don't you wait until the morning and get an early start? You'd be there for him when he gets out of surgery."

"I'd like to see him before that. Besides, Vanessa and PJ are probably already headed this way." He didn't want to say that he was about to do something even more dangerous than driving in the middle of the night.

What an angel Vanessa was, offering to stay in the house with Ellie for a few days while he was in Colorado, and with everything going on with her business. She assured him that she could handle the issues just as successfully from Destiny Springs, and the rest would get done as soon as she returned to Cheyenne. But still, it was weighing on him.

"Well, okay. As long as you promise to drive carefully. Don't go too fast," Ellie said.

Again, he knew his grandma was talking about driving, rather than the thought that popped into his mind. Specifically, that he was running out of time and could no longer go slow with his and Vanessa's possible future.

Together, he and Ellie tidied up the two guest rooms, at her insistence. He took care of putting fresh linens on the beds while she ran a feather duster over all the easily reachable surfaces.

Once done, she said, "I need your help with something else."

He followed her to a hall closet. She opened the door and pointed to the highest shelf.

"The blue one," she said.

That blue blanket brought back memories. It had been his when he'd come visit as a little boy. It had to be the softest blanket on the face of the earth. He pulled it down and held it close. *Still is.*

Ellie took the lead to the utility room and extended her hands. "I'll take it now."

"What are we doing, Grandma?"

"We're washing it for PJ, of course. It's been up there a long time and is probably a little musty. Plus, I want to dry it just before he goes to bed so that it will be nice and warm for him."

Austin felt the familiar warmth, as if she'd draped it over him instead. His mom had heated the blankets, like Ellie. Bath towels, too.

"You're going to spoil him, just like you spoiled me," Austin said.

"That's the idea. Maybe he'll beg his mommy to come visit us in Colorado. If that's okay with you." She gave him a good long stare as if urging him to do what he knew he had to do. Tonight.

"I think you know the answer to that," he said.

She smiled and proceeded to pour in the detergent and start the washer. "Let's just hope the blanket doesn't disintegrate."

Let's hope my whole world doesn't disintegrate.

He exited the utility room first, but Ellie turned the opposite direction, toward the big, empty room instead of the den. He made a U-turn and followed.

"I'm going to listen to some music for a while." Instead of sitting down, she flipped through the albums, selecting the one he now recognized as her favorite, placing it on the turntable and positioning the needle.

Once he made sure she was secure in the ladder-back chair, he headed to the den to listen for Vanessa and PJ's knock. His stomach was in knots, but he managed to pour a glass of sweetened iced tea for Ellie. By the time he got back, Tango had joined her and was eyeing the woman's lap.

"I know what you're thinking, and don't worry. I'll make him get down," she said in a loud voice over the music.

He believed her. After all, she'd asked him to retrieve that blanket, which was something she otherwise would have attempted by herself. It was as if she knew she needed to cooperate now more than ever, because their little family couldn't handle any more accidents.

"He'll choose PJ over me anyway," Ellie continued. "In fact, I was thinking of seeing if Vanessa would want to take him back to Cheyenne. He might be happier there."

Austin could practically feel his heart breaking for her. For all of them.

"Don't do anything rash, Grandma. We'll talk about it when I get back from Colorado."

"You don't need to rush back," she insisted.

Except he did. The question was, would he be able to?

As he made his way back to the den, there was a tiny knock on the door. He opened it to find PJ clutching a stuffed tiger and already in his pajamas. Vanessa was carrying a small overnight case.

Austin rubbed the tiger's ears. "And who is this?"

"Sylvester. I wanted him to meet Tango 'cause they're both cats and they would like each other."

Vanessa had her hair in a ponytail and was dressed in white sweatpants and a matching hoodie. Those black boots of hers didn't go with the outfit at all, but somehow it worked. She'd never looked so beautiful and relaxed.

And he'd never been so scared.

"Grandma is in the back room, in case you couldn't guess. Tango is with her," he said, which sent the little boy flying down the hall to see both of them.

Austin eased the suitcase from Vanessa's hand and led her to the guest room that he and Ellie had prepared.

"This is yours. PJ's is right there." He pointed to the room directly across from hers. "Ellie agreed to keep the bell beside her at night. You should be able to hear it."

They headed back out to the den. "I'm not worried," Vanessa said. "She's doing great. And you don't need to worry either. I know you'll have a lot of decisions to make once you know more about your dad's prognosis."

She settled onto the sofa, and he eased down next to her. His heart was beating too fast, and his stomach was churning.

"Lots of decisions. For everyone," he said.

Just say it.

"How would you feel about coming to Colorado?"

Vanessa blinked. "What?"

"To the Happy U."

"Who would stay with Ellie?"

Austin let out a nervous laugh. He was already messing this up royally, but he hadn't really thought out what he would say. Sure, he'd been thinking about it since their first kiss. He'd simply thought he had a little more time.

But that was the same thing he'd thought about his mom. He didn't want to miss out on any more time with Vanessa.

He shook his head, reached for her hand and squeezed it. "I meant to say, how would you feel about living in Colorado? Someday." He stopped short of saying "soon" because there was so much that both of them were dealing with. No one needed the pressure of a time line. And he wanted his marriage proposal to be special and happy. Not stressful.

Not to mention, he wanted to have a reasonable amount of certainty that she'd say yes. This had happened so fast, yet it felt so right.

She visibly gulped, then shook her head and looked down at their intertwined fingers.

"You know that isn't possible," she said.

A fair response. His initial reaction might have been the same if the tables were turned.

"Someone's being a pessimist," he said, then squeezed her hand a little harder and smiled, even though he was a quivering mess of emotions on the inside.

That earned him a nervous laugh. He knew that now wasn't the time for joking around. Yet he didn't think the whole thing was impossible.

"I don't mean to be, but I'm a realist. I have to be for PJ's sake. And you're under an incredible amount of stress right now."

True, but that wasn't why he was saying any of this. Austin knew what he really needed to tell her in this moment, even though he'd wanted those words to be special. Not that it would make a difference, but she needed to have the indisputable facts and know exactly how he felt.

He took a deep breath, looked into her eyes and mustered every ounce of courage that remained.

"Vanessa. I'm in love with you," he said.

Judging by her expression and hesitancy, it clearly wasn't enough to convince her. Besides, there was one more thing she needed to know.

"I need you in my life."

If only he hadn't said the last part. Those words cast a long, familiar shadow across her objectivity.

Before tonight, and for a few brief moments, she thought that maybe it was possible for them to have a future together. Of course, it would have to look a lot different than the one she knew he had in mind, based on what she knew about him from their brief time together.

But being in love with someone wasn't enough. Neither was being needed.

Even though Austin was like a father figure to PJ, she didn't want her little boy growing up on a remote ranch, like she had. Besides, he had friends and a former life that he loved in Cheyenne. And she had a new life for herself waiting there. One that revolved around her precious son. Moving to Colorado and being part of an extended family would mean giving up all of that.

Most of all, her attention would, once again, be divided. PJ would get a smaller portion than he deserved, because there was no way she'd let Austin do all the caregiving for his father and for Ellie. It might not even be possible for him to do it without any help, even if he wanted to. There was only so much one person could do in a day, much less week after week. Nonstop.

Yet she was in love with him. But his teasing accusation that she was a pessimist challenged her.

"How would you feel about living in Cheyenne? Someday."

Austin stared, unblinking, as if he hadn't considered the possibility. Then he blew out a long breath and looked away.

"Ellie's improving," she said. "She'll need help with a few things now and again, which could be easily handled by friends or ranch hands. Doesn't have to be family."

Austin finally looked at her. "I can see that. It's just…"

"You *want* her to live with you and your dad?"

He paused. "I really do. You've met her. Can you blame me?"

Funny thing was, she wouldn't blame him for wanting such an arrangement. She hadn't wanted to admit it to herself, but she was starting to picture an extended family. Except, as with a husband, it had to be one who loved her more than needed her. PJ needed to be a child, while he could. Because once that innocence was gone…

"I can't blame you at all. Then there's your dad, but it's a temporary setback. He's still pretty young. I don't know much about him, but I bet he will manage just fine for possibly several more years. Maybe the injury isn't as bad as it sounds."

"He's having surgery tomorrow. The break wasn't clean."

She knew what that meant. The man would need help for more than a few weeks. Possibly a couple of years, although she didn't want to scare him by saying it. But perhaps he already knew about the worst-case scenario. Maybe that was what prompted the urgency and his words.

I need you in my life.

Vanessa felt the familiar sting. That familiar doubt.

"I'm so sorry. I'd help if I could. I know you'll find a caregiver, though. It's a growing profession, with people living longer and longer," she said, struggling to offer a professional perspective while experiencing a very personal one, because this whole situation was cutting deep and furious.

That didn't seem to comfort him.

"I'm not looking to hire you as a caregiver. I'm asking you to share my life," he countered.

Translation: unpaid caregiver. That was pretty much what she'd been all along, and she was the one who had insisted upon it. But they weren't talking about a temporary situation.

"You want to be there to not only make sure he's okay, but to spend time with him," she said, as if she even needed to clarify anything at this point.

Austin nodded. "Sounds like you know me too well."

Unfortunately, it was looking as though she did. And it broke her heart. He probably did believe he was in love with her. Her first husband did, too. But she couldn't—wouldn't—go back to that life if she didn't have to. And she certainly wouldn't take PJ with her.

Whether Austin believed it or not, he would still need help. If he didn't realize it now, he would soon enough.

And even if he didn't ask her to help, she would still end up being the one taking care of everyone. Because that was who she was.

Austin dropped his chin and inhaled deeply, as if reading her thoughts.

"I kept telling you that Vanessa needs to take care of Vanessa. You're finally starting to listen." His voice quivered.

She wanted to tell him that he was wrong. That Vanessa needed to take care of PJ. Give him the normal life he deserved and that she had never gotten. Give him 100 percent of her available attention.

They looked into each other's eyes as if a solution could somehow be found there. But even the possibility of a long-distance relationship was off the table. With their priorities and other commitments, it would be too difficult to juggle. They both needed less of that in their lives. Not more.

The bottom line was, their respective vision for the future was too different. No one was right, and no one was wrong. They'd fallen in love so fast, with eyes closed. But all eyes were open now, and they couldn't deny the truth.

"So it's settled," he said.

She teared up at the finality of it. They sat in the silence, his hand still secure over hers yet disconnected. No reassuring squeeze. No musical crescendo to accompany the pain.

No music coming from down the hall.

The silence was broken by someone clearing their throat in the background. How long had Ellie been standing there?

"I've changed my mind, Austin," the woman said. "I'm not moving to Colorado or selling my ranch. I'm staying right here. Ellie can take care of Ellie."

He released Vanessa's hand and stood. She got up, as well.

"How much did you hear, Grandma?"

"Enough. Maybe there are things about me that are falling apart, but my hearing is just fine. You need to get on the road and check on your father. And don't hurry back. Leave the name of that couple who looked at the house. I'll let them know it's definitely not for sale, and I'll accept the blame for wasting their time."

Vanessa's heart sank to her feet. She'd never seen this side of Ellie.

"Before you say a word, Vanessa, as of tomorrow, you're officially released of any caregiving duties. I'm of sound mind and am legally empowered to make such decisions."

Austin shook his head. "Please don't do this."

Vanessa resisted the urge to do the same. She'd dealt with her fair share of stubborn seniors, and she was always able to successfully put her foot down when reasoning failed. But this had become very personal.

"If you don't want to move to Colorado, I understand. But you're not staying here alone until you're ready. I love you too much to allow it," Austin said.

"I'll be fine. I'll have to be a little more careful than usual, that's all."

"You both know I don't like to take sides, but I'm afraid I have to agree with Austin on this," Vanessa said.

Austin cast her a look of appreciation that she couldn't describe, except that it had something to do with those expressive eyes.

"Who said I'll be alone? That nice physical therapist who stops by all the time told me that if I ever needed help in a pinch, to give her a call, she could use some side work as a caregiver. I'll get in touch with her first thing in the morning."

"And what if she can't make it that soon?" Austin asked.

"I'll still be here," Vanessa said.

"Except I fired you, my dear. Vern and Sylvie said they'd help, too, if I ever needed it. This will be a good way to test 'em. Besides, I have Tango. He offers all the company I need."

"So you're kicking us both off the property," Austin said.

"You can both come visit anytime. Destiny Springs is about the same distance from Cheyenne as it is from the Happy U, give or take. Unless you want to meet each other halfway and leave me and Destiny Springs out of the equation, in which case halfway between Cheyenne and River Rock would be around Golden Gate Canyon. PJ helped me measure it on a map."

Halfway isn't good enough.

"Where is PJ?" Vanessa asked.

"He's asleep in his room with Tango. The minute I put that warm, freshly washed and dried blanket over him, he was out."

"You should have let one of us help," Austin insisted.

Again, Vanessa would have to agree. Probably required more bending than was good for her at the moment.

"And you should have been on the road by now, Little Buckaroo," Ellie countered.

Austin looked to the ground and shook his head. What would have ordinarily been funny was anything but. She could picture them both, twenty or thirty years ago. A grandmother taking care of her grandson. Now the roles were in the natural process of flipping, and Ellie wanted nothing to do with it.

That brought Vanessa back down to reality

after a few brief minutes of being on the same page with him when it came to Ellie. Knowing how much she meant to him, and how it was going to cause him to worry about her for the rest of her life. Now Vanessa was sure she was going to worry, too. The thought of having Ellie somewhere safe had been more comforting than she wanted to admit.

So much for being the strong advocate for keeping the elderly independent. It was a new twist to an impossible situation. For all of them.

"I'll get my things," Austin said, then disappeared down the hall.

"And I'm going to check on PJ." Not that she was worried about him. She simply didn't know what to say in the moment. It felt as though she was not only losing Austin, but also Ellie. And PJ was about to lose Tango.

She tiptoed into the guest room. PJ looked so warm and cozy beneath a soft blue blanket. Tango was quite content sleeping on the pillow beside him.

Vanessa sat at the end of the bed and watched him breathe, hoping they'd both get through the pain, because there was a new and beautiful life waiting for them in Cheyenne. School field trips and, eventually, football games and dances for him. And maybe some dancing for her, as well.

Except she couldn't imagine dancing with anyone other than Austin. The problem had never been the two left feet he claimed to have. The problem was the two of them weren't in step as far as the future.

She closed her eyes and willed the tears not to flow. When she opened them again, the night-light was eclipsed by someone.

Austin.

He tiptoed to the bed and sat on the opposite edge. His eyes looked sadder than ever, as if he'd been crying. Like they had after he'd watched *Love Story* with Ellie.

"I'm going to miss this little guy," he said.

"I know. He'll miss you, too. But you'll be visiting Ellie at some point. Maybe we could come up from Cheyenne the same weekend."

Even to her, that sounded like it might be more hurtful than it would be helpful. Not only for PJ, but for her.

"Maybe." He swallowed hard, then nodded.

She stood and felt a little dizzy. No wonder. She'd barely eaten all day. She wavered for a moment, but he didn't witness it.

Would he have swept in to help, if she had fallen? She would never know.

And that was for the best.

VANESSA EASED OUT of a light sleep and pulled the toasty blanket up to her chin.

Blanket?

She shot up into sitting position, temporarily disoriented before remembering where she was.

"I'm sorry, dear. I didn't mean to wake you up. It's drafty out here, so I brought you a blanket until you're ready to go to bed." Ellie was standing next to the sofa, her walker within reach.

"Is everything okay? Can I get you anything?" Vanessa sat up completely and tried to collect her thoughts. She remembered making sure Ellie was safe in bed, and then she came back out to the den and plopped down on the sofa instead of getting ready for bed herself. And that was it.

"Not a thing, dear. I couldn't sleep. Too busy worrying about Austin being on the road in the middle of the night. But worrying doesn't change anything, does it?"

Funny, it had taken Vanessa so many years of worrying about her relatives' and clients' health and safety for her to reach that same conclusion.

"You're right about that. I'd say it shows how much you care about someone, though."

"I could tell you some stories of worrying about outcomes that aren't within our control." Ellie maneuvered her walker around and sat on its narrow bench seat.

Vanessa scooted over to where she was as close to the woman as possible and draped the blanket across both of their laps. The thing was still warm.

"You put this in the dryer, didn't you?" Vanessa asked.

Ellie simply smiled. "And no one stopped me. But I did very little lifting and hardly any bending."

"Okay. I trust you," Vanessa said, even though she wasn't so sure anymore. "That was a super-sweet thing to do."

"I suppose it's the mother in me. Or the grandmother, considering my advanced age," Ellie said.

"You aren't old. You just feel that way right now. Like I said before, you're healing beautifully, from what I can tell. That's my professional opinion, which I can give since I'm still your caregiver until morning. Even though you're the one doing the caring right now."

Let Ellie try arguing with that.

"And you're definitely sweet. Maybe a little too much at times," Vanessa continued. "You never wanted to sell your ranch and home, did you?"

Ellie gave her a good long look. "Please don't tell Austin that. It was just that he inherited the worrier gene. I love him too much to let him worry about me so much. I certainly love him more than this old house or ranch. But after I overheard your conversation, I decided that ordinary love wasn't enough. This situation called for tough love."

Vanessa had to laugh. "I have to say, you're awfully good at it. How much of our conversation did you hear? And what made you change your mind?"

"When you proposed he move to Cheyenne, and he clearly wasn't going to so much as consider it. Really ruffled my feathers."

Why? "I hate that it upset you. I didn't really think it out. It was selfish of me to even suggest such a thing, with everything going on in his life. You probably heard the part where he asked if I'd consider Colorado."

"Yes, I did. And I thought he wasn't being selfish enough."

Vanessa closed her eyes and shook her head. For a moment, she thought Ellie was on her side and had expected that she'd say Austin was being selfish, too. "I'm not following you."

"Austin was letting worry make the decision for him. In doing so, he was making the biggest mistake of his life. He should have been supremely selfish in that moment and taken you up on your suggestion because he's in love with you, Vanessa."

"Did he tell you that?"

Ellie laughed. "He didn't have to. He showed me. The way he smiles when your name is mentioned. The way he admires you when you're not looking. The way he would stand at the window when he knew you were coming over, like a little lovesick puppy."

Vanessa couldn't help but smile. But then the familiar doubt set in.

"Maybe that's what he feels. Puppy love," she said. "And everyone knows that puppies grow up very fast and become much smarter about who to trust."

Not a bad argument, in her opinion, but Ellie simply smiled.

"I couldn't agree more. They also become fiercely loyal to those they love, don't they? Love grows with time, but that doesn't diminish its power in the puppy phase. Or its importance."

Vanessa sank back into the sofa. Ellie was right.

"You should have suggested a wager on this discussion, because you have clearly won," Vanessa said.

Ellie laughed. "Nobody wins in love unless everyone wins."

The wisdom just kept flowing.

"I have a confession," Vanessa said. "I'm not so sure I shouldn't move to Colorado. I hate to say this, but if I wasn't worried about how such a drastic change of plans would affect PJ, my answer might have been different. I love the business I'm starting, but I love Austin even more. But PJ is on a pedestal of his own."

Ellie nodded. "A child's happiness and well-being are naturally a parent's top concern. I don't know what he'd be leaving behind in Cheyenne, but I've seen how happy PJ is around Austin and Tango."

"And you." And their home in Cheyenne, and all the friends that he had there.

The extended family that would probably make PJ the happiest included way too many people and creatures for any house to hold.

Ellie stood, and Vanessa resisted the urge to jump up and spot her. But then Ellie pulled the blanket off Vanessa's legs and placed it on the seat of the walker.

She assumed that was her cue to go ahead and get ready for bed. But before she had a chance to stand, Ellie put her palm out to stop her.

"You stay right there. I'm going to warm up this blanket for you again. You can stay here or go to the bedroom, but I want you to get some sleep and stop overthinking this. Your heart knows what's best. You just need to trust it. Austin does, too."

Vanessa's first instinct was to insist she could warm the blanket herself. Or, better yet, warm one up for Ellie. But in this moment, she felt like a little girl again, before she was forced to grow up too fast. One who had always warmed the blankets for others.

She was convinced that Austin really did love her more than he needed her. She also realized something even more enlightening.

She needed *him*.

CHAPTER SIXTEEN

AUSTIN BEGAN UNPACKING his toiletries at the Happy U, then stopped cold.

Last night was such a blur that he didn't even remember what all he'd placed inside. At the bottom of the bag was one of those full-size toothpastes PJ had picked out for him in the drugstore. The day when people assumed the little boy with the painted cat face was his son. From that point on, Austin's heart had wished it were true.

He tried to gulp back the unexpected tears but failed.

The Happy U didn't feel happy anymore. Not because his dad was facing a long recovery period, but because Austin had lost everyone else who mattered to him.

The ranch didn't feel like home either. He'd been so determined to hold on to the property and be there for his dad—and admittedly lasso those feelings from his past—that an even better future slipped through his fingers.

His heart had chatted up a storm on the drive

back from Destiny Springs as to what and who truly made him happy. And what his options were moving forward. Austin couldn't let his grandma live alone. Not until she was ready. Or, make that, not until he was *convinced* she was ready. The physical therapist could stay with her temporarily—at least, for extended periods during the day, as needed—so that was of some comfort. But then what?

For the next week or so, he'd have to trust that enough people could pitch in to help his grandma, because he had to make sure his dad would be taken care of until the man could somewhat take care of himself. How Austin could make that happen was the question. Short of hiring a full-time caregiver, it seemed impossible. He couldn't care for Ellie and his dad.

Upon his return to Destiny Springs, he planned to give Ellie's ranch a proper name: the *Happy Us*. It was the best apology he could think of to make up for the pressure he'd put on her to do something she clearly didn't want to do. It was also in hopes of the *us* his heart was stubbornly refusing to give up on. He just hoped Vanessa felt the same way about giving their love a fair chance and a little more time for him to figure everything out while Ellie finished healing.

For now, a more urgent apology was in order, right here in River Rock. There was no way to let his dad down gently. Austin wouldn't be there to supervise the man's care beyond the short term. Perhaps even worse: the family business would have to be put on hold. Indefinitely.

Austin tried to formulate his words as he finished getting dressed. He'd seen his dad briefly last night—or more like before the crack of dawn—as soon as he got into town, then came back to the ranch to catch a couple of hours of sleep before returning to the hospital. He wanted to give his father a little time to recover. Partly for selfish reasons.

His dad was always a bit grumpy after the anesthesia wore off. Never wanted visitors. This wasn't their first rodeo with surgery, what with all the ranch-related injuries.

Austin checked in at reception when he arrived and headed to his dad's room. When he got there, Randy was standing outside the closed door, Stetson respectfully in hand. He nodded as Austin approached.

"Is everything okay?" Austin asked, thinking that a nurse was probably in there doing vitals and blood work and whatnot. Unless something else was going on.

"Oh, yeah. He's doing great, according to him," Randy said. "I'm waiting for Ms. Harris to finish her visit before I go in to say hi."

"The client who kept pressuring him?" And he'd caved to her demands.

"Yep, although 'pressuring' might not be the best description for it. I'll let him tell you what's going on."

Austin didn't blame the woman in any way for what had happened, since his dad was riding alone at the time. But she was very likely the reason he'd ended up breaking his promise to not ride in the first place.

He stepped around the ranch hand, tapped on the door and opened it without being given permission.

"There's my boy!" his father said. The man was in uncharacteristically good spirits.

Ms. Harris stood and nodded. She was an attractive woman, about his dad's age. Maybe that was the "going on" that Randy was talking about. The man might not have been able to say no to her. Yet his father was going to have to learn how to say it now. Otherwise, Austin would be forced to say it for him.

"You must be Austin. I'm Linda. Wes has told me so much about you."

"All good, I hope," he said, for lack of a better response to a rather awkward moment.

She had a warm smile—he had to give her that much. And there was nothing about her that screamed "pushy."

"Only great things. I'll leave and let you two talk." She grabbed her handbag, smiled at his dad and patted Austin on the arm as she left.

It wasn't lost on him how the man had a smile on his face the whole time. Still did.

"That woman is an angel," he said.

Austin picked up the thermal water jug and offered some to his dad, but he refused.

"I'm sure she's very nice now, but how will she be when you tell her you can't teach for a while?"

"She already knows. And she's been even nicer," Wes said.

Austin sat in the chair that Ms. Harris had vacated and scooted it even closer to the side of the bed. It looked like they now had more than one thing to talk about.

"Sounds like teacher has a crush on his student," Austin said. Might as well call it like he saw it.

"Oh, it's more than that," his dad insisted.

"Don't get mad at him, but Randy told me she's been a little insistent that you teach her, and that she's been over a lot. You can do whatever you want, but you *did* promise you'd wait until I came back."

"Randy only knows what I've told him. I wanted to tell you first."

So there *was* more to this.

The man looked so weak and vulnerable, what

with all the tubes and needles and monitors. Austin had a sinking feeling that Ms. Harris was trying to take advantage of him somehow.

"She isn't exactly a student. She's a cutting-horse trainer," Wes said.

What? "I don't understand."

"She came looking for a job. She has several years of experience."

That was an unexpected twist. Austin struggled to wrap his mind around it but could only reach one conclusion.

"Are you planning on replacing me?" Austin asked.

"Not exactly. I thought it would be a good idea to have a third trainer anyway. In case something like this happened to one of us," he said, pointing to his injured ankle.

That was actually better news than Austin could have hoped for. Maybe Linda could keep the business up and running while his dad was healing, and while Austin was in Destiny Springs taking care of Ellie. However, one thing still needed to be discussed.

"About your care when you get home. I'm going to wait here for the doctor and see what we need to do for you."

"We? No." Wes shook his head. "I'm handling this. You're going back to Destiny Springs. Or maybe Cheyenne?"

How did the man know about his plans to

help Ellie? Even *she* didn't know about them. And Cheyenne? That could only mean his dad somehow knew about Vanessa. He'd barely even thought that far ahead regarding moving to her city, but he was no longer ruling it out. Not by a long shot.

"With all due respect, I want to make sure things are handled and you're taken care of before I so much as go to the grocery store. I didn't do that with Mom," he said, although he hadn't meant to bring up the subject. But that was his only defense in trying to "micromanage" his dad, as Vanessa would say.

That was enough to wipe the smile off his dad's face.

"You're blaming yourself for that?" his dad asked.

"Yes. No. I don't know."

"Then I'll tell you the answer, and it's *no*."

"Except—"

"Except nothing. We all take a chance when it comes to love. And we all deserve another chance when the first one ends, for whatever reason. You deserve it. I deserve it."

Austin had seen his dad tear up only one other time in his life. At his mom's funeral.

He stood, leaned over the bed and gave his dad a hug. It was becoming so clear now that no matter what Austin thought of Linda or her motives, she clearly made him happy.

Austin pulled away and sat back down. "Tell me about Linda. Just a trainer, huh?"

Wes shook his head and dabbed at his eyes. "She's my second chance at love. Which brings me to what I needed to tell you."

"You mean that wasn't it?" Austin asked.

"I want the new love of my life—and future wife, if she'll say yes—to be happy at the Happy U. I get the feeling she wouldn't be into the whole extended-family thing," his dad said. "And that's a good thing, because I'd kinda like for it to be just the two of us. At least for a while."

"Are you booting me out of the house?" Austin asked.

"I sure am. The good news is, Linda is gonna take good care of this ankle. You won't have to worry about that."

And to think he'd been concerned about hurting his dad's feelings. The whole thing was so abrupt and unexpected that it hurt his instead. Not only was he being replaced as a trainer, he was being replaced in his dad's life.

"You're welcome to come back anytime. Your room will always be your room. I'm not changing the locks or anything," Wes said.

Austin's head was still spinning. "Gee, thanks, Dad."

"And bring your girlfriend with you. Vanessa, is it?" A smile spread across the man's otherwise pained face.

Ellie.

"You've been talking to Grandma," Austin said. So that was where his dad had gotten the information.

"She called to check on me before I got prepped for surgery this morning. We had a nice long chat."

Austin didn't ask about what. He already knew. He decided to keep the focus on his dad instead.

"So, the future Mrs. Cassidy is an angel, huh?" Austin asked.

I have one, too. Or at least he had one. With any luck, and perhaps some helpful intervention from some other angels he knew, he could have her back in his life again.

With that, Austin was suddenly sure he could have it all, like his dad was on the cusp of accomplishing. Except his "all" had to include Vanessa and PJ. But it had to start with an apology.

In the meantime, Ellie's ranch had plenty of work possibilities until he figured out where this new journey would take him. In Destiny Springs, he'd have to settle on being *halfway* happy.

The other half would require moving to Cheyenne.

Talk about anticlimactic.

Vanessa had fantasized about a certain special moment every morning for so long. Specifically, the moment she first opened the doors to her very own business and stepped over the threshold and into her new life.

Yet there she stood. Already inside before realizing what she'd done. She hadn't even checked the freshly painted logo on the door to make sure it was what she'd approved, to make sure Forever Home Caregiving and Recovery was spelled correctly and no words were transposed.

Instead, she'd been preoccupied with the idea of a whole different forever home: the one she walked away from.

Her assistant practically ran over to her from the reception area. The woman was all smiles.

"Can you believe how fabulous everything looks? All because of us," Beth said.

Us. Another common word that took her all the way back to Destiny Springs.

Vanessa finally took a moment to do a three-sixty. So far, so good, although this was only the first room.

"I know what you're thinking," Beth said when Vanessa failed to match the woman's level of enthusiasm.

"I bet you don't," Vanessa teased.

Beth cocked her head. "The sofas?"

Vanessa looked at the sitting area, but it looked pretty much how she envisioned. Except she did see it now. They were more turquoise than navy. Definitely a detail she normally would have noticed.

Beth seemed to be holding her breath.

"They look better in that color. If the supplier was going to make a mistake, they made the right one," Vanessa said.

Her assistant exhaled a sigh of relief. "Thank goodness, because I have a confession. I changed the order while you were gone. I really felt the turquoise was cheerier."

Funny, but that didn't bother Vanessa in the least when ordinarily it might have. Made her wonder what other improvements Beth may have made without Vanessa's consent. But there really was only one thing she cared about in the moment.

"Did the deliveries arrive?" Vanessa asked.

"Yes. And I *love* your idea."

Another good one that wasn't Vanessa's. Ellie deserved all the credit.

Vanessa glanced at the wall clock. "We have ten minutes until the doors open."

"Everything is taken care of. Except your delivery is still in the box, but only because I know you wanted to do that yourself. I can get bingo started, once we have enough folks."

"That would be terrific…boss," Vanessa said with a wink.

"I like the sound of that," Beth said. Vanessa suspected she wasn't entirely kidding. The woman had even joked that she planned to open a rival caregiving center one day, and she wanted the "best in the business" to show her the ropes.

Vanessa visited each room, and sure enough, everything seemed to be in place. Then she reached the room that had caused her so much grief earlier, but which now was destined to be her favorite.

She unpacked the turntable that Ellie had sent via delivery service, along with records that the woman had generously donated to get Vanessa started. She thumbed through the albums and landed on the one with the prettiest sleeve.

Couldn't say whether she'd made the best choice, but it might be nice to have something pleasant piping throughout the rooms during the open house. Not only that, but it would be classic music played on a vintage turntable.

She set the needle down and was immediately rewarded. The scratchiness of the sound only lent to the charm. It filled that big, almost empty mistake-of-a-room with an undeniable nostalgia and mystery.

It also made her miss Ellie and that big, empty room of hers. Among other things.

Among everything.

Although she'd yet to hire a dance instructor, she wasn't concerned. She was using Ellie's idea as a placeholder. In fact, after the one night that Vanessa spent with her before leaving Destiny Springs, she was convinced the woman could make the trip to Cheyenne in due time. If that was the case, Vanessa could have a "guest teacher" who was once a national ballroom dancing champion.

Maybe it was wishful thinking, but it made Vanessa believe that perhaps nothing was impossible after all.

The past week had been a whirlwind of activity and emotion. What had been an estimated three-day leave had turned into a week after Beth started worrying, rationally or irrationally, that it might be the last time she got to see her grandparents. They were both seventy-eight, after all. Vanessa understood the need and desire to put family first. Perhaps now more than ever.

The important thing was that Beth had returned in time for the grand opening, and with more energy and enthusiasm than Vanessa had ever seen. In fact, her assistant insisted on taking charge of greeting existing and prospective clients, and their families, as they arrived. She was now showing them around the offices and activity/recovery center, and introducing them to the caretakers and physical therapists who would be meticulously matched and assigned to the clients, before attempting to corral them into the bingo room. All the things Vanessa had envisioned being a part of.

But her vision for the future beyond this day was no longer so clear. She couldn't stop thinking about Austin, and Ellie. Even Tango.

This music…on this vintage turntable…was taking her back in time.

Then there was PJ, whom she'd left at home with a new babysitter. A bold step, but one she knew she'd have to eventually take.

"Mind if I join you?" someone asked from the doorway, somehow loudly enough for her to hear over the music.

Vanessa turned to look.

"Mr. Lake! Not at all." Harold Lake was her favorite client. Well, one of them. She could confidently say that they were all her favorites. Of all of them, he reminded her the most of her grandpa Vern, though.

She walked over and gave him a hug. "Is your daughter here?"

"Oh, yes. I couldn't convince her to do something else today. I think she's interviewing the babysitters."

It was so cute how some of them had latched on to calling the caregivers "babysitters." In some ways, it was accurate. At a certain point, the child became the parent, and the parent became the child. Not an easy transition for either party.

"Tchaikovsky. 'Waltz of the Flowers,'" Harold said as he shuffled to the center of the room and took it all in.

She glanced at the album cover, which she'd placed on the console next to the turntable. He was right. "Waltz of the Flowers."

Before she could ask if the song had special meaning for him, a few of her other clients wandered into the room. Simon Dauchy, Beatrice Abrams, Isabelle Beaumont. All unaccompanied by relatives or friends. And all of whom had been relieved of their driving privileges, so she knew they hadn't come alone. Yet they'd found their way to this room.

Without her having to so much as explain its intended use, Mr. Dauchy asked Mrs. Abrams for a dance. That left Mr. Lake and Ms. Beaumont, who both stood there like awkward teenagers. But not nearly as awkward as she felt.

She walked up to Mr. Lake. "You should ask Ms. Beaumont for a dance."

He shook his head and blushed.

"Oh, Isabelle wouldn't want to dance with me. I have two left feet," he whispered.

Vanessa's breath caught in her throat. Such a common saying. Such uncommon special memories it evoked.

She whispered back. "I heard that she has two right feet."

That seemed to tickle him. Of course, she wouldn't have suggested it if Ms. Beaumont hadn't been looking longingly at the man.

"I don't know," he said.

"The worst that could happen is that she says no," Vanessa said.

She could speak with authority. She'd said no

to Austin's suggestion that she consider moving to Colorado. Someday. And her hasty answer was turning out to be the worst for her. But it ultimately came down to what would be best for PJ. Even that, however, had come into question.

"That's what I'm afraid of," he said.

"And if that happens, you give her a little time to think about it. She'll realize her mistake," Vanessa said.

That got a bit of a smile out of him.

"Okay. You've convinced me." Harold straightened his bow tie and walked over to Isabelle, who used a walker to get around.

It suddenly dawned on Vanessa that perhaps she needed to make sure her business was insured for any dance-related accidents. She could suggest they try their luck at bingo down the hall after this song. Yet they all looked so happy. Harold asked, and his invitation was well received. He was careful to hold her steady as she abandoned the walker for the safety of his arms.

When the album finished playing, Vanessa promptly returned the needle to the beginning.

In the meantime, a few of her other curious clients had wandered down the hall. Unescorted. They were either pairing off and dancing or waiting on the sidelines for their turn. Or simply unable to dance but wanting to be a part of it anyway.

If only Ellie could be here to see it. The final night in Destiny Springs was an evening that Vanessa would always cherish. How Ellie confessed that her grandson was head over heels in love with Vanessa. In turn, Vanessa confessed that she felt the same way and harbored some serious regrets.

Problem was, once she returned to Cheyenne, she felt the need to confess her love for Austin to anyone who would listen. Her precious clients didn't even have to coax the whole story out of her during their final one-on-one meetings that she'd managed to work in as soon as she'd returned. Instead, they couldn't be more interested or excited. She ended up breaking her rule about keeping all client relationships professional.

When the record finished, the couples all clapped. A few left on their own, while others were located and retrieved by loved ones. But the original four remained. One of them walked over to the door and closed it. That was when they surrounded her, concern etched into their faces. Were they unhappy with someone they'd met this afternoon, or something else about the business? Her heart sank at the thought.

"What's going on?" she asked.

"I believe it's called an intervention," Harold said.

"For me? Why?"

"We've been thinking about this whole business you got going here. We don't think it's going to work out," Isabelle said.

Ouch. She hadn't seen that coming. She'd consulted with each of them, more than once, to get their input. Sure, there were a few glitches. But, all things considered, Vanessa thought it had turned out pretty great.

"I'm open to more suggestions," she said. "I want this to be a place you will enjoy. And if you have any problems at all with the caregivers or physical therapists, let me know immediately and I will step in. Okay?"

With both hands, Beatrice enveloped one of Vanessa's. "It isn't that. All of us couldn't be happier with what you're doing for us here. At the same time, we couldn't be sadder. For you."

Vanessa gulped. She'd done her best to remain upbeat for everyone's sake. Even during the chats she'd had with many of them, she'd insisted that she had made the right decision to come back to Cheyenne.

That was what she got for getting involved with her clients and treating them like family.

"You need to walk away from all this and straight into the arms of that man you're clearly in love with. Otherwise, you'll get to our age and regret it," Simon added.

They all nodded in agreement.

"You do realize that you're suggesting I give up something I've worked very hard for," she said, stating the obvious.

"We realize that. But this business of yours isn't gonna love you back, is it? Of course, all of us do, which is why we wanted to talk to you about it. Not that we have the answer, but we're not just gonna sit around and watch you let true love pass you by."

All of a sudden, she was back at Ellie's. Being lovingly lectured to on the ways of the world. And, specifically, of love. All that was missing was a warm blanket. At the same time, she was blanketed by the genuine love and caring of these people whom she'd been a caregiver to.

No, they didn't have the answer. But they offered something just as valuable: life experience. She would be smart to take their advice—otherwise, she'd never hear the end of it. If only it were that easy. But there was a world of difference between something being difficult and it being impossible.

Their certainty made Vanessa wonder what she'd already begun to ponder: Did the Happy U hold the key, as its name promised? Compounding that was Austin's stubborn refusal to give up his own dream, which was making Vanessa question hers.

Plus, she missed Ellie. So did PJ. He'd chosen to video chat with the woman and Tango over going out to the movies and getting pizza on two separate occasions already. The unlikely duo's chats alleviated some of Vanessa's concerns about Ellie's well-being. Vern and Sylvie had also agreed to check on her regularly, which was huge.

In fact, Vanessa would love to join their chats. But she enjoyed watching their special one-on-one connection even more. She was only now able to admit to herself that she may have been wrong all along about what would be best for PJ in the long haul.

Someone knocked on the door, then opened it. Harold's daughter walked inside before Vanessa could issue an invite. Right behind her was a string of other concerned relatives.

"There y'all are! We were starting to get worried," the daughter said.

"Nothing to worry about here," Simon said. "We just wanted to spend some time with this young lady while we had a chance, because it might be a while before we see her again. Right, Vanessa?"

All eyes were suddenly on her.

"Right. No worries," Vanessa said.

Maybe just one big worry in the form of a tiny six-year-old. Despite what was obviously the best decision for her, she was still committed to doing what was best for him. That was what she'd tried to do all along. At least she probably wouldn't be seeing her clients for a while since her whole plan was to stay out of the trenches, which meant she wouldn't have to get into the details of why she chose to ignore their advice.

At that, she left that big, empty room of her own behind. Despite being all but devoid of furniture, it had been the fullest room in the place.

She waited until everyone had left before collecting her purse and fishing out her keys. Beth was still there, doing some straightening up. Throwing away the stray paper cups and whatnot.

"Let's go home. I can take care of the rest tomorrow," Vanessa said.

"Oh, no, you won't. I'm coming in early to make up for bailing on you," Beth said. "Besides, I enjoy this part of it as much as the rest."

"You actually did me a favor."

Beth cocked her head. "How so?"

She opened her mouth to confess that if Beth hadn't left, the grand opening would have played out a little differently and she might not have realized which one of them would be the better boss after all.

"I lost a few pounds from the stress," Vanessa said, instead of explaining what her heart and mind were both suggesting.

"Then would you please do me a favor and bail on me for a week? I have an old swimsuit I'd love to fit back into," Beth said with a smile.

Vanessa bit her lip. "What if I bailed on you for longer than that?"

Beth looked stunned. Maybe her instincts weren't very good at the moment.

"Are you saying that you'd rather be with that cowboy you fell in love with and are going to ride off into the sunset instead of running this business? Because if that's what you're thinking, then I'm pretty sure you know what my answer would be."

Vanessa blinked. How did Beth know about Austin?

Then again, she'd pretty much blabbed her feelings to anyone who'd listen, once she got back into town. Her precious clients had made a bold intervention, so of course they'd told Beth.

Lots of details to work out in either case. She and Austin would have some details of their own to work out, assuming he still felt the same way.

Beth remained perfectly still. Vanessa hesitated, the words on the tip of her tongue, but it seemed too early to say them:

That's exactly what I'm thinking, boss.

CHAPTER SEVENTEEN

"I MISS YOU *soooo* much, Miss Ellie. Tango, too!" PJ said.

"We miss you even more," Ellie countered.

"Nuh-uh, 'cause I miss you *this* much!" PJ said.

At that, Vanessa looked up from her laptop. Her little boy had spread his arms as wide as he could manage.

Ellie did the same, from what Vanessa could tell from such a distance.

"I say we're tied. How about a virtual goodnight hug since our arms are already open?" Ellie asked.

PJ took it a step further and actually embraced the laptop.

It both warmed Vanessa's heart and shattered it. Not that it wasn't fractured already. Started with the whole intervention earlier and ended with her doubting practically every decision she had ever made in life, but daring to hope for a different future than she'd been envisioning.

But nothing had been decided yet, and Austin

may not want to try. Yes, Ellie had told Vanessa how Austin really felt. But that was before.

In the end, Vanessa hadn't "popped the question" to Beth about buying her out, but she had bought herself some time to figure things out. In the meantime, she wasn't about to abandon the business. She focused once again on the spreadsheet. With the popularity of the dance hall concept at the center's open house earlier, she needed to ensure there was adequate seating moving forward. That meant she'd need to find money in the budget for some chairs. And at least one velvet love seat, like Ellie had.

Didn't need to be anything fancy. But not all her clients had enough physical ability or energy for even one dance. She wanted them to have the option to simply relax and listen to music.

One of the available caregivers could help in changing out the albums. Or perhaps the clients might want to handle the task themselves and pick out their own music. In fact, they would probably love it. There would always be someone around who could lend a hand.

By the time she logged out of her own laptop and mustered the energy to uncross her legs and get off the comfy sofa, PJ and Ellie's video chat had ended. That created the opening she'd been waiting for ever since returning from the event and settling with the babysitter.

She swooped in to collect a hug of her own.

"How would you feel about a quick trip to Destiny Springs? Then you could get a real hug from Ellie," she said in the little boy's ear.

And I could see if Austin has mentioned anything about me. Or us.

Not that she couldn't get the same type of information over the phone or from a video chat of her own, but she could use a hug from the woman. As well as one from her grandpa Vern while she was at it. The man had spoiled both her and PJ in that regard.

Vern was equally generous with giving good advice. She was still afraid that Austin needed her more than he loved her. Of course, the only way to find out for sure was to take a chance. But it would help to know that her grandpa would be there to catch her when it all fell apart.

"*If* it fell apart," she said, self-correcting her thinking. If she was going to go through with this, she needed the glass to be at least half-full.

PJ wiggled out of her grip and looked up at her with those blue eyes. "I could go to school there with Max and we could live with Pawpaw and see Miss Ellie and Mr. Austin every day."

Vanessa blinked. She'd expected him to like the idea, but not enough to want to move there.

"You don't like our house here?" she asked.

He used to. In fact, when she'd first brought up

the idea of going back to Destiny Springs for another couple of weeks, PJ had claimed he didn't want to go. Fortunately, he quickly got over it as he reconnected with Max and then got to know Ellie and Tango. But *this*?

PJ shrugged. "It's okay."

Not much of an answer. She'd bet he would be more enthusiastic once first grade started. She'd been looking forward to living vicariously through him, having been homeschooled herself. She'd missed out on all of it: field trips, school lunches, a recess playground with swings and slides and spinners.

And friends her age. Lots of them.

"The only problem with your plan is that Mr. Austin lives in Colorado. Maybe we could go visit him, though. Would you rather do that than go to Disney World?"

Now, *that* was a choice he had to think about.

It was the next big trip on their official vacation spreadsheet. A real getaway would be a first for her little two-person family.

His whole demeanor brightened and he sat up straighter. "We could all go to Disney World together. Miss Ellie and Pawpaw could come, too."

Within that innocent statement, Vanessa found answers to the questions that had formed in Destiny Springs, and which were weighing heavier and heavier on her mind.

In her desire to give PJ her idea of a normal childhood, was she denying him something even better?

Yes.

If she'd had a different kind of childhood herself, would she have found her calling?

No.

She gave herself a moment to see if her heart raised any arguments. It didn't.

Then it's settled.

AUSTIN WALKED UP behind his grandma and placed a tall glass of lemonade on the table beside her.

"Can I get you anything else?" he asked. "Some *Karaage*?"

Maybe sneaking up on her wasn't the best idea, because the woman nearly fell off her walker seat.

She placed a hand on her heart and turned her head. "You scared the living daylights out of me. What are you doing here?"

He walked around so she wouldn't have to twist, then removed his Stetson and sank into the velvet love seat.

"I came to Destiny Springs to apologize. I'm in the right place, aren't I? Isn't this the apology room?"

Ellie shook her head, took a long sip of lemonade and closed her eyes as if savoring the unexpected treat.

"I already told you, dear, an apology isn't necessary," she said.

"Maybe not for you. But I owe someone else one. And I'm not leaving this room until you reveal its secrets, because I need all the help I can get. Besides, I figured I wasn't welcome back in this house until I came to my senses."

At that, Ellie opened her eyes and studied him as if to make sure he wasn't teasing. "You're here for Vanessa."

"Yes, ma'am. Besides, I didn't have anywhere else to go. Dad kicked me off the ranch. But you already knew that, didn't you?"

She offered up that coy smile of hers. "I had an idea something like that might happen."

"I thought so," he said.

"Where's my therapist?" Ellie asked.

"She went to town to get some chicken thighs."

"That's not her job."

"Neither was staying with you so much while I was gone. I'm paying her extra for it."

"Then you weren't joking about the *Karaage*."

"I'd never joke about something that serious. I can't guarantee it will be as tasty as when Vanessa and I made it together, but it will at least be good practice, because I'm planning to stay a while. If it's okay with you, that is."

He wasn't joking about that either. Might even

need to pick up some more full-size tubes of toothpaste.

"Didn't the therapist tell you? I'm recovering even faster than expected," she said.

"I know. I wouldn't be staying because *you* need *me*, but because *I* need *you*. And who knows how long it will take to win Vanessa back. The sooner I do, the sooner I'll be out of your hair and on my way to Cheyenne," he said, even though his feelings hadn't changed about wanting all his family under one roof. His heart and mind simply made a more compelling argument.

There was a tap at the door frame. The therapist.

"I have your chicken thighs," she said, holding up the grocery bag. "Should I come back tomorrow?" she asked, looking to Austin. But he would let that be his grandma's decision.

"I don't think that will be necessary," Ellie said. "I can take care of my grandson all by myself."

The therapist got the joke and smiled. "Okay, then. You know how to reach me if that changes."

At that, the woman left, and it was down to the two of them again.

It was also time to get down to business.

"Tell me how this apology room works. Please."

Ellie folded her hands on top of the lap blanket and stared out the window.

"Shelton added this room to the house when we got married. Said it was his apology to me for my having to give up dancing to become the wife of a rancher. He wanted me to still have a place to practice, if I ever wanted to get back into it."

Now it all made sense, although he never would have guessed it. How this room could ever help him, he didn't have a clue.

"Did you ever try?" Austin asked.

Ellie shook her head. "I didn't want to. That would have meant finding a partner, and there was only one man I wanted to dance with from that point on. But that only made Shelton feel like adding this room wasn't enough. So I told him that he could apologize by dancing with me, and all would be forgiven."

"So...the dancing was the apology," he said, which still didn't help his cause with Vanessa.

"Exactly. But it wasn't easy for him. He had two left feet, you see."

Oh, boy, did he ever. "So do I, Grandma."

"Shelton was determined to improve, however. He even started picking fights with me so that we'd have to come to this room. Our unspoken rule was, we wouldn't stop dancing until we'd forgiven each other. And it worked. Of course, the fights he'd pick were never anything for me to get upset about. Didn't take long for me to catch on. I started doing it, too."

"Did he pick a fight with you before he passed? You'd mentioned that you were waiting for an apology. I can't tell you how much that worried and confused me."

She laughed softly as tears formed in her eyes. "Yes, he did. He told me I'd been too good of a wife by spoiling him rotten."

Austin looked at her for an extended moment. "What an awful thing to say."

When she looked at him, he offered up the most sympathetic expression he could manage, which made her laugh.

He couldn't help but laugh himself, even though there wasn't anything funny about it.

"Maybe you can help me think of something equally awful to say to Vanessa so I can persuade her to come all the way to Destiny Springs for a dance. I'll tell her the story behind the name. She's always been curious."

"Vanessa actually came very close to guessing. She wanted you and me to get together here to apologize. I told her that wasn't quite the way it worked. I didn't tell her that it was for romantic couples exclusively. I've only tested that theory with one other couple—Vern and Sylvie. It seemed to work."

"I'd say it's time we do further testing. But I'll need some dance lessons first, if you know of any professional dancers who could give me some pointers. Even if your theory turns out to be wrong and she doesn't accept my apology, I want to at least dazzle her with some fancy footwork."

"I don't think it's necessary, but why take any chances?" Ellie said.

Austin smiled and nodded while silently disagreeing.

He was about to take the most important chance of his life.

CHAPTER EIGHTEEN

"YOU DON'T HAVE to do that," Vanessa said to Vern.

When would all the pampering end?

She already knew what her grandpa's response would be, so she leaned against the kitchen doorway and soaked in the memories instead. All of a sudden, she was five years old again, with her grandpa making her favorite snack. The visits had ceased a few years after that, when her mom got sick. Vern's luck hadn't been much better as he struggled to keep his ranch afloat.

Tough times all around. Not that what she was going through right now was easy.

Vern swatted in her general direction and proceeded to finish making her a peanut-butter-and-banana sandwich. It was a little late to eat, but he'd correctly picked up on the fact that she hadn't done nearly enough eating lately. The stress of everything had killed her appetite. Her looser-than-usual flannel pajamas were barely hanging on her hips.

She couldn't wait to get her appetite and curves back. PJ, on the other hand, was eating enough for the both of them. If she stared at him long enough, she would swear that she could see him growing taller and broader right in front of her eyes.

Vern cut the sandwich in half and handed her the plate.

"I'm not sure I can eat all of this." As delicious as it looked, if PJ wasn't already fast asleep upstairs, she'd give him some.

"That's why I cut it in half. I'll help you with it and make another one for you tomorrow. A whole one for PJ, too. Now go sit down and relax. I want to know why I have the pleasure of seeing you again so soon. All I can say is it better not be because you're checking on me. I'm doin' just fine."

"That's not the reason, although seeing you again is a major perk. PJ was super excited. But it's Ellie I came to talk to," she called out as she settled into an overstuffed chair in the den.

Vern emerged from the kitchen carrying two glasses of milk. One for each of them. He set them on the table shared by the chair and sofa and took a seat nearest her.

"You may want to call Ellie before stopping by. She has company in from out of town. A relative."

"I had no idea." She hadn't bothered to let the

woman know she was coming back into town. PJ had wanted to surprise her.

In retrospect, alerting her would have been the polite thing to do. At the same time, she was glad that other family members were finally stepping in to help as she continued to heal. Vanessa, for one, was going to sleep a lot easier with that knowledge.

"How long is her company staying, do you know?" She took a bite of the sandwich. It was as good as she remembered. Although she'd made these sandwiches dozens of times for PJ and herself, it tasted so much better when someone made one for her. With love.

"She didn't say, but it sounded like he might be there a while. She made some joke about him bringing a full tube of toothpaste with him, and that meant he wasn't going to leave anytime soon."

A knot formed in her stomach. During one of the video chats between Ellie and PJ, Vanessa had overheard them talking about toothpaste and how PJ had picked some out for Austin. She'd thought it was odd at the time, but no stranger than all the zombie talk PJ managed to squeeze into their conversations.

The toothpaste purchase must have happened during their first outing to the diner, which was also the first time a man had ever brought home lunch for her, anticipating that she'd be hungry.

Except for her grandpa, of course.

Such a small gesture, but a telling one. And Austin's attentiveness had continued from there, which meant the steak fingers hadn't been a one-off favor. So exactly why did she doubt that he loved her more than he needed her, after all the ways he demonstrated the opposite?

"Does this relative have a name?"

"He certainly does. And I suspect, like you, he's not here to take care of his grandparent."

She set the sandwich down. Couldn't take another bite if she tried. That knot in her stomach had dissolved into a swirling mixture of fear and anxiety and hope.

"Were you going to tell me that Austin was in town? You and Ellie seemed to be scheming to get us together the whole time I was here before, so I would think you'd both pounce on this coincidence."

"You're right about the matchmaker part." Vern reached over and grabbed half of the sandwich and winked. Before she could ask him to elaborate, he took a huge bite.

That was okay. She'd wait, because this discussion wasn't over with yet.

He washed the bite down with milk, then wiped his whiskers with a napkin.

"But you're wrong about pouncing," he continued. "You need to decide what's best, without the benefit of Ellie's and my combined experience and wisdom of more than one hundred and sixty years."

She couldn't help but smile. When he put it that way, how could she have any doubts at all?

But he was right. This had to be her and Austin's decision. Still, she wasn't sure what his decision might be.

All she knew was that she wanted to see him. Now, even though it wasn't practical. Most of all, she wanted to dance with him. For the rest of her life. Broken toes would heal. Her heart, however, would not. And that terrified her. Only one thing could help in the moment.

Vanessa stood. "Will you do me one more favor, Grandpa?"

He finished taking a long sip of milk and set the glass down.

"You do realize you don't have to ask. The answer will always be yes," he said.

"Good." Vanessa extended her hand. "Dance with me."

She'd only seen her grandpa get teary-eyed once, and that was when Sylvie accepted his marriage proposal. This moment marked the second time.

He allowed her to help him stand. Then he lifted a finger. "We need music."

Vern walked over to his album collection and selected one, then put it on the turntable. Whatever it was, it was beautiful.

She put her arms around his waist and her head on his chest, and they embraced as they swayed. Just like that, Vanessa was five years old again. Except this time she didn't stand on top of his feet.

"I'm scared, Grandpa."

"I know, sweetheart."

By this time tomorrow, she'd know the fate of her future with Austin, because she wasn't going to leave until it was settled, once and for all. She just wasn't sure she would be able to convince him that she all of a sudden had no more doubts about his intentions. It didn't make sense to her either, but it was true.

You just know.

She also knew for certain that if he decided he didn't want a future with her at the Happy U, the resulting fall would be the most painful of all.

If only her grandpa could be there to catch her if it happened.

"WOULD YOU ANSWER the door, dear? Must be Vern with the egg delivery," Ellie called out from the den.

That was odd. His grandma was doing more and more around the house. Was her hip hurting? She'd promised to say something if she ever felt bad. In return, he promised not to bug her about anything. So far, it seemed to be working out.

Austin set the *Karaage* recipe on the counter, wiped his hands on a dish towel and went to the den. Thankfully, he hadn't gotten to the deep-fry part yet, because he needed to watch that carefully to make sure the chicken didn't burn.

"I thought Vern came early in the morning. And to the side door," he said as he walked by.

"He usually does, but he called earlier. Said he was running late."

Austin remembered that Vern had called—he'd picked it up—but he'd just as quickly handed the phone over to his grandmother, as he'd been busy setting up his bathroom for another potential long-term stay.

When he opened the door, it wasn't Vern at all.

All of a sudden, he couldn't breathe. He blinked a few times to make sure he wasn't seeing things, even though his heart started galloping toward a hopeful answer to the only question he had. "What are you doing here?"

It must have come out wrong, because Vanessa looked away.

He'd tried to imagine a moment like this a million times since the realization of what he really wanted in life had dropped on his thick head like a ton of bricks. But he knew better than to predict how she might feel.

"I didn't mean that the way it sounded. I'm just surprised. Pleasantly, of course," he said.

That earned him some kind of softer look. Hopeful, perhaps?

"I'm here to drop off these eggs," she said. Instead of a crate, she handed him a plate covered with plastic wrap.

They were eggs all right. Deviled ones.

He opened the door wider. "Please, come in."

"Is that who I think it is?" Ellie asked.

He already suspected she knew this was going to happen. They'd obviously coordinated something more than simple egg delivery logistics.

Vanessa walked over to his grandma, set the plate on a coffee table and gave her a hug.

"I brought these over for you and Austin. All the whites are intact. I still can't thank you enough for the recipe," Vanessa said. "Vern will bring over the whole, raw ones in the morning."

Ellie grabbed both of Vanessa's hands in hers and squeezed.

Austin shifted from one foot to another. His stomach was doing somersaults at the thought of what he would say. He wasn't prepared. At the same time, he was more than ready.

His grandma released Vanessa's hands.

"I'm glad I have both of you together. I need you to help me with something in the apology room," Ellie said.

The woman didn't wait for their responses. She stood and took the lead down the hallway. They both seemed to know they'd better do as they were told and follow.

Once inside the room, Ellie searched her albums and put one on the turntable.

"When this record reaches the end, all you have to do is lift the arm and place it at the beginning again." With that, Ellie turned the knob on the player, dropped the needle to the record and headed to the doorway.

"What did you need for us to do, Ellie?" Vanessa called out.

In that moment, Austin knew exactly what he needed to do.

"Why, dance, of course. I'll let my grandson explain. And don't come out of this room until you've offered any apologies you feel you need to offer."

His first thought was, Vanessa didn't owe him an apology. His second thought was, what if she didn't accept his? Could they keep dancing until she did?

Ellie walked out the door and into the hallway, lingering long enough to give them both a stern down-the-nose look. "When you're done, you'll find me in the kitchen, finishing the *Karaage* Austin started," she said. "And don't worry. I won't reach too high or bend too far."

He smiled and shook his head as he walked out to the middle of the floor.

Vanessa stayed behind. "We probably don't have to do this if you don't want. We can just talk. I doubt she has any hidden cameras in here."

"You saw that look on her face. She means business."

"I thought so, too. She kind of scared me."

That made him laugh. Only because Ellie had the ability to scare him, too. The only times he'd ever been on the receiving end of that look from her was when he'd gotten into something he wasn't supposed to get into, and he'd better make it right. Which was exactly what he intended to do now, with Vanessa.

"You may be right that she isn't somehow watching. But I *want* to dance with you." He offered his left hand.

She hesitated before joining him and accepting it.

He invited her in and placed his right hand on her left shoulder blade. She rested her hand on his upper arm. He then adjusted his body alignment so that no toes would be in the way. And he proceeded to lead her in a waltz.

The look on her face was priceless.

"You said you didn't know how to dance, even though you did just fine with our slow dance at Renegade. But this?"

"I had a good teacher," he said. "And I'm a fast learner when something is important. And this is important."

At that, she turned quiet and followed his lead.

"I wanted to apologize. For trying to get you to change your whole life for me," he said.

Vanessa shook her head, and for a moment she shifted her position just enough that he almost got her toes. He course-corrected by stepping slightly to the left, just like Ellie had taught him to do.

"As it turns out, it's a good thing you rejected my offer," he continued. "My life has changed more than you know. I'm officially homeless. I was thinking Cheyenne might be a good place to settle down."

"But your family ranch isn't there. Neither is your dad, who probably needs you."

"Not as much as I need you. And what I mean by that is that I need you to let me be there for you. I need you to love me, despite my clumsiness with words sometimes. And with toes. Most of all, I need you to keep making those deviled eggs for me, because I'm only staying here until Grandma can take care of herself."

"And you're really thinking of moving to Cheyenne?"

"Not just thinking about it. Looking forward to it. A special little boy lives there with his mom, and I'm thinking of asking her to marry me. That is, if she feels the same way and doesn't mind a long-distance relationship for a while. Or a life with a hopeless cowboy who is hopeful he can make her as happy as she makes him."

"Does this woman have a name?" Vanessa asked.

"Yes. Angel something-or-other."

"I know Angel personally, and I don't think that arrangement will work out."

Austin swallowed hard. He was so sure this proposal would be perfect.

"She's been considering the Happy U, because she's in love with the stubborn rancher who lives there with his dad," Vanessa continued.

"Lived there. He kicked me out. I wasn't joking about being homeless."

Vanessa stopped midstep and dropped her hand to her side. "Did he really do that?"

"Sure did. But it saved me the trouble of telling him that I wouldn't be living with him anyway." He pulled her in close this time, wrapping both arms around her. She did the same, replacing their imperfect waltz with the perfect sway.

"I'm sure he didn't mean it," she said.

Of course his dad hadn't meant it. The door to the Happy U would always be open to family.

"Sounds like our problem is unsolvable, with you wanting to go to Colorado, and me wanting to live in Cheyenne. If there was only a place where we could both be happy," he said.

A problem for sure, but one with a brilliant solution. One that Ellie herself had unknowingly suggested.

"Destiny Springs," they said in unison.

She pulled away and looked at him. "PJ and I can be close to Vern and Ellie. And Tango. And his *best* best friend, Max. Seems as though PJ would rather grow up here than in a proper city."

"What about your business?"

"I did what I set out to do. But there's someone who would be even better at running it. Besides, my clients don't want me there anymore."

Austin stopped abruptly. "What?"

"They felt I wasn't putting myself first. Mainly, they worried that I'd be missing out on a chance at true love if I stayed in Cheyenne. Enter my loyal assistant, Beth, who has been eyeing my job since I hired her. She wants to be in charge. I haven't asked her to buy me out, but she's pretty much already said yes. Long story short, there would be some negotiating."

"But you worked so hard for it."

"I did, and I proved to myself that I could do it. I could always start a business here, now that I know what's required to pull it off. Or anywhere, for that matter. My clients helped me see that. They helped me see a lot of things, especially when it came to us."

"So your clients were playing matchmaker?"

"They advised that I follow my heart. That's

what I get for not keeping those relationships professional."

He pulled her back in. "I get it. Look what happened when you got too close to Ellie and me."

"I fell in love with a cowboy."

His heart could have exploded right then and there. She was pressed so tightly against him, she must have felt it beating faster.

"I like your idea of starting a business in Destiny Springs," he said. "Ellie is going to eventually need more help, and I'd like to hire a caregiver from someone I know and trust. And love."

Furthermore, Austin would always take care of Vanessa. For better or for worse. If it took a lifetime to convince her of that, then that was how much time he'd spend.

"I'm sorry, too," she said.

"For what?" he asked. She didn't need to apologize for having doubts about his intentions, after everything she'd been through in life. He'd meant it when he'd said, *Vanessa needs to take care of Vanessa.* Now that they would be together, he'd make sure of it.

"For even suggesting that you move to Cheyenne and leave the family business, for starters."

"Who says I'm leaving? I'm merely expanding, if Ellie will agree to let me stock her ranch with cattle and horses again."

"I think that's a wonderful idea," she said.

"One of our future sons or daughters can join me. Carry on the family tradition long after I'm gone. Just thinking ahead," he said with a grin.

"Maybe there's already one who might be interested. He keeps surprising me. But before you get too excited, it would be totally up to PJ. I'll hold off on his pre-applications to law school and medical school. And I won't start prepping him for his CPA exams just yet," she teased.

If she kept this up, she was going to make him cry.

"I have one more thing to ask, though. Just to make it official," he said.

"Oh, yeah? What's that?"

"Will you marry me, and how soon?"

She pulled away and smiled. "That's two questions. But the answers are yes, and as soon as we decide where and when."

It couldn't be soon enough for him, although he could have continued dancing like this forever. Nothing but the sound of the needle scratching against the label of the record that had long ago finished playing.

Another thing they hadn't talked about was, where would they live? With Ellie? Vern? Or get a place of their own?

Not that it mattered. He was already home.

EPILOGUE

Three months later

"Isn't there some rule that female guests aren't supposed to outshine the bride?"

His grandma looked so lovely from where he stood. She'd been wearing warm-up suits since the surgery, and he told her she could wear one today. But she insisted on an elegant long-sleeved velvet floral dress instead.

Ellie turned to face Austin, except no smile was forthcoming. Instead, tears streamed down her cheeks as the fireplace flickered behind her.

Oh, no.

Austin rushed over to her and gave her a hug, all but forgetting about the single white rose pinned on the lapel of his black tuxedo jacket, which he'd paired with jeans and his cowboy boots. He and Vanessa had decided on a whatever-makes-you-happy dress code for their guests and for themselves.

"Are you okay?" he asked.

Being in this bedroom with the fireplace again most certainly brought back memories of being curled up in furry blankets next to Shelton while they took a nap.

Having their wedding at the Happy U ranch had been Vanessa's idea. She didn't think his dad should try to travel to and from Destiny Springs with a broken ankle that was going to take months to heal.

Inviting extended family only had been Austin's idea. But that list quickly grew to include PJ's best friend, Max. The two little monsters were already terrorizing the guests, which also included Max's parents, Becca and Cody Sayers. Georgina, their assistant, was left in charge of the B and B while the family was in Colorado.

"These are happy tears, I promise," Ellie said. "I was thinking how I would still love to steal this fireplace. Do you think it will fit into the back of your truck?"

He offered up his best coy smile. "Maybe."

She shook her head as if she thought he was teasing. He wasn't. Not entirely.

Ellie wasn't the only one who could keep a juicy secret, as she had with the apology room. He'd already been looking into ways to bring the fireplace to her. Just like she always wanted. Wasn't going to be easy. It would have to be torn down, transported in pieces and put back together. But it would be worth it.

After all, there was an empty exterior wall in her bedroom suite, waiting to be filled. She could come stay with him and Vanessa and PJ at Fraser Ranch—their temporary home until they got situated in one of their own—while the fireplace was being installed at Ellie's. At least, that was one idea. Her grandpa Vern and his fiancée, Sylvie, had entered serious negotiations about the wedding date. She'd wanted Valentine's Day; he'd wanted it to happen yesterday. He finally realized that he'd be willing to wait forever for her, so perhaps a few extra months wouldn't kill him. And she conceded that perhaps a few extra months was too long. At least they agreed that the wedding would be followed by a two-week honeymoon in Hawaii. There was already plenty of room there for Ellie, but she'd have more privacy if she stayed over only while they were away.

Surprising his grandma with the fireplace was something he was looking forward to, but not nearly as much as this moment right in front of them.

Austin took a deep breath. "It's time."

That got Ellie's tears flowing again.

His, too, except he was doing a better job of keeping them at bay.

Ellie took hold of his arm as they walked out

of the guest bedroom and toward the living room, where an even bigger fireplace had been lit and was keeping everyone warm. Vanessa insisted they open all the French doors that led to the patio, where champagne and deviled eggs and *Karaage* would be served at the reception that immediately followed.

His dad was already seated in front, in his wheelchair. The soon-to-be Mrs. Wes Cassidy was sitting right next to him. Every empty chair and sofa was occupied.

Finally, a full house of loved ones. Like he'd always wanted.

Make that, *used* to want. He was now looking forward to focusing on Vanessa and PJ, exclusively, once they moved into a place of their own. The number of bedrooms was the current sticking point. They both wanted plenty for family visits, but their combined budgets weren't cooperating. Vanessa was sure it had to be an error on her spreadsheet. But Ellie looked it over and the numbers checked out. The woman could balance the national budget if they'd give her a chance.

But such endeavors weren't in Ellie's future. Instead, she volunteered to teach dancing in Cheyenne once a week, at the business Vanessa used to own, and where she now acted as a consultant. And friend.

Vanessa insisted on remaining in her former

clients' lives by driving Ellie to the facility and back to teach a dance class. The seniors there were tickled pink to have a champion ballroom dancer as an instructor.

As soon as Austin and Ellie entered the hallway, they were nearly knocked over by a pair of adorable zombies.

"PJ," Austin called out.

The little boy slowly turned around and headed back to Austin, his head hanging low. Must have thought he was going to be reprimanded. As if that had ever happened to him. Yet he knew PJ understood how important today was. The little boy had even started referring to him as Daddy.

"I'm sorry," PJ said.

"For what? I just wanted to tell you that you forgot your tie." *Son.*

PJ's eyes widened, and he grasped at his neck.

"I had it, but I think it fell off while I was a zombie," he said.

A strong possibility with a clip-on.

"Retrace your steps. If you can't find it after a quick search, then meet us in the living room without one."

"Okay!"

When he and Ellie entered the den, ranch hand Randy scurried to the side of the room.

A moment later, it was obvious why. Music.

The same waltz he and Vanessa had danced to in the apology room.

As he led Ellie to the high-back chair reserved for her nearest the fireplace and his dad, he asked, "What is this song?"

"'La valse d'Amélie,'" she said.

"What does it mean?"

"It's the dance of love. A wedding dance."

And she had been the one who had picked it out for him and Vanessa that day. When he looked at her, she offered up that coy smile that he loved. That was when he just knew. Her choice had been intentional.

He stood nearby as she eased into the chair. He leaned over and whispered, "Thank you," but didn't wait on a response.

Austin took his position, front and center, and nodded at the officiant. Instead of an aisle, the guests had formed more of a circle.

PJ ran back into the room, having found his clip-on tie but not putting it on straight. He took his place beside Austin as instructed. His little best man looked up at him with the biggest smile. Instead of pointing out the wardrobe malfunction, Austin gave him a thumbs-up.

A few minutes later, Vanessa appeared on Vern's arm.

He wasn't sure whether it was the warmth that was radiating from the fireplace, or from the smiling faces of this family of theirs. But with the way her white layered chiffon dress was billowing in the occasional strong breeze even as she stood perfectly still, he would have sworn that—at least for a moment—Vanessa had wings.

Not that it would surprise him. She really was an angel.

My angel.

* * * * *

Don't miss the next book in Susan Breeden's
Destiny Springs, Wyoming miniseries,
coming December 2025
from Harlequin Heartwarming.

Harlequin® Reader Service

Enjoyed your book?

Try the perfect subscription for Romance readers and get more great books like this delivered right to your door.

See why over 10+ million readers have tried Harlequin Reader Service.

Start with a Free Welcome Collection with free books and a gift—valued over $20.

Choose any series in print or ebook. See website for details and order today:

TryReaderService.com/subscriptions